Also by Douglas Brunt

Ghosts of Manhattan

THE MEANS

DOUGLAS BRUNT

A Touchstone Book
Published by Simon & Schuster

New York   London   Toronto   Sydney   New Delhi

Touchstone
A Division of Simon & Schuster, Inc.
1230 Avenue of the Americas
New York, NY 10020

First Touchstone hardcover edition September 2014

TOUCHSTONE and colophon are registered trademarks of Simon & Schuster, Inc.

For information about special discounts for bulk purchases, please contact Simon & Schuster Special Sales at 1-866-506-1949 or business@simonandschuster.com.

The Simon & Schuster Speakers Bureau can bring authors to your live event. For more information or to book an event contact the Simon & Schuster Speakers Bureau at 1-866-248-3049 or visit our website at www.simonspeakers.com.

Interior design by Robert E. Ettlin
Jacket design by Jason Heuer
Jacket photograph © Ethan Myerson/Vetta/Getty Images

Manufactured in the United States of America

10   9   8   7   6   5   4   3   2   1

Library of Congress Cataloging-in-Publication Data

Brunt, Douglas.
The means : a novel / Douglas Brunt.—First Touchstone hardcover edition.
pages cm

1. Politicians—Fiction. 2. Political corruption—Fiction. 3. Political campaigns—Fiction. 4. Political fiction. I. Title.

PS3602.R868M43 2014
813'.6—dc23   2013049797

ISBN 978-1-4767-7257-8
ISBN 978-1-4767-7260-8 (ebook)

For Megyn

Democracy is the worst form of government except for all those other forms that have been tried.

—*Winston Churchill, 1874–1965*

PART ONE

Print is dead.

—Dr. Egon Spengler, 1984

SAMANTHA DAVIS

1

"There's been a plane crash."

Samantha had expected the receptionist to ask her to wait a moment or to offer her coffee. People are running in all directions around them but the receptionist sits in place, redirecting phone calls.

"Where?" Samantha asks.

"In the ocean, just beyond Staten Island. About five minutes ago."

"Passenger jet?"

"Yes, I think it was one of the big kind. International."

"Oh, no."

"I'm sorry, but Mr. Mueller is not going to be able to conduct your interview today. He's heading to the newsroom now. I can try to reschedule you."

"Of course, I'll just call you later. I'm sure you're all busy," says Samantha.

"Erica, cancel everything for the rest of the day." A man has come around the corner from behind the receptionist at the speed of an Olympic power walker. He looks about fifty and has extra weight around his middle and face. He has a cell phone and his jacket is flapping behind him from the other hand. His tie is on but loose with the top button of his shirt undone and his hair is brown and full and looks like it hasn't been cut for some time.

"Yes, Mr. Mueller."

"Make sure Paul Becker gets in Control Four and tell him no commercial breaks until he hears from me. Send only emergency calls for me to Control Four."

"Yes, sir," says the receptionist.

David Mueller stops next to them but his manner keeps a hurried pace. "You Samantha Davis?" Gorgeous brunette with green eyes. He remembers hearing the deep voice with gravitas. He sees in person that she has kind of a big head with a little body and he knows from experience that translates well to TV.

"Yes."

He looks at her for two seconds, making a decision. "Come with me."

He moves from reception to the elevators without looking at her or thinking about her again, like she's something he tucked into his pocket for later. Samantha follows behind.

Mueller continues yelling into his phone. "Is Ken Grant in the studio yet? Good. I want Jeffries and a crew out on Staten Island now. How far offshore did this thing go down? No? See if you can get any of our guys on a police or rescue craft. And charter our own boat. Divert our traffic helicopters out to the scene and get some visuals on it. Get a crew to South Street Seaport, and put a crew on Ellis Island. We can get some coverage of the rescue boats coming and going. I'm stepping into the elevator, I'm going to lose you. Reach me in Control Four."

Mueller lowers the phone and they step inside the elevator. He pushes 1 and looks at Samantha. "You're going to see a newsroom in high gear. Stay next to me and observe."

"This is the best interview I've ever had." She worries this sounds insensitive but sees that Mueller, for the moment, is not as concerned with what happened as he is with covering what happened.

"Ken Grant is great on breaking news. He's also a pilot for Chrissake. He's perfect for this." Mueller is a general content with his battle plan. "It's Rolling Thunder now. News rundowns are in the trash and it's breaking news, live as it comes. This is what reporters live for. It's going to be nuts in there."

Samantha nods. They step out of the elevator and walk thirty paces to an escalator that takes them a level below ground. The security guards recognize Mueller and he and Samantha pass by into the newsroom.

The room is the size of a football field. The ceiling is about ten feet, which feels low in a room that stretches so far. Plain, square columns that are drywall around load-bearing beams look skeletal. They mark the perimeter of different pods of news teams.

The room is full of people sitting, standing, and running, holding up printed computer paper and yelling for each other's attention. Phones are ringing, everyone has one or two small TVs at their desk. Unlike usual, today the volumes are up. News people develop the ability to talk and listen at the same time.

To Samantha's left is a twelve-by-twelve-foot stage raised one foot off the ground, under studio lighting that hangs from tracks in the ceiling. It's an island of glowing TV lights in the darker newsroom. In a chair on the stage is a blond reporter in a red dress. She's reading notes and getting her makeup retouched.

Samantha has gone from the stark white lighting and quiet of the hallway to the newsroom full of spotlights and accent lights, desk lamps, and in any direction the glow of more than a hundred television and computer screens competes for her eyes. She's dazed and her senses work to catch up.

Mueller keeps power walking and she chases him. He cuts through the aisles that are created by the kind of desk furniture that connects to make rows and corners so the workers can have their own space for computer and phone but are crowded together.

A younger version of Mueller with no tie runs up to them. "CNN is reporting no survivors."

"Do we have that?"

"Jeffries is calling all his contacts at Port Authority."

"Tell him to move faster."

Thirty yards farther is another twelve-by-twelve-foot space, this one enclosed in glass walls. Standing inside under more tracked studio lighting is Ken Grant. His suit and hair are perfect. Samantha recognizes the evening news anchor for UBS-24. His makeup is more obvious in person.

They're taking a reporter hit from outside the studio and Ken Grant and Mueller exchange a nod. Mueller gives a thumbs-up and keeps walking through the pods of newsmen and women who are chasing information. In thirty yards more they reach the back wall of the newsroom and a set of doors. Mueller turns left then opens the door marked Control 4.

The hypnotic mix of the thousand noises in the newsroom behind her is cut by a single, violent voice from inside the control room. "Get that feed back now! We're taking her remote in thirty seconds!"

Samantha and Mueller enter and close the door behind them. Everyone senses Mueller has come in but goes about their work. The far wall is covered by a grid of 10" television screens, many showing live footage they can pull into the broadcast, others showing the broadcasts of competing networks. One screen is larger than the others and shows Ken Grant in the live chest-up shot that the rest of the world can see. In front of the wall of screens are three rows of six people each, seated elbow to elbow in front of computers and phones. Standing behind them all is the man who screamed and Mueller moves beside him.

The man leans down into the desk in front of him, presses a button then speaks into his headset. "Ken, in thirty we're going to Pam Roberts in Staten Island with an eyewitness to the splashdown." He uses an unnatural voice of forced calm.

He turns to Mueller and Samantha and nods. He looks about forty with short hair and ears so tight to the side of his head you can't see them when he looks straight at you.

Everyone talks in a hushed voice except this man. The room is lit only by screens. It is dim and closed like a submarine.

Mueller steps forward to a seated woman who just put down her phone. He taps her shoulder. "Get someone from Airbus and someone from Air France to come on with Ken. If Airbus won't come on, then get someone from Boeing and tell Airbus that's what we're going to do if they don't give us someone. It was an Airbus craft that went down so this is their chance to get their narrative out. May not go as well for them if it's Boeing doing the talking. And get someone from Homeland Security to cover the terrorist angle."

The woman has the phone back to her ear and nods yes.

"Where is Pam Roberts?" yells the man.

"Trouble with the feed. We need another minute," says a small but efficient voice.

"Shit!" Bodies shift in front of the voice as though shoved. He leans down to the same button then says, "Ken, I need a minute. Stretch."

The only screen with audio on in the room is Ken's and he starts a new thread that appears a natural transition.

"Typically in this sort of craft, the pilots will transfer control to the autopilot at four hundred feet, so at the altitude and distance traveled at the time of failure, the plane could easily have been on autopilot. Boeing and Airbus differ in philosophies regarding piloting and aircraft controls design. Boeing favors more pilot involvement. When the autopilot adjusts engine thrust, or speed, the manual controls on a Boeing craft will move while Airbus bypasses all manual controls." Ken Grant continues about cockpit design.

"Jesus Christ, get me Roberts. Grant can only do so much. We're losing eyeballs."

"Pam's good." The TV monitor marked REM 3 beneath it now shows an attractive black woman with a middle-aged white man in a flannel shirt by the Staten Island coast.

He leans in. "Ken, we have Pam."

Less than a second later. "Right now we're going to our own Pam Roberts in Staten Island, who is with an eyewitness to this tragedy. Pam?"

"Thank you, Ken. I'm here with Al Moses, who is a roofer in Staten Island." The broadcast TV that had shown Ken now shows the picture from REM 3. One of the smaller screens on the wall shows the same image of Ken Grant, who is now reading papers and glancing at a live screen shot of Pam Roberts in front of him. "Mr. Moses, you were on a roof when Air France Flight 477 flew overhead."

"That's right. I've been doing the roof of this oceanfront home the last week. Three-story home and beautiful vistas. Beautiful." Every viewer has their first experience with the word *vistas* in a Staten Island accent. "Sometimes I take a moment up here to watch things like birds and planes. Just for a moment, you know, but this one I watched the whole way 'cause I noticed it was at this funny angle, like." He raises his forearm with his fingers straight and pointed up. "The nose of the plane was up the whole way, like it wanted to climb but wasn't climbing much, just sort of plowing through the air."

"Did you see it hit the water?"

"Oh my God, I did. It slammed right down in the water, right out there."

"What did you see?"

"It wasn't much of a landing. No disrespect. It just fell out of the sky. Normally, you land a plane, you're moving forward faster than down. This thing was moving down more than forward."

"Could you hear the impact?"

"Nah. Probably too much noise around here what with the beach and waves breaking and all. I could make out the white water kick up when it landed."

"Could you see anything else? Flotation devices that released?"

"Nah. Once the white water settled down, it was just flat horizon from this far away. Couldn't see nothing more then."

She turns back to the camera. "Ken, back to you."

"Pam Roberts in Staten Island. Thank you, Pam."

While Pam and the eyewitness had been speaking, someone in the control room had started screaming about a statement from Homeland Security. People had gotten into the ear of both Ken and Pam to wrap the interview. Ken reads the written statement for the broadcast that says there is no evidence of terrorism as yet, that the department is investigating and, along with the FBI and NTSB, are headed to the scene to assist local law enforcement.

"Where's Airbus? Where's Air France?" yells the man. Samantha has learned his name is Paul and he is the executive producer for this news hour.

"Paul, I've got a call from the husband of a flight attendant who was on the Air France flight." It's a male voice from one of the rows in the darkness in front of them. "He has a voicemail recording from the flight attendant, recorded as it was going down."

People in the room shout hows and wheres and expletives.

"Verify it," says Paul.

"He says he played it for authorities who are coming to his house. He wants it out to the media to make sure nothing gets buried in the investigation."

"He called us? We need to verify this guy first," says Paul. "Get the roster of the attendants on the flight, see if this guy can match the names. Have the Research Room get a phone listing for the flight attendant. Call the number back and see if the guy answers."

Mueller steps to an available landline on the desk in front of him. "I can get you the roster. Give me three minutes."

"Thank you, Dave. If we put that guy on the air and he starts yelling Ba Ba Booey, I'm going to kill somebody."

Samantha looks around the control room. Half the people are on phones in low voices, lining up experts and eyewitnesses to come on the newscast. The rest are preparing graphics and data for the show, researching information, typing editorial into the prompter to be read by Ken, after Paul has read it over first, though it is mostly just the names of the upcoming guests on the show. There are no scripts for breaking news and the anchor is ad-libbing.

The door behind her is solid metal with no window, so she can't see the newsroom where Ken is seated in the glass box but she can hear him talking about Saint Elmo's fire. "A luminous glow appears in the cockpit. It is generated by an electric field, often due to a thunderstorm or volcanic eruption. Sailors through the centuries have talked about it as an omen of bad luck as it would throw off compass headings."

"Jesus Christ," says Paul. "Get me somebody from Airbus."

All of Samantha's senses are devoted to the absorption of events and none to calculating the passage of time. Then she remembers to tap a text message to the associate lawyer assisting her on the two cases she's currently working. She's a litigator and new partner at Davis Polk. She had budgeted ninety minutes for the interview at UBS and now clears more room on her schedule.

A faxed page is handed to Mueller who hands it to the woman who is speaking with the husband of the attendant. Mueller turns to Paul. "You better screen this guy yourself."

Paul walks around the desk and down the aisle to the woman and takes her phone. He crouches over the paper with the phone to his ear.

Three seconds later he drops the paper from his left hand and raises that arm, clenched fist with extended thumb.

Mueller is standing with arms folded in front of him as though he's surveying it all from a much greater distance, a faraway hill over a battle fought in preindustrial times when no weapon can reach him. "Jesus, this is TV gold." Only Samantha hears him. She looks at him, then back to the room.

The room has a heartbeat. The newspeople are having a different experience than the people to whom they are speaking. Under pressure, there's a shorthand between them, everyone must perform and no mistakes can be made, and it's when they're at their best and love their job the most.

Paul sprints up the short aisle, around the corner, and back to his place. He presses the same button in front of him. "Ken, we have a voice-mail recording from a flight attendant to her husband in the last seconds of the flight while it was going down. Tease the recording, we'll have it in one minute."

Ken responds on air like a nickel in a jukebox. Samantha can't believe how smooth. He emphasizes the husband-wife relationship and their last words on earth.

The production reminds her of the image of a duck on water. On the surface, calm and beautiful while beneath the surface the bony, orange legs are thrashing like mad.

The pace, intensity, the spoken and unspoken teamwork to make a product with instant gratification. Millions of people not only watch it, they depend on it.

Samantha has the feeling people get when they find what they think they're supposed to do. Whether the feeling is real or rationalized, it's the idea that their whole life has been a practice for this calling.

Ken Grant continues. "I must warn you that in a few seconds we will play the recording of a voice message from Sarah Friar, a flight attendant on Air France Flight 477, to her husband, David Friar, in the final seconds of the flight. This recording is tragic and horrifying and you may want to turn down the volume or leave the room."

No viewer will move and Ken knows it. The screen cuts to a photo of Sarah Friar from her Facebook page and the lower third of the screen reads "Final Words of AF 477 Flight Attendant."

David, it's me. If you're there pick up. I want to talk to you. [pause] *Something's wrong here, on the flight. It might be nothing. But it might be bad. I went to deliver coffee to the cockpit. They were . . . confused in there. Some sort of fight, argument. They ordered me out right away and I couldn't tell what they were fighting about. Now the plane is flying funny and I have a bad feeling. We're only a few minutes out but we're over water.*

The recording goes silent for a few seconds.

Oh, God! David, there was a thud. Something banged against the cabin door. I'm on the flight crew phone outside the cockpit. It sounded like a body ran against the cabin door from the inside.

There is a beep as the message ends and a mechanical voice says "Next message."

David, please get this! We're not at altitude but we're standing at sharp angles to the deck. The passengers are starting to realize something is way off.

There is a crack of hard plastic on hard plastic and many voices jump on top of each other but no words can be understood, only that there is fear and distress.

David! [She is yelling now, over yells in the background that are constant and more panicked.] *The plane jolted. We're too low. We're getting . . . I think we're getting lower, it's hard to tell looking out. Mark, can you reach the captain? Try knocking on the door.*

A "No" comes through more clearly than the screams.

David, I love you, I love you, I love you. Kiss our little babies for me. You kiss them, you love them. Take care of them. Help them remember me.

There are seven seconds of quiet. Nothing from Sarah, just the dull screams from the cabin around her. Sometimes a voice rises then falls back into the rest but words are never intelligible. The seven seconds feel much longer than that. There is the sound of a catch of breath near the phone then all noise cuts out. There is no sound of a crash, no explosion. Just silence.

Ken Grant holds the silence. He knows that silence propels the mind of the viewer. Cut off from sensory input, the mind is forced to become metaphorical, to conjure the scene for itself which is more powerful than to be provided the scene. The absence of noise from the television set creates a vacuum, the bodies of the viewers sucked toward the screen and the strange quiet, no longer propped up by Ken's voice.

Ken lets it run on for ten seconds. The control room is silent and unmoving. "David, are you there?"

"I am." The voice is a whisper.

"Thank you for sharing this with us. Our deepest sympathies. This is a terrible tragedy."

No reply.

"How are you holding up?"

"I'm not."

"I want to tell the viewers that you contacted us with this tape. Can you tell our viewers why you did that?"

"I want a full investigation into what happened. I want the media to make sure there is a full and open investigation."

Ken ends the interview.

"My God," says Paul.

"I have a spokesman from Airbus."

The hum returns to the control room and Paul is yelling orders again.

Mueller remembers Samantha is standing next to him. "Let's take a walk."

They exit the metal door and turn right to a conference room with a window out to the newsroom. Mueller opens the door and walks in. There is an oval table that seats eight and Mueller waves her to a chair. She pulls it back from the table to face him. He sits first but not because she waited for him. He raises his arms to say, Look around you.

This is her third interview with UBS News. Mueller is president of the news division and the last hurdle. She reminds herself of all the men in power she's dealt with and impressed as a lawyer. She's handled depositions of Fortune 500 CEOs and litigated cases in front of juries for billion-dollar settlements. She's only thirty-four, but she's been excelling in powerful circles for years already.

She has just told her senior partner that she's considering a move out of the law. He's still mounting an argument as to why a move to journalism is a mistake and waste of her talents. As gifted a litigator as he is, Samantha knows she'll be immune to his protests. She loves the law but hates her life as a lawyer.

"I remember you from *Latch Key* years ago. I was too old for that show but my niece loved it. How old were you then?" asks Mueller.

She was a child actor from the age of eighteen months. First baby commercials, most of the time playing with dolls and toys. Then toddler clothes. At seven years old came her break—Sally, the seven-year-old daughter with attitude to a single, working mother of two daughters on the show *Latch Key*. Samantha had a deep voice that was so incongruous with her little body that the writers of the show used this voice as a tool in most episodes. *Latch Key* ran six seasons in prime time, made her famous, made her money, and made sure she was homeschooled by her real-life mom until she was thirteen, when Samantha insisted on a break from acting to attend an actual school for a while. "I was seven in the first season and it ran for six seasons."

Humans form lasting memories as early as three years old. Samantha didn't have the opportunity to remember getting her SAG membership card. Clearly it wasn't her idea. Nor was it about her at all. It was about the nineteen-year-old girl who was waiting tables in Santa Monica and taking acting lessons who had given birth to Samantha and who then had the idea that her baby could be a child actor when she saw what a pretty face her baby had. And the nineteen-year-old former waitress turned stage mom was right. With enough force and will and compulsion, she was right.

When Samantha was a child, her face was rounder and people called her very cute. In her last seasons of *Latch Key* her bones started to show up as the flesh melted away. Bones in her cheeks and jaw made her face seem longer and less girly, bones in her shoulders and hips pushed aside her youth and prepared for the transition from child actor to real actor. Her mother controlled her exercise and her nutrition, brought in a special breakfast, lunch, and dinner, and Samantha ate with her mother by the set and not the other actors so that her mother could critique the acting skills and weight gain of the others.

Her mother didn't complain about the bulimia in her twelve-year-old daughter until Samantha's weight dropped below what was attractive on screen and the show's director asked if Samantha was sick. But by that point the disease was caught. The years of psychological damage had taken hold. Her mother could find equal success in mentioning to a person with diarrhea that he ought not to crap so much.

"Any acting after that?"

"Just some smaller stuff, commercials mostly. By the time you become a teenager, you need to decide whether or not you're all in. I wasn't." Samantha takes a breath. She didn't expect to be nervous for this interview.

By seventeen, Samantha had left acting and gone to college. From college it was law school. Three more years to prove she was more than a child actor. With each year, her relationship with her mother was more estranged.

Her first seventeen years in acting were about her mother. The next seventeen years in law were a reaction to her mother. This is her first choice driven neither by her mother nor by the damage her mother inflicted.

"Columbia Law. Impressive." Mueller smiles. "Partner at Davis Polk?" She nods.

He leans back in his chair, interlocks his fingers, and rests his joined hands on his belly. "Samantha, why are you here?"

She knew this was coming. Lots of lawyers turn to journalism but most don't turn their backs on a successful law career in order to take an entry-level news job. But this question had been asked and answered by herself. "I want this job and I'll be great at it."

"You're a partner at Davis Polk. You're probably making a million bucks a year. In a few years, maybe two million. For a first-year news correspondent at UBS, I can maybe pay you six figures, barely. And that's if I think we're going to use you a lot." He pauses. "That's a big salary change. How are you going to pay your bills?"

"I'll manage." She has no family money, modest savings since she only just made partner, and a mortgage on a new apartment that is too big for a hundred-thousand-dollar salary. "Let me worry about that. All I'm asking is that you make a bet on me. A small bet."

"I've seen your tape," says Mueller. With TV broadcasting, it doesn't matter much where a person's degree is from. It's the resume tape.

Samantha paid a thousand bucks to a cameraman who is an old friend from L.A. to shoot her doing a fake news story. She scripted a hurricane disaster site and got herself in the mode of delivering closing arguments and appealed to the viewers of her tape to relate to the plight of the victims in the way she would appeal to the jury to award damages. "I'd appreciate your advice. What did you think?"

"It's rough as hell but there's something there." Mueller knew after watching it the first time that he wanted to hire her. She has that intangible star quality. You never know what makes it come across. You just know it when you see it.

He wants her and he'll pay more than a hundred grand if he has to. His mind was made up by the end of the initial handshake, as it is in all his interviews.

Mueller's manner changes as his internal timer for the meeting has gone off. "Anything else?"

"No, thank you. If I have any questions I'll email your assistant."

"Great." He stands and they shake hands. "I'll walk you out of the newsroom." He leads her through the hive and to the security guards.

"Thank you." They have another handshake which is an awkward one because neither feels it is necessary or is sure it will happen until Samantha decides it will just be easier to get it over with and she sticks her hand out.

He walks back toward the control room.

She takes the escalator back up to ground level and steps outside into the heavy, wet July air. She decides she wants a drink to celebrate and contemplate whatever the hell just happened in there. Whether it leads to a job or not, it was a moment. It was a step toward change. Real change to make her life happy again.

Heavy drinking is the one thing about a lawyer's life that sits well with her. As is too often the case, it will be drinks alone. Sometimes to blow off steam or after a good verdict she'll get drinks with the legal team. But if it's something personal to celebrate, she has no one to go to.

I want this job, she thinks. Litigation to broadcast journalism is a proven path. If it isn't UBS, it'll be someplace else. I won't stop.

She cabs to the Time Warner building, walks past the statue of the fat man and up the escalator to Stone Rose. It's 4:30 p.m.

A waiter comes right over wearing a starched white button-down shirt and black pants. He's deciding whether or not to flirt.

"Vodka martini up, slightly dirty."

He nods. He decides to hold off on flirting until he has a better read.

Samantha's cell phone rings. It's Robin Paris, her friend and college roommate. "Sam, if I didn't call you we'd never speak."

Samantha laughs. This is not said with judgment, just an observation. "I swear I've been meaning to call you."

"Thank God one of us is a pampered housewife," says Robin.

"I knew I chose the wrong major."

"Did you get the job?"

Samantha says, "I don't know yet. He seemed to like me but it wasn't much of an interview because they were busy covering the plane crash. It was more like an introduction to the news business and he was challenging me to like it."

"What's next? Another interview?"

Samantha says, "There's no one left to meet. He's the one who decides. Now either I get it or I don't." She sips her martini, drawing the vodka up from the glass more than pouring it past her lips.

"You'll get it, Sam. You'll be the smartest, prettiest badass lawyer on TV." Robin is the only daughter of a wealthy Boston family and she went to Andover, so admission to Harvard was not as significant as a rejection from Harvard would have been. She married a childhood friend and managing director at Goldman Sachs. She's the rare person who's taken advantage of an easy draw in life to be a happy person and not expect even more of the world.

"I may not get this one, but I'll get something."

"When are you giving your notice at the law firm?"

"Tomorrow. I'm sad but certain about it," says Samantha.

"Good, Sam. We get one go-around on the planet. Don't spend it filing legal briefs." Robin plays tennis, goes to lunch, shops, manages two nannies for her two kids, and has the time to be a considerate friend. She carries the bigger part of the burden for nurturing the friendship and does it without real complaint because she loves Samantha. They have a curiosity for each other. There is the unusual combination of a separation of their lives mixed with institutional knowledge of each other's lives that makes them perfect confidants.

Call waiting beeps on Samantha's phone. She holds the phone back to look in case there's an emergency legal filing required of her at Davis Polk, which is probable. The caller ID says unknown.

"Robin, I need to take this. I'll call you later." She presses to hang up and accept the incoming call. "Samantha Davis."

"Samantha, it's David Mueller."

"David, hi." She pauses while her brain runs scenarios of why he could be calling and prepares her answers. Legal training. "Nice to hear from you."

"Well, Ms. Davis. Do you always get what you want?"

"It feels like never, but that may be a neurosis of mine."

"I'm calling to offer you a job." Mueller knew he was going to hire her. He just wanted a few minutes to decide on the salary and terms. "It's a three-year deal. One fifty year one, one seventy-five year two, two twenty-five year three. General assignment news reporter based in New York." Mueller had upped his number because he wants to put a condition on it. He knows there are still people smart enough at his competitors to hire her if they see the resume tape. "One more thing. I need to fill this spot, so you have forty-eight hours to accept."

"Okay." She decided earlier that she would take any offer without pushing a negotiation on terms. Now that she has an offer, her instinct to drive a better deal is kicking in. She knows she'll be a success. She can push either for more money or fewer years. "Is the three-year commitment negotiable?"

"We like three-year deals." He pauses. "You don't have an agent."

"No."

"Friendly piece of advice. Get one."

I tried, she almost says and doesn't.

"I've got a forty-eight-hour window for you, so it won't matter for this deal, but you should get one soon. He'll tell you that three years is standard." He continues. "Today was a plane crash. That's newsworthy but not consistent. The only consistent news we do is politics. Are you political?"

"Not really."

"Bone up. Get steeped in the news, especially politics. I'll email you a few websites that you should read every day, and watch cable prime time. Bounce between channels and start with ours."

"Got it."

"Alright."

"David, I appreciate the call. Can I call you at close of business tomorrow?"

"Sure. One more thing I want you to think about. This is UBS News. You can work packages for the network morning show and for the network evening news. No show has bigger ratings. Bigger exposure. Nobody. I also have UBS-24. Twenty-four-hour cable news where you can do legal, political, and general news reporting. There's a lot of real estate to cover here. Nobody has more real estate than I do. That kind of opportunity for growth and exposure is an important thing for you to think about as you start your career in this business."

He's selling me! I can't believe this, she thinks. "I appreciate that, David. I also appreciate the opportunity."

"Talk to you tomorrow, Samantha." He hangs up.

"I got the job," she says to her martini.

2

"Samantha, it's Megan Ruiz from booking." Samantha has met Megan in person twice now and likes her. When meeting other female on-air talent, she always gets an up-and-down from them the way she would from a drunk guy in a bar. Whether it's from a place of competition or benign curiosity, it's second nature to them. Megan isn't that way. She doesn't preoccupy herself with things other than getting the bookings done. She seems like a nice, hardworking person.

"How are you?"

"Good, thanks." She seems rushed, which she is. "*Sunrise America* wants to use you for a piece tomorrow. Their booker asked me to get in touch with you. A Bronx couple won the largest lottery payout ever, over one point two billion. We're going to roll a truck for you in an hour to do a pretape with them to air tomorrow at seven forty-five a.m. You need to be back on location tomorrow morning to intro the package and do some banter with Mike."

"Great. Tell me where to go."

"Stop by hair and makeup in studio if you want. You should have time. One of the show producers will get you and take you out."

"Okay, thanks."

"Samantha."

"Yes?"

"You're doing good work. You're impressing people and they want to use you. That's a good sign for you. A package for the network morning show is a big deal."

"Thanks, Megan." I love compliments from other women, she thinks.

An hour later she's in a truck with six other people heading to the Bronx. She doesn't even know what they all do. The *Sunrise America* staff is huge, more than a hundred people.

She learns one of the guys is a writer for the show and he's giving her the story background. A retired mailman and his wife living in the Bronx claimed the single winning ticket for the $1.2 billion lottery three hours ago, making them the largest single-ticket lottery winners ever. They're active in the local church, have one son and one grandson.

"Yellow Ledbetter" by Pearl Jam comes on the radio and the driver turns up the volume. "Pearl Jam rules."

Samantha laughs and says, "Don't say anything rules. You sound stoned or twelve years old. And anyway, they don't rule."

"Then they dominate." He smiles. He balances cocky and unoffensive.

"Don't tell me you're one of those surfer geeks who feels an obligation to love Pearl Jam. You realize how ridiculous that is?"

"Okay, old lady. Who's bigger, Pearl Jam or the Who?"

"The Who, by far."

"Wrong. Please. I can tune my Sirius Satellite Radio to a Pearl Jam channel," he says. "Can I do that with the Who? I don't think so. Case closed, Your Honor."

Samantha's enjoying this. "You can't go by that."

"Why not?"

"Because the passage of time and taste matters. To Sirius, that matters."

"So what?"

"There's no Beethoven channel either. Anyone bigger than Beethoven? In his day. The Who was doing comeback tours in the eighties. Pearl Jam is still out touring with a following that tunes in to Sirius. You can't compare."

"Elvis has a channel. He's dead."

"I will stipulate that Elvis is bigger than the Who."

"There's no arguing with lawyers."

The van pulls up to a six-story white brick apartment building just as a GBS News van is pulling up across the street. It will be a race to get to the story first.

"How fast can you parallel park this thing, Ron?" the writer calls up to the driver.

"Screw that," says Samantha and she opens the sliding side door while the van is still rolling. Ron hits the brakes and they come to a full stop. Samantha steps out onto the pavement and turns back and points in the van at the person she thinks is the cameraman. "Come with me. What's the apartment number?"

"Four G," someone yells from inside the van.

"The rest of you meet us there." Samantha looks at the GBS van and sees faces pressed to the side windows like kids at an aquarium. She and Alex, who is in fact the cameraman, jog into the lobby of the apartment building. "Stairs!" she yells.

Alex takes this like a jolt of adrenaline. He's no longer taping a package for a morning show, he's deployed to a forward position. He moves ahead taking stairs three at a time with only one thing in mind. Get to 4G first.

The elevation of the heels on Samantha's shoes won't allow her to take more than two steps at a time. As she rounds the third-floor landing she hears a knock on a door above her. As she makes the fourth-floor landing she hears the clamor of dropped equipment and shouting from the lobby below. Her team and GBS arrived to the lobby at the same time. She imagines a dozen people bouncing off each other and pulling each other back as they go up the stairs like football players after a fumble.

She looks down the hall in time to see the door of 4G swing open, and her colleague bends an arm to her like a waiter presenting wine. "This is Samantha Davis with UBS."

A little, round, gray-haired man in a cardigan sweater and slacks is at the door with an arm around his wife's waist, who is of matching shortness. They both look to be early seventies. Her hair is nicely combed in a short perm and she's wearing a pink blouse. It's clearly her best and has been for twenty years. "A pleasure to meet you," Samantha says during an exhale that she can't yet control.

"Come in, come in!" says the man. He's beaming. He's in the middle of a life-changing moment and a steady state of elation.

"I'm Alex Pierce," says Samantha's colleague, and they walk in and the man closes the door.

"I'm Ned Prince. My wife, Frankie."

Ned shuffles them into the living room where there's an emerald-green felt sofa with three seat cushions and a matching one with two. "You two take the big one," he says.

It's an old person's home. There could be more natural light than there is but for the blinds and the heavy green curtains that match the sofa and are far older than Frankie's pink blouse. There's no art on the walls but some old photographs and a few patterned plates with wire mounts. There are some table lamps that are too large for the tables they're on and a few limp potted houseplants that sell for $2.99 at Walmart. The whole thing is cute, thinks Samantha, though nobody under seventy would live this way.

As they sit, there is a knock at the door that is more urgent than it needs to be.

"Excuse me," says Ned, and he walks back to the door.

He opens the door and about a dozen people push through, knocking Ned on his heels and to the side while they stream past him.

Samantha stands. "We're in the middle of an interview."

Samantha's producer Ron turns to one of the GBSers. "You guys need to get in the hall until we're through."

"We're on a timeline. You guys go ahead. I'll stay and the rest of my team will go to the hall while I set up for our shot for when you're done."

This seems to be a producer-to-producer discussion. Ron doesn't like the idea of this guy sticking around but says, "Fine. Get the rest of your team out."

All of GBS but one leave while Ron and his team set up. Samantha takes the interview on a journey from the Prince family's humble roots to the plans they have to stay in the community and put the money to good use. She learns that not only was Ned a mailman, but their son is a mailman and their grandson was a mailman for Halloween last year.

"Do you have a picture?" asks Samantha. This will go over great in the package, she thinks.

"I'm sure we do," says Frankie, and she disappears to the next room. The UBS team working on the shoot doesn't notice the GBS producer follow Frankie out.

Ten minutes later Samantha starts to wrap up the interview. They have plenty of good material for a ninety-second package. Frankie has been back on the two-seater for several minutes and Samantha asks her, "Were you able to find a Halloween photo?"

"Oh, yes. I gave it to that gentleman there." She points to the GBS producer who looks nailed to the floor.

Samantha stands and walks to him with her hand out.

He takes it from his shirt breast pocket and gives it to her though his expression is defiant rather than embarrassed, as though she should know he had to try it and it was a good effort and she should respect that.

"Asshole," she says loud enough only for him.

Back at the van, Ron helps Samantha step up through the sliding door. She appreciates the gesture and notes that he hadn't done it on the way over. "You did a great job in there," he says, and he holds eye contact and nods, trying to make sure she knows he's not just saying this but really thinks it.

"Thank you. That GBS crew is such a bunch of assholes."

"It's not just that crew. That's GBS. That's how they are. You know how some basketball coaches will teach their players to step on a guy's shoe when they're on the free-throw line going for a rebound? It's dirty. That's how they coach them at GBS from the top down. That's why they're a culture of assholes. I know people who weren't assholes when they started working there but they're assholes now."

"What do people say about UBS?"

Ron laughs. "Not as bad as GBS but none of the networks has a reputation for kindness and goodwill. It's a tough industry all the way around." She's seated now and he's about to slide the door closed. "Try to find somebody who's honest and not in the industry and make a deal with them to let you know if you're ever becoming an asshole. So far, I can tell you you're not." He smiles and closes the door.

The next morning Samantha is back outside the apartment building and ready for her live shot. She's with a smaller team this time. A producer, one cameraman instead of two. She's already been to the studio for the full hair and makeup treatment.

The line producer from back in the studio says through her earpiece, "Thirty seconds!"

Live TV is different from her childhood work. She's about to go live on the biggest show in the country and she doesn't know the names of the people around her. She misses her mother. An impossible feeling but she's having it. Her mother always made sure her makeup was good and they did her hair in the right way, that the lighting and camera angle were how they should be, that she had rehearsed her lines. Her mother was her team, doing all the blocking and tackling. Whatever the dysfunction, Samantha used to have someone protecting her, telling her she had talent and just had to let it shine.

Most child actors can't transition to real actors because at some point they become conscious of what they're doing. At seven years old an actor isn't trying to make it work. He just goes out on the set and it either works or it doesn't. It's unconscious. Soon an actor needs to treat acting like a craft and hone his talent. Many discover they never had any talent, they were just great at being unconscious.

She hears Mike Lord laugh at one of his own jokes then introduce the segment about the massive lottery winners in the Bronx. "Samantha Davis is in the Bronx this morning to tell us about it. Samantha?"

She sees the red light on the camera. She's live. On *Sunrise America*. Holy shit, don't freak out. "Good morning, Mike. I'm outside the Bronx apartment of Ned and Frankie Prince. Ned, a retired Bronx mailman, and Frankie, his wife of forty-seven years, have big plans for this local community and their new fortune."

The program cuts to the pretape package. The cameraman signals they're off. "You're back in sixty seconds."

Samantha waits for red. It pops on and she hears Mike Lord, "Wow, one point two billion. My lord. Samantha, what would you do if one point two billion dollars landed in your lap today?"

Without thinking she says, "Obviously, I would start with world peace, then I'd cure the common cold. If there's anything left over, I'd buy a private island and a case of rum and you'd never see me again."

Mike laughs. It sounds like a real laugh that he's trying to stop so he can say something else. They're having a TV moment. It's a mini one, but this is the kind of thing that makes highlight reels and careers. "Well, that sounds great. You better save a little for a bathing suit. I'm sure you'll want that on your island."

"I said it's a private island!"

"Well, this is a family show, but even so, I'm going to say that sounds like my kind of place. Thank you, Samantha. Reporting from the Bronx."

The red light goes out. Wrap.

Back in the studio, they cut to commercial and the executive producer explodes down the open mic, "That woman is dynamite!"

This goes into Mike's ear but he doesn't respond other than to nod and say, "Book her on something tomorrow."

The female coanchor and female newsreader are both watching Mike. Neither thinks this is good news.

Samantha can feel that she is being developed and knows that it is Ken Harper who believes in her. Harper runs all political coverage for UBS and has been putting Samantha on more political stories. Now he's introduced her to the network morning viewers. He's letting the UBS audience get to know her.

Ken Harper reports directly to David Mueller. He's more slick in appearance than Mueller. His hair is gelled and combed, his suit is pressed, and he makes an effort through the day to keep it all looking that way. He looks more like a PR guy. He has a constant busy energy that seems manic to people that don't know him well, and a high voice that sounds strained even when he isn't straining it.

Harper had called a meeting with Samantha three months earlier, where he had said, "Samantha, I'm going to give you two pieces of advice." He raised his eyebrows and cocked his head to one side to make sure she understood he was about to deliver a gift. "Number one, it really is about hustling when you're not on the air. Develop relationships. Politics gets a lot of coverage, so pick politics. Meet with senators, governors, political advisors, lobbyists, pollsters. You name it, take them out to coffee. Get to know them, and eventually you might get access to something worth putting on the air. Over time, those relationships will be important. You're an attractive reporter at UBS. Most of those people I just mentioned are men. They'll meet with you. They may not say much at first, but they'll meet with you."

"Okay."

"Number two, find a big story and stay on it. Dig in, be relentless, be the network's expert on it and we'll use you across the network."

This made sense but Samantha wasn't sure how to put it into practice. "Do you have an example?"

"Yes. O. J. Simpson. Several anchors made their bones on that story. They were small fries, but all they did was eat, sleep, and breathe O. J. When a network covered O. J., they went to their expert reporter. And every network covered O. J. wall to wall. By the time that case was over, stars were born."

Samantha nodded. Again, it made sense, but not something she could get started on right off.

"Look, O. J. was a once-in-a-generation sensation, but there are smaller events that resonate with mass viewership, and you need to be able to see which ones will do it. Look for the key elements. Celebrity, death, class warfare, social or racial injustice. When you see it, get on it. I'll support you."

The last sentence was the one Samantha wanted to hear. The advice was terrific and she took it. Just as important was getting to the front of Ken's mind and letting him know she was ready for more, but without pestering him and getting labeled a pain in the ass. Time to get out of bounds, she thought. He had a lot of people asking him for air time. "Ken, thank you. I appreciate the advice, and believe me, nobody in this building is going to outwork me."

"I believe you."

Samantha stood to go.

Ken liked her more than he'd expected to. He also liked to have the last word in meetings and he had another observation to share anyway. "Samantha. One more, and this really is the last thing, then you can go."

"Sure."

"I see a lot of lawyers make the jump to TV and most of them suck."

"Okay."

"Now, how you carry yourself on TV is more Mueller's area. I'm editorial, but I'll tell you why I think it is that most of these lawyers tend to suck."

She nodded.

"Lawyers are trained not to make mistakes. Especially a fancy lawyer like you from Davis Polk. You have to be perfect. You can't embrace your mistakes and you certainly can't laugh them off."

"That's true."

"But here, that's exactly what you need to do. Nobody's perfect. A fact of life. Be human on the air and cop to your mistakes. That's relatable. If you go on air trying to act like little Miss Perfect, viewers will smell a phony and they won't like you. Viewers like authentic and they know it when they see it. And when they don't."

Samantha nodded again.

"That's the trouble with most of these lawyers. They're not authentic. Too worried about mistakes."

Samantha was concerned this was meant entirely for her and Ken saw that in her face.

"You're better than most in this area. You seem naturally fun, so run with that." He paused. "Okay, that's it from me."

Samantha walked to the elevator digesting all the information from Ken. She thought how much easier it is to get advice when you're on your way up.

The week following the *Sunrise America* piece Samantha is at the Delta Shuttle terminal at LaGuardia on her way to DC to meet with Republican congressman Tom Cone from Florida. She's trying to build her contacts and finding that people are increasingly willing to take a meeting. By lunchtime after her first *Sunrise America* hit she had voicemails from four agents asking to represent her, including one from CAA.

With Cone, she's planning to talk about president-elect Mitchell Mason and how the Republicans view the upcoming four years of a Democratic White House.

She clears security and walks toward the gate. "Samantha!" She turns to see a man in a suit waiting at a gate for a flight to Boston. He's about her age and okay-looking. "Samantha!" He yells and waves.

She changes her direction to head toward him and tries to place him, hoping she can do it before they're face-to-face. "Hi!" she calls ahead.

He looks confused and stops waving. She thinks, He has my name right. It would be too much of a coincidence if I'm not the person he thinks I am. Who the hell is he?

"Hi," she says again. "How are you?" They're close enough to shake hands now but he doesn't move. "I'm sorry, what's your name again?"

"Mark," he says, but all his enthusiasm is gone. He's flat and nervous.

Mark, she thinks, but comes up empty. "Mark," she says out loud. "I'm sorry," and she smiles with her eyes squinted in frustrated apology.

"I'm a big fan," he says. He clearly didn't expect her to come this close and now seems regretful.

"Thank you," she says, now more embarrassed than Mark. Jesus, she thinks. Things are changing.

TOM PAULEY

3

Tom Pauley walks down the steps of the Durham County Courthouse. There are only eight steps. It's nothing like the scenes from *Law & Order* where the ADA walks past marble columns down dozens of gorgeous marble steps into a swarm of media, police, and other lawyers.

But for the first time ever for Tom Pauley, there is a media scrum waiting for him at the bottom of the eight steps. National media, and there's a smile on his face that is beyond his ability to influence. It is happiness and pride beaming through an otherwise modest and subdued countenance.

People draw conclusions from faces whether they know it or not—even if they try to avoid doing so, it happens. Pauley is aware of physiognomy but has never been concerned with trying to manipulate it to his advantage. People happy in their own skin never do. They just go about their lives and trust that people will see them for who they are because they've never tried to be anything else.

Tom Pauley has a handsome and boyish face for forty-three years. People who smile a lot seem to age better. He's six two, which makes him more universally likable at first meeting. Many have an impression that a short person will have an edge and that a very large one will be stupid.

People have always been drawn to Tom Pauley. Kids and animals love him. Juries love him. And he takes it all in stride, which makes them love him more.

His wife emerges through the line of reporters and cameramen, and her knees pump to lift her the few steps up and into his arms. Her smile matches his and they kiss. The cameras catch the moment, then the questions start.

"Mr. Pauley, were you surprised at how quickly the jury returned a verdict?"

"No. Over the course of the trial we made it very clear my clients are innocent. Fortunately, the jury was paying attention. They did their job."

"What did your clients say to you when they heard they are free to go?"

"They said thank you and God bless you. I wished them luck now that they have their lives back."

"What will your clients do now?"

"They'll probably talk to an anchor at one of your networks. You should pay them well for that. Then they'll go back to their families, to school, to their lives."

Tom Pauley thinks it is gracious of the Reverend Don Whiskers to give him the initial time with media alone. It isn't Reverend Don's usual method but Tom and Don have become friends over the previous few months, at first out of necessity, then genuine mutual respect. Don knows what a caricature he's made of himself but he's a genius in his way and he gets results.

Terence and Todd Darby had been picked up by police in downtown Durham, two miles from a home invasion, rape, and quadruple homicide. In the shoddiest law enforcement work since the Duke lacrosse rape case, the state charged the sixteen- and eighteen-year-old brothers with the crime.

When inconsistencies in the prosecution's case first emerged, the Durham DA managed to keep it out of the media, but Tom Pauley heard about it and took the case pro bono. With his reputation came local media. Within twenty-four hours of his taking the case, Tom's office had a call from the Reverend Don who had just landed at the Raleigh-Durham International Airport.

Watching the reverend at work was impressive. He didn't just fly in, get in front of a camera and wing it. He met with the family, the lawyers, the local politicians and made sure there was good camera footage of everything for the media to access. He determined what was the essence of the offense to the black community and articulated it in a way that could be repeated in a sound bite. He called his contacts in national media outlets, the Black Panthers, religious organizations, civil rights organizations. All of this was done in stepwise fashion like following a baking recipe. The people around Reverend Don know his system and go about their work quietly. He's the only one making noise.

The reverend's work was all to the benefit of Tom's clients, so Tom cooperated with him. The evening of Don's arrival in Durham, stories about the case ran on GEAR, CNN, UBS-24, and Headline News. The following morning, *Mornings* and *Sunrise America*. Nancy Grace devoted all or some of her show to the case for seven straight weeks. Reverend Don has his critics, but he knows how to bring a national spotlight to the issues he cares about.

"What's next for you, Mr. Pauley?"

"I'm going back to being a private citizen. No more peanut gallery lawyers critiquing my work on the evening news." He says this with a smile. He's had a decent relationship with the peanut gallery and given them access when it advanced his cause, and all the news coverage hasn't bothered Tom. He knows it's part of the job on a high-profile case, and his job he takes seriously. Himself he does not, and it helps to be humble in his business. Sometimes he needs to act like a hard-ass but for him it is only an act. When he was eight years old, his middle-class family went through a trauma that pushed them into poverty. Specific memories are mostly faded but the period formed his approach to life. As long as his family is safe and provided for, there isn't much that can rile or scare him. He's irreverent. Everyone has irreverent thoughts, but not everyone expresses them. For Tom, as long as it's away from the courtroom, it's fair game. He already has an arm around his wife's shoulders and he pulls her in tighter. "Alison and I are going to have dinner together tonight. We have a five-year-old boy, Patrick, and a three-year-old girl, Olivia. I haven't seen as much of them as I would like lately, so I'm going to focus on family time." He looks at his wife. "What's that train set we just got for the kids?"

"Thomas the Tank Engine."

"Right. We're going to play with Thomas. And I think I saw a box for a Barbie Hybrid Cadillac."

The media laugh and Reverend Don appears at Tom's side. He gives Tom and Alison a hug, then takes several steps to the side away from them. He wants the cameras to have a clear solo shot. The shift in media focus is immediate, like a torpedo acquiring a new target.

The reverend speaks. "I have just prayed with the Darby family. We prayed for the victims and their relatives. We prayed for this community. We prayed for God's healing hand to come down and touch our lives, that a lesson can be learned here today."

Tom thinks how different it is to listen to Don over lunch and to listen to him now. It's the same rhetoric, but here he performs it. Don would have made a hell of a litigator. "Let's slip out of here," says Tom to his wife. "I have a meeting at the Washington Duke and Donnie looks like he can go another thirty minutes."

With minor fanfare, Tom and Alison get to her BMW sedan where they kiss again and Tom opens the door for her. Alison drives home and Tom walks to his Chevy Suburban to drive to his meeting.

It's a brand-new car and enormous. It gets ten miles to the gallon in city driving, thinks Tom. Money isn't a problem, though. Tom doesn't get paid in the Darby case, but he'll make out okay from all the good press. He started a general litigation practice, and he rarely does criminal defense. He's usually suing someone for millions.

Those poor saps from the top law schools who go to big New York firms, thinks Tom. They slave the decades away. Being partner at a big firm sounds fine but in the best years they make a million or two. Nobody gets silly rich that way. The only way to make big money as a lawyer is to be a plaintiffs' attorney. A good one. Win a hundred-million-dollar lawsuit, earn thirty percent, lather-rinse-repeat. John Edwards got very rich doing that.

Tom didn't get into law for that reason, though. He got into law for cases just like Terence and Todd Darby. He was just very effective, though, and now at forty-three is making as much as the partners in the fancy firms. In a few years he'll be making more. He had started out with Davis Polk in New York for the first seven years of his career, so he appreciates how much better he has it now.

The Washington Duke is one of the nicest hotels in Durham and is on the edge of the Duke University campus. As long as it isn't a reunion weekend there are usually rooms available but the place always does a nice business because it has a great golf course, a good restaurant and bar.

Tom has a meeting scheduled with Benson Hill, who is affiliated with the Republican Party of North Carolina. He's a bundler. He rounds up money from wealthy North Carolinians to contribute to Republican presidential candidates and he also helps the state GOP candidates.

Tom thinks his numerous TV appearances with the left-leaning Reverend Whiskers would throw people off the scent, but it's easy enough to see with a web search that he's contributed money to the GOP presidential candidate in each of the last four elections. Benson wants my money, he thinks, but these kinds of connections can't hurt.

Tom pulls onto Cameron Boulevard. The Duke campus is on his right and he makes a left into the parking lot of the inn. "Jesus," Tom says out loud. If this guy picked the Washington Duke, he must be a Duke fan.

People in North Carolina support either Duke basketball or UNC basketball. Everyone's a fan and everyone takes a side. Eighty percent of the state are for UNC. Tom went to undergrad and law school at UNC, so he's more than a casual fan. Tom has friends who are Duke fans, but he can't stand to be near them during the season. All those asinine cheers and fight songs.

Tom steers around the circular drive up to the front of the inn and valets the car. He walks through the lobby which he thinks is full of too much Duke crap, then into the Bull Durham Lounge.

On the left is a long bar made of dark wood. To the right are windows overlooking the golf course. The far wall is mostly a massive fireplace that is not lit. The carpet is dark blue and throughout the room are small round bar tables with bowls of nuts and leather chairs that are wide and look heavy.

A burly, balding man who looks like a drinker gets up from a chair by the fire. He moves with athleticism as though his gut is something he just carries around for exercise.

He makes for Tom Pauley and starts his handshake from behind his ear, something Tom noticed Obama always used to do that he found annoying and dramatic. The man swings his hand around like throwing a football and clasps where Tom has simply put his hand out.

He seems like the kind of guy who greets all his friends by slapping their backs and calling them old sons of bitches. He says, "Benson Hill. How the hell are you? Your mug looks just like it does on TV. A pleasure to meet you."

"Nice to meet you, Benson." Tom decides he likes him already. He likes people who are characters, people who put themselves out there.

"Congratulations on the Darby case. Big win."

"Thank you. Sometimes the system works."

"Good for you. Good for you. Drink?"

"Gin and tonic."

"Good man, good man."

Benson orders with a waiter and they drag two leather chairs closer together by the fire.

"You really poured yourself into their defense. All pro bono."

"Yes."

"You're a real servant of the people."

"It feels good to do good." Tom toasts the air and drinks. "Somebody said that."

"Right. Tom, I'll tell you a bit about me, then I'd like to learn a bit more about you. Is that okay?"

"Sure."

"You know who I am?"

"You're with the Republican Party of North Carolina."

"Correct."

"Exactly what is the Republican Party of North Carolina? Besides just you."

"It's not even me, really. I'm just a rich guy. Full-time, permanent staff in an off-election year? Maybe four people. The chairman and a few people answering phones. It's just a place to receive fund-raising. In election years it balloons to twenty full-timers or so. We're like a traveling circus. After the show we fold up tents and everyone disperses."

"I see."

"My day job though is dry cleaning. I have thirty locations throughout the Research Triangle Park area. This is the last bastion of non-Korean dry cleaners on the planet." He laughs and his belly moves like a kid shifting in a sleeping bag. "Dry cleaning is a very scalable business. Any businessman trying to grow is going to be Republican."

Tom nods. He lines up mostly with the Republican platform on economic issues but he's never been very political and doesn't like talking about it, certainly not out of the home.

"So tell me about yourself, Tom. Why did you get into the law?"

This is surprising to Tom. It feels like an interview but it isn't. It's a stranger asking personal questions. His face doesn't show that he's annoyed because Tom's gift is that it takes much more than this to annoy him. He rolls with it and decides to answer and Benson thinks they're having a nice conversation. "My uncle is the whole reason. Thirty-five years ago he was wrongly convicted of murder. It nearly bankrupted my family in every way possible, money being the least significant." Tom pauses, not for effect but just to gather his thoughts. Everything about him is sincere and understated. "It's a powerless feeling to know in your heart and your head what is right but not be able to get there. Not be able to make anyone else see it even though it's in plain sight to you."

"I'm sorry."

"He was cleared twelve years later by DNA evidence."

"Thank God."

"Yes, thank God. He could still be in there, but for twelve years it was no picnic."

"I'll bet. Well, that's a noble reason to enter the law. I like that." Benson's body language is celebratory and inappropriate.

What an odd thing to say, thinks Tom. One drink with this clown will be enough.

Benson picks up on the sentiment and makes a lasso motion with his right hand to signal the waiter for another round. "Tom, I know you've given some money to the GOP in the past. Do you mind if I ask you a couple more questions?"

"Shoot."

"Position questions. In confidence."

"Shoot."

"Okay, let's start there. Gun control."

"I duck hunt from time to time. I'm okay with guns but I certainly don't think people need a grenade launcher in their closets either."

"You hunt. That's good. Let's stay with social issues. Abortion?"

This guy is getting offensive. "I'm the son of two liberal Democrats. I grew up pro-choice. Once I had kids I became pro-life, but I can see both sides."

"Death penalty?"

"Against it."

"Are you on the record as having that position?"

"What's going on here?" Tom runs a hand through his hair.

Benson looks at the hairline Tom has exposed and studies it. "That looks like it has plenty of years left on it."

"Excuse me?"

"Male pattern is easier to deal with than receding hair from the front, but you look okay."

This crosses even Tom's line. "Benson, this is the strangest meeting I've ever had. I've had some strange ones. I think I'll show myself out.

Take care of yourself." Tom puts his hands on the armrests with his elbows up to push out of the chair.

"Hang on a second, Mr. Pauley. I'm sorry. No more beating around the bush."

Tom stops but his hands and elbows are still in position. The waiter returns and delivers the two drinks. Everyone is silent until the waiter is back out of earshot.

"My GOP colleagues and I have watched your trial with great interest. We've also asked around about you. We've learned about as much as we can about you without actually contacting you."

"This isn't making our conversation less strange."

Benson decides he needs a moment to organize his pitch. "Tell you what. I'm going to do two things. First, I'm going to go to the bathroom. Second, I'm going to give you my thoughts on a plan."

"There's something synonymous about those."

Benson stands and smiles at Tom. "You're some kind of card, aren't you." He walks to the restroom. Tom works on his drink for a few minutes until Benson returns with his sales pitch ready.

Benson sits and picks up his drink again. "I'll get to the point. We want you to run for governor. On the Republican ticket. You'd have our support."

Tom brings his hands together to have a place to rest his chin. "I'm not a politician. I'm barely political."

"After John Edwards, the Democrats are still very vulnerable in North Carolina. We have a real chance to take the governor's mansion. If we have the right candidate."

Most of Tom's brain function is digesting this information and only a small part is formulating responses, so his mannerisms seem detached and sedated. "Why me?"

"Because you can win."

"I don't know anything about running a campaign."

"You don't have to. I do. The party does. You're a natural. You get out, give speeches, get on TV, do debates. We'll build the organization, raise the money, get out the vote. You just be you. We do the rest."

Tom looks into the fireplace, trying to find a starting point to evaluate what he's hearing.

"Tom, North Carolina isn't so blue as people think. Historically it was as blue a state as there is. The Dems were black people plus the unions. In the seventies when all the manufacturing jobs went overseas, North Carolina got wiped out and so did the unions. In the nineties, the New South started. Banking and technology took off, places like Research Triangle Park. The Dems here now are still black people and unions, but now it's public unions. The teachers and municipal workers. Demographics are different and the Dems aren't so strong."

Tom's mind is catching up with the conversation and his voice regains authority. "Look, all of that's fine, but this is a career decision. A life decision. It's never been something I wanted."

"What we're offering you is an opportunity of a lifetime. Here's the timeline. In December, you declare, and I'll make sure you have about eight million bucks you can announce with it. That should scare people off and make for an easier primary. Primary vote is May. By then, I'll have another six million for you, plus a lot of the eight will still be there. If you're looking good, which you will be, in late summer the national Republican Governors Association will drop a few million more your way. They want this state. That's almost twenty million for your campaign, and that matters. There are three major media markets here— Charlotte, Raleigh, and the coastal area around Wilmington. But a hell of a lot of this state is rural. You can't reach it with ads on cable and the Internet hasn't changed everything here. You need to buy broadcast advertising and that's what's expensive. At twenty million, you're likely to have double the funding of everyone else. And you'll have organization. You'll have a chief of staff, campaign director, communications director, press secretary, maybe three spokespeople, finance director. You'll have a director of advance to scout out all your event locations and do setup for you. You're going to have early money. Early money is key to getting office space and infrastructure. You need to be built out ahead of time to be able to accept the volunteer help when it comes. We're going to do this right for you, Tom."

"Jesus," says Tom.

"Tom, you have nothing to lose. Let's play out a few scenarios. In all scenarios, I raise a few million bucks for your candidacy, build an organization, and we run a strong campaign. Scenario one, you lose the race but your celebrity and profile in the state are much bigger and your law practice benefits. Plus, you've had a chance to articulate what you believe to be sound political positions for the state. Scenario two, you win and you're the goddamn governor. Maybe you hate the job so you serve one term and you return to your practice, but now you're an historical figure in the state. Scenario three, you win and you love the job."

"Benson, I have young kids, a law practice. And politics is so ugly. Call me vain, but I like people to like me. Right now, there's nobody out there running around saying they hate me. That would all change."

"You sue people for millions of dollars all the time. You think those people don't hate you?"

"Insurance companies pay the settlements."

"They still hate you. And so do the insurance companies."

"It's different. Politics is nasty. And personal."

"Tom, the party and I are offering you fame, market power. You'd have it, win or lose. You just have to say yes, and then you can leverage it any way you want. You could do some real good. That's why you got into law in the first place."

Pauley is no dummy. He knows everything Benson Hill says is self-serving and he knows he'll owe somewhere down the line. But it also makes some sense. "My wife would have to support this."

"Of course. She'd be important to the campaign."

"We need some time to think it over. Don't give me any crap about twenty-four hours."

"How about a week?"

Tom knows all he's committing to is a conversation with his wife about a crazy idea, but it's an idea he likes. He doesn't yet know if he likes it enough to do it, but he likes it. "Alright."

"Tom, can we round back to the position questions? I need to take this back to the party."

"So, I'm not definitely your guy?"

"We think you're our guy. Just diligence."

Tom is too distracted to go through a punch list of questions and wants to talk with Alison. "Here's the overview of the three legs of the stool. On economic policy, I'm for lower taxes, less regulation, and smaller government. Even though I'm a lawyer I support tort reform, and the British system of loser pays is the only thing that makes sense. The good lawyers will still make money. On foreign policy, I'm for a strong military to deter conflict and to handle small, regional conflicts abroad to keep us safe at home. On social issues, I'm center. I'm pro-gun and pro-life. I'm also pro gay marriage and anti death penalty and it doesn't matter which of these positions is on the record because I won't change them for a campaign."

Benson nods. "You sound like a candidate already."

"You should know that now, Benson. I won't change them." Tom feels this is a stand he needs to make now to set the tone if he's really going to do this.

Benson looks back at him. He knows he's just flipped Tom's world around. This guy can win, he thinks. He's so freaking naïve, but that's the beauty of it. "Of course, Tom. It's your call. You're the boss of the campaign." Benson has seen uncompromising men before and that trait never lasts once they step inside politics. The first time they give away their principles is hard to watch, like seeing a homeless mother parting with her last morsel of food to feed her child. But soon they become real politicians who understand sacrifice and the larger picture. Tom Pauley can say whatever he wants today. Years from now he'll look back at this moment and have a laugh at himself. Benson looks at him as though Tom is a child. "We do it your way," he assures him again.

Tom mistakes the look for admiration, a rare misinterpretation for him to make. "Good."

"You a Duke fan?" asks Benson.

"Carolina."

"Damn. Well, nobody's perfect. How the hell can you stand Roy Williams, though?"

"I don't like Roy much. He made his bones coaching at Kansas and he should have stayed there. Now that whole state hates him because he's got no loyalty and I don't like him for the same reason."

Benson nods. *If this guy gets the job, he has a lot to learn. I think I can get him the job, though.* "I hate him because he's tough to beat."

"In North Carolina, you're not supposed to talk politics or basketball in polite conversation. Look at us doing both."

Benson laughs. "Tom, this is not polite conversation. This is the start of your campaign."

4

Tom pulls out of the Washington Duke lot and his cell phone rings. He answers and puts it on the car speaker. The Reverend Don says, "Well done, Counselor."

"I thought you'd still be dazzling the media."

"They're saturated with dazzle so I stopped."

"I see," says Tom.

"I wanted to ask you about Harold Wallace."

Something's wrong. The reverend's tone of voice tells Tom he's caught. It's the tone used with the name Harold. "Okay."

"His testimony was very important."

"Eyewitness testimony is compelling," says Tom.

Harold Wallace was a witness for the defense. Six months earlier he had walked into Tom's office and told Tom that he was not Harold Wallace but Harold's older brother Bobby. Bobby has two prior felonies and is on parole, and when approached by the police as the witness to a homicide, Bobby panicked and told them he was Harold, his one-year-younger and similar-looking brother. Now Bobby wanted to know what to do.

Cleaning up this confusion might replace a strong witness for the defense with a parolee who has two felonies and who has already once been dishonest about the case. And to what purpose? Tom had worked with his clients several months already and was convinced of their innocence.

Tom had replied to this man in front of him, "I don't know what you're talking about, Harold, but when I go to trial, I want you, Harold, on that stand with a driver's license in your pocket that says Harold Wallace, and nothing else you've said in here today makes any sense to me."

The Reverend Don says to Tom, "It sure is nice to have a credible eyewitness."

"Sure is."

"Not like his brother, Bobby. Same height, same weight, same home address, just felony convictions."

"I guess so. I don't know much about Bobby," says Tom.

"Of course not, Counselor. I just called to say that you did great work and you got the right result. Justice was served today, any way you cut it."

Tom realizes that Don is the type to keep a file on everyone. The reverend makes a business of attacking what he finds to be unjust, so he always has a target, and a person on offense so much needs to think about defense too. "Nice knowing you, Don."

5

Alison is better-looking as a woman than Tom is as a man. Smarter too, but she doesn't have the fearlessness in life that he has. Like many people, she was drawn by something her subconscious realized she lacked.

They knew of each other as undergrads at UNC, then met as first-year law students and dated off and on. She never wanted to be a litigator. She never wanted to be at a big firm at all, where sharper elbows are required to get ahead. From law school, she took a job at Duke Energy as inside counsel and started working her way up. Tom went to New York and they were out of touch for several years.

When Tom moved back to North Carolina to open his practice they went on a date and were married a year later. Alison had their first baby a year after that and Duke Energy allowed her to work part-time from home as deputy general counsel. The company feels like a second family to her now. She loves to watch Tom try cases, but making the arguments is not for her.

"I have something interesting to tell you about my meeting at the Washington Duke today."

Alison pours them each a glass of white wine. The kids are both asleep. "It's a high bar for interesting around here these days."

"This clears it." They clink their glasses in a silent toast and hold eye contact. Eye contact during the toast is something that they've decided as a couple matters, and it makes a moment of feeling connected when they do it. "I told you Benson Hill is with the state GOP?"

"You did."

"He was doing diligence."

"On what?"

"Me."

They hardly talk politics at all so there's no context for her to make the leap so quickly. "Why?"

"They're vetting me. They want me to run for governor."

She's stunned and processing. "You think that or he told you that?"

"He said they think I'm their guy."

"Tom, that's incredible!" Her emotion is pride that the man she loves has been tapped on the shoulder for something this big. She's consumed by the honor of it and not what the honor could mean.

Tom tries to bring her there. "I don't know what to do. What do you think?"

"Let's save that for the second glass of wine. My little Tar Heel law student has just been asked to run for governor. I want to celebrate that for a minute first." She comes around the table and behind his chair. She leans down so her chest is against the back of his shoulders and she hugs his neck. "I love you."

"I love you too, honey. Thank you." He tops up both their glasses. He's already had time to absorb the news and is on to whether or not it's a good idea. He wants to give her some time as well but has never had a lot of patience. "Should I do it?" He reaches up to hold her forearms that are wrapped around his chest with her hair draped over them. She kisses his cheek. He says, "We're happy now. We can go on being happy like this. This might make us unhappy."

Tom already decided he wants it. On the drive home with the music loud enough to vibrate the steering wheel and drown out his screaming voice from his own ears he decided fuck yes. But he wants to keep that out of this discussion. He wants to play devil's advocate to see if Alison can independently want it also.

"What's the commitment?" she asks.

"I guess a year for a campaign. If I win, four years on top of that."

"What would your firm do during that time?"

"They'd adjust the caseload. They'd be fine, and when I come back I'm a bigger asset, win or lose."

"So no problem there. Just good things." Alison's tone is positive.

"The problem is the unknown. I don't know anything about a campaign or even politics, really. I could embarrass myself. I could hate it. It could be hard on our family." Tom needs to say all these things even though he fears none of them.

Alison straightens up her back and steps around to sit across his lap and hug him from the front this time. "We can do anything as long as it's time-limited. This will be one year, or five years max if we don't like it. How bad can it be?"

This is what he needed to hear.

6

Tom is unopposed in the Republican primary. He imagines Benson Hill and some of his old sons of bitches had something to do with that. His eight-million-dollar war chest helped. North Carolina still has an element of the early-twentieth-century political boss machine, and the machine is either with you or against you. That's not the way in national politics, but local politics is different.

"Jesus, you could hang meat in here." Tom has gotten irritable with the grind of the campaign. He's on his plush campaign bus that is skimmed on the outside with "Pauley for Governor."

Tom is seated next to Peter Brand, who yells to the front of the bus, "Lighten up on the AC. We can't move from ninety degrees outside to forty in here."

Over the last week, Brand has taken over as the chief of staff for Pauley. Brand was always involved but was splitting time, also trying to help win North Carolina support for the GOP presidential candidate, who is now hopelessly behind in the polls to the Democratic candidate, former New York governor Mitchell Mason.

"How you doing, Tom?"

"I'm fine." They're leaving a campaign event on the UNC campus at the Dean Dome and traveling Route 15-501 to the Duke campus for an event at Cameron Indoor Stadium. "Doing Duke and Carolina back to back, there'll be plenty of fodder for jokes about being able to work across the aisle."

Brand is on his BlackBerry. "Just got new polls in." His thumb sweeps over the face of the BlackBerry to scroll through the data. "Mason is killing Wilson. Real Clear Politics average has Mason up nine points in the national polls. The latest poll on North Carolina has Mason up ten."

"Damn."

"Mason is creating an obstacle for us. It could be a problem. It's the blessing and the curse of the gubernatorial races that sync up with the presidential campaign. Many people just vote party down the line, so there's a lot of drafting the state candidates can do behind the top of the ticket. If they have a winner. Mason's going to be the winner, so it's an uphill battle for us."

"I thought we're up in the latest polls."

"That's the amazing thing. You're up five points."

"Good." Tom nods and looks away from Brand and out the window. Brand is in the aisle seat and flags an aide for a couple bottles of water. There are eight members of the press on the bus which is twice what they had three weeks ago and they're all in the back of the bus and out of earshot. "How do you explain that?"

"It's all guesswork but I'd say it's a few things. Republicans are motivated now, so you have that locked up. The Whiskers endorsement and all the TV footage of you with him during the trial have added some independents and Democrats."

"I'm amazed he endorsed me."

"He likes friends in high places. Maybe he decided a Republican in a high place would give him some credibility. Or maybe he's getting moderate in his old age."

"That wasn't my experience."

"I guess not. I couldn't believe the endorsement myself. Nobody could, so those headlines were effective." Whiskers made the announcement three weeks ago, which was exactly when the number of press people on the bus doubled. Whiskers said Pauley was a champion of good causes. "That would have killed you in a primary but it's great for a general." Peter hands him a bottle of water. "The other reason is you're putting in the hard work. You have to get out and see as many people as you can. Especially a person like you who has charisma. If a person shakes your hand and has a word with you, they'll vote for you. It's not that way with every candidate. It's not that way with Derek Wilson." The GOP candidate for president has a reputation for being stiff.

Peter has been in DC the last few days meeting with the Wilson campaign. He's now back with Tom full-time for the next six weeks until the November election.

"Thanks. It started out as real fun, but it's so damned exhausting. November can't get here fast enough."

"Now's the time to pour it on. The benefit of Wilson getting his ass kicked so badly is you can expect more help from national. If the poll numbers hold like this for another couple weeks, support for Wilson will start to fall away and move to the state elections where we have a shot. Like yours. You'll get more money, more staff. Talented guys. Starting today you already have me for the duration." He sips his water. "Sorry I missed the Maiden Creek event." Tom had visited a retirement community in Charlotte two days earlier for a campaign event.

"I started the speech saying I wouldn't leave until I spoke with everyone who wanted to speak with me. They all did. Every single one."

"Did it take long?"

"In geological time? No."

The bus takes 751 to Cameron Boulevard to the campus. It's a beautiful day and typically hot for late September in North Carolina. So far the bus has been a campaign prop. Tom meets the bus at various events around the state. He might stay in a hotel for a night here and there but usually gets a short flight home. From the end of September on, it's not just a prop anymore. He'll be on the goddamn bus and in crap hotels for weeks straight at a time. The bus takes Wannamaker to Towerview Road then pulls into the lot next to where the Duke students camp out for days and weeks to get into the basketball games. "My God," says Tom.

Brand is also a Carolina fan. "I know. Sickening. Try not to think about it."

Cheers go up as the bus pulls to a stop. About a thousand people have turned out for the event which was well publicized in advance and gave an opportunity for citizens to have a seat inside Cameron. Most have signs or campaign swag in support of Pauley and the crowd looks to be a mix of half students and half Durham residents.

"Let's do it," says Tom.

"Kick ass." Peter stands and steps back to let Tom pass into the aisle and walk forward ahead of him. They can both walk at their full height in the bus. The junior staff has gotten off the bus already to clear a path for Tom. To the left of the bus are the Duke tennis courts and nobody's on that side. To the right, the side the bus door is on, is the lot and the stadium behind it and the crowd which has synchronized in a rhythmic chant yelling "Pauley, Pauley, Pauley."

Before Tom is off the bus he turns over his shoulder to Peter. "Nice greeting though I thought these Duke kids were more creative than that." When he turns back he sees a throng that is more Durham than Duke and at the center of it, making a determined push for the bus door, is an enormous transvestite. A fiftyish man turned woman with puffy, unhealthy-looking skin under heavy powder. The shoulders are broad though the belly is broader and the legs are thick. The wig isn't exactly crooked, it's just too small for the bloated head and the hair of it some-how has qualities that are both greasy and straw-like. In heels, she's taller than Tom and is getting closer.

Tom is two steps from the pavement. "Jesus, Brand, would you get a load of that?"

"Wow. What's happening there?"

"Ugly as a man. Outrageous as a woman."

Tom steps to the ground and starts shaking the hands that are thrust toward him. Young, eager faces with big smiles that say they are big supporters and have been following the campaign. Several volunteer their services and Tom makes sure his aides follow up. He has a burst of energy in response to this and is enjoying himself though without looking he can feel the transvestite's presence closing the distance from the right. He keeps his gaze away but like the shark music in *Jaws*, knowing and not seeing is scarier. He keeps pushing left, hoping he can outrun her. He has a bad feeling.

He's no longer responding to people with words but only shaking hands and moving to the next hand to the left so he can take a step with each one. He wonders if Brand is sensing anything at all, but doesn't stop to look for him.

He takes another hand from the left and another step but it's no use. He looks into the broad chest covered in a pink dress that looks like it was sewn at home. "Hello," says Tom with a smile and he extends his hand, seeing now that the transvestite has not put a hand out to him.

Their eyes meet, then in a flash her hand comes around from behind her back. Tom sees but can't react. She's holding a plastic cup and the contents shower Tom. It's glitter. The densest part of it hits Tom in the chest and creates a powdery cloudburst around him. Glitter is in his hair, his ears, his mouth. It has a static cling quality and his suit is decorated.

Tom tries to spit the glitter from his tongue and looks up at his assailant. "What the hell was that for? I'm pro gay marriage, you moron."

"Is that right, honey? Good for you. Taste the rainbow!" The voice is deep and terrifying.

Peter Brand gets between them and with a hand on Tom's shoulder pushes him up to the sidewalk toward Cameron, away from the crowd and the television cameras which have caught the whole thing.

As they step into the Cameron lobby, Peter points to an aide. "Get Mr. Pauley a new suit off the bus." He turns to Tom. "I'm sorry, Tom. Damn."

"Jesus Christ. Is that just because I'm Republican? Doesn't anybody read anything about my positions?"

Peter helps Tom off with the jacket which is raining glitter on the floor. "Tom, try not to say words like *moron* when you could be on camera."

"Well, what the fuck!"

"Try not to say that either."

"Jesus Christ, Peter, I'm not going to say *fuck* on camera."

"Good. Right. Look, politicians get glittered all the time. It's some sort of weird movement. It doesn't even mean they don't like you, they just do it to get on TV. Let's just get you in a new suit and put this behind us. No more close-up stuff today. Just the podium."

Tom looks up to see a life-sized cardboard cutout of Christian Laettner and a Duke National Championship trophy. "This fucking campaign."

7

The glitter incident puts Tom's campaign in the national news for the second time in three weeks. Every cable outlet has the video teed up for their prime-time audience. As is the way when things are rolling in a person's direction, the pundits, left and right, take Tom's side. They're fed up with the disrespect of glittering, but more than that, they love that Tom got a little pissed off. They love how human that is. The following day, Chris Stirewalt writes in an op-ed:

> Yes, folks are all a little tired of the glittering of the good people who make the personal sacrifices to run for public office and serve our country. It's immature, disrespectful and distracting. But yesterday showed that it may be a small part of our political vetting process along with debates and campaign speeches.
>
> Glittering strips a candidate of his produced and rehearsed behavior. For a brief moment we see instinct, not automation.
>
> Rick Santorum met glitter with a plastic smile. His instinct was to cover up, not to reveal. To say, "You can't get to me," even though we all know that horse has left the barn. He's pissed off! Everyone

watching wants to tell him to show that a little. Don't show a temper, but show something real! Nobody actually thinks he found it amusing and something to smile about. He's not fooling any of us watching, he's just making himself look more ridiculed in our eyes. And it makes us wonder, what else does he cover up on instinct, and possibly do a better job of covering up?

But Tom Pauley showed us something different. He showed us a little fire. Not only did he get angry, but he defended his position to his assailant. He called her a moron.

That's human! The folks applaud him, and more than that, they find him to be someone they can believe in.

8

Tom's Democratic opponent is Terry Mills, who stepped down as state attorney general to get into the race. Attorney general is an appointed position and Mills has never run for elected office either. His campaign managed to raise only four million dollars, which is bare bones for a gubernatorial or Senate race in a state the size of North Carolina. Mills is outspent four to one through mid-October.

They have two debates, which are notable only for extreme boredom. Both candidates are intelligent and well prepared as good lawyers are, but they both get deep in technical aspects of issues that viewers don't understand and so don't care about. Neither lands a kill shot and both carry themselves well. By October twentieth, Tom is up two points in the polls.

Tom's staff has finished the briefing on fund-raising and polling data so he adjourns the meeting. He leans into his chair and closes his eyes. He never naps but he needs thirty minutes a day to think in quiet and to let his mind wander.

With closed lids Tom visits his childhood as though he's an adult come back, peering through a window at the boy he was. But even as a boy he felt outside himself, watching the scenes in his family happen to them.

The young Tom blows out all ten candles on his birthday cake with enough air left over to shout "I got 'em." He looks up at his mother who has her palms pressed together under her chin and tears in her eyes. Tom knows these are not tears of happiness but of sadness and that they are not for him but for his uncle, her brother in a jail cell.

Tom's mouth stays in the shape of a smile but the vibrations it had been sending through his face stop. The room sees Tom's face go plastic and the birthday party goes lifeless. No one can find the enthusiasm to fool the rest into being happy.

Tom doesn't feel wronged or cheated of this moment by his family. He stands with his family against this outrage and he feels more of a grown-up to be also sober about it with them. He is angry, and more than that, he is scared.

It is one thing to know as a child that there are ogres and trolls and bad guys but that good guys help us and that our parents, our heroes, are always there and unafraid. It is another to learn the good guys can't be trusted, that the biggest danger on the streets is from those whose job it is to protect and who have the authority to do whatever they want. The cops and the lawyers speak a language we don't understand and we watch our parents, our first heroes, cower powerless and afraid.

Two days after the party is visiting day at the prison and Tom goes to sit in front of soundproof glass with his mother and across from his uncle. He's come many times the last two years to say hello.

His mother holds the kind of heavy black phone that is in public phone booths and she gives a factual update of the appeals process and conversations with lawyers. There isn't much to report. Then they sit for a while with no noise, touch the glass a few times, look at each other then look away, look at Tom. The phone drifts down from her ear to rest on her shoulder like a cradle and her fingers rest on top.

Uncle Neil motions to speak with Tom. Tom's mother hands over the phone and Tom presses it hard against his ear.

"Jeez, buddy, you're getting big."

"Hi, Uncle Neil." His uncle's eyes are always wet and he wonders whether or not he just has wet eyes.

"You're filling out too. I see the muscles popping out from under your shirt."

"I'm playing football. We're working out pretty hard now." Tom feels neither brave nor afraid. He is too confused to know how to feel and that insulates him from acute emotion at the time. He just wants his family to be happy and his uncle to be free.

"Good for you, Tom."

"How are you?"

Neil takes a long breath. "I'm doing okay." He nods and looks pensive as though this is a real and thoughtful conclusion.

Tom is unconvinced but knows it's just conversation.

Neil says, "You know, Tom. When each of us is born we're all given a big shit pie. And every once in a while we have to cut off a slice and eat it."

A tear falls from Neil's left eye and he pretends to scratch an itch on the side of his nose. Tom sees his uncle trying to be brave which makes Tom less confused and so less protected and Tom starts to cry too.

"I'm just having a slice now, buddy. That's all." Neil's voice breaks up over the words. He lowers his phone, presses a palm to the glass then stands and walks away and Tom watches the drab green smock disappear behind a prison guard.

"Time to go, honey." His mother's face is a disaster.

They stand from metal folding chairs that scrape the cement floor when the backs of their knees push against the seat.

They walk along the visitor's bay to a heavy metal door where a uniformed guard is standing with thumbs in his belt.

To Tom's ten-year-old body the prison is huge and cold. The walls are cinder blocks covered pale yellow and haven't been painted in years. The floor is cement with throw rugs and the lighting is the hanging fluorescent kind that is in school cafeterias.

The guard is unmoved by Tom's mother's face, like a numb Manhattan pedestrian passing the innumerable homeless.

The admissions room is just as cold. More metal chairs and people behind thick glass, though these people are showered and uniformed, armed and with combed hair.

They walk faster now, both in a silent cry, knowing that sunshine and an end to claustrophobia are one set of doors away.

The doors open out. Tom puts his back into it and leads the way for his mother. In the sunshine Tom stops crying. The sidewalks are all at right angles so Tom and his mother zigzag the beige walkways to the blacktop of the parking lot.

"Goddamn lawyer." It's rare for his mother to swear but she does it again. "Hasn't moved things a damn bit."

She's still crying but Tom is done and not close to tears anymore. He's thinking about something else. Something hopeful. "Mom, I'm going to be a lawyer."

She pats his shoulder and smiles a real smile.

"I'll start some reading up on it today. I'll help Uncle Neil."

"That would be nice, honey."

9

Benson Hill rents out Crook's Corner for a private dinner with Tom, Peter Brand, and the top twenty RNC donors in North Carolina who are all looking forward to an evening with the man they expect to be their next governor.

Benson picked Crook's Corner so Tom would feel more comfortable on his home turf of Franklin Street in Chapel Hill. As a student Tom would take his dates here when he had enough money for more than pizza and Schaefer.

The restaurant and bar has hubcaps on the outside and a pig theme decorating the inside, also a pink pig on a platform and red post high above the roof. It has charm that seems accidental and the cooking is real Southern.

The tables have the hard, reflective tops of diner tables and the chairs are metal and plastic. The restaurant reconfigures the tables to accommodate the party and at Benson's insistence Tom is at the head of the table, though Tom has already become comfortable with taking the lead in a room of big shots without any assistance.

Peter Brand sits at the far end of the table to spread out the campaign insiders with the paying guests. Benson is on Tom's right and the other donors sit next to Tom in descending order of amount contributed.

"How's your wife holding up?" asks Benson.

"She's holding us both up. Alison's amazing."

"It's vey potent, have a guh woman," says Bubba Greenhouse, seated to Tom's left in the number-one-donor chair. "Vey."

Most North Carolina accents in the major cities and university towns are mild. A twang and a few y'alls here and there. Bubba sounds almost Cajun. "Where you from, Bubba?" asks Tom.

"Nawlens." He smiles. "Rigley. Now ah live in Duck Beach. Been theyah twunny yeeahs."

"Bubba has substantial farming and hunting properties. He was very happy to learn that some of that property is home to enormous natural gas deposits. Isn't that right, Bubba?"

"Bettah lucky dan guh."

"As you know, Tom, Bubba's one of our biggest supporters, both for you and nationally. Of course, now that Mason is running away with the White House, you're our only bright spot for the season."

"We still have a couple weeks' work ahead of us."

"We gone git out da vote," assures Bubba. "Den you gone git in theyah and do da rahyt tings."

"Tom's a fiscal conservative, Bubba. You know that. Balanced budgets, debt reduction, lower corporate tax rates. This'll be the most business-friendly state in the Union. Hell, that Boeing plant in South Carolina may relocate all those jobs up here when Tom's through!" Benson smiles and slaps the table. He's a crony who knows how to round up other cronies.

Tom's happy to discuss policy. He knows it's his obligation to his donors, but he wants to make clear they don't own a piece of his platform. "That's right. When elected, I intend to reduce the corporate tax rate from six-point-nine to five percent. On the expense side, there are some small pickups in waste management, water, but the main thing to address is education reform. Education is almost a third of the total budget."

"Thass rahyt, Tom."

"Bubba, the catfish amandine here is the best thing on any menu anywhere," says Tom. He knows he has an entire dinner of policy talk ahead but would like a short break to talk about food.

"Awrahyt." Bubba puts down the menu and picks up his glass of bourbon on ice. "Dem unions, Tom. Dey killin dis state."

"The teachers union has a sweetheart deal. No question."

"Kaynt go on. Dat dealz no guh."

"We're going to look at it. I won't have a full legal review until I'm in office. If and when. But we'll try to get the teachers union to the table and do the sensible thing for the state."

"Trah? You gone haf do moh dan trah, boy. Ah know doz union pricks. Crooks don't pahrt wit dey money."

"It's all a negotiation." Tom smiles. "Life is a negotiation." Tom doesn't like being called boy and he hopes this sounds dismissive in return.

"No, suh. Noo bahginin. You say how gone be. Das dat. Dee end. No uddah way wit dem."

"There's another way. We'll get around a table."

"Tom, Tom. Dis has to be yo job wun. Firs ting. Dat stupid deal. An git it dun from yo desk in yo mansion. Not round sum tabah."

Tom glances at Benson to give him a few seconds to intercede. When he doesn't, Tom looks back at Bubba and says, "Bubba, I didn't like being told what to do before I ran for governor and I don't like it now. You know very well the platform I've run on. I'll have a lot of jobs to do, if elected. If you have some suggestions, I appreciate that."

"Tom's going to move this state in the right direction, Bubba. No worries there," says Benson. He picks up his own glass of bourbon and drinks, hoping to punctuate the conversation.

Benson realizes he's been a step behind in the conversation and should have stepped in earlier but now it's too late. Tom's back is up and Bubba's pissed and Bubba ignores Benson. "Lookie heyah, Tom. You heyah by the guh graces oh my wallet."

"I'm also here by the good graces of an endorsement from Donnie Whiskers." Tom lets the name sink in like a slap across the face. "Should I also be taking policy direction from Don?"

The obvious answer is no but Bubba isn't going to verbalize the concession.

"I didn't think so." Tom's taught himself a trick during the campaign. Whenever he feels he isn't calm, he forces himself to think of what a calm person would say. "Look, Bubba. You and I want very similar things. We may not agree exactly on the path, and I admit my path may be a bit longer. We can debate all night whether that's a good or a bad thing. But in the end, you and I are aligned."

"Amen," says Benson when what he really wants to say is Holy fuck what a disaster.

Bubba's still pissed but Tom is feeling very good about being his own man.

10

"The *Herald Sun* says 'Pauley in a Squeaker.' The *News & Observer* has '2 a.m. Concession Gives Pauley the Win.'" Alison holds up a newspaper in each hand under the frame of the open front door. Tom sees her from his chair at the kitchen table and wishes he had a photo image of her at that moment to keep with him. He smiles and commits to remembering.

The election was so close that Mills refused to concede until most of the state was asleep in bed. He had made the call to Tom just in time for the papers to get the headlines correct in the morning.

"Get over here and kiss your governor."

"Yes, sir. Is it sir? Your Excellency?"

"For Bubba and Benson, I think Your Excellency will do. The First Lady of North Carolina can call me whatever she pleases."

The article below his in The *News & Observer* has a report on the Air France Flight 477 crash near JFK from a few months earlier. There had been signs of mechanical failure and now the black box recording indicates that one of the pilots was hungover or drunk or both.

The article credits reporting done by Samantha Davis at UBS. Tom recognizes the name. He pushes the paper across the table and kisses his wife.

11

Tom drinks from the marble water fountain of the Old Well. He takes Alison's hand and turns to deliver his victory speech in the heart of the UNC campus, just three hours after Alison read the headlines. Because Mills had not conceded the night before, Tom's team rushed preparations for the speech at his alma mater.

Thousands have gathered and more swell into the brick walkways around the old landmark like blood gathering behind a clot. The student body knows Tom is an alumnus and he appears young enough that he seems recently one of them.

The Old Well is a small rotunda more than a hundred years old. There are eight columns and it is only a few steps across. The top is twice the height of a man. It used to function as the sole water supply for the Old East and Old West dormitories. Now students drink from the fountain on the first day of classes for good luck. Tom wipes a drop of water from his lip and waves to the crowd.

Standing on a bench are two young girls in bikini tops and tiny jean shorts that match. They each hold over their heads a bottom corner of a sign, the kind they use in the stands at the basketball games. This one reads, "Finally a HOT Governor!" Another sign held by two girls Tom assumes must be from the same sorority reads, "Luv the Guv."

Tom scans the growing crowd and sees there are many more females than males. From farther back comes a scream—a sorority-aged voice that has the raspiness and edge of a girl who is not the prettiest but is pretty enough to be bold without a chip on her shoulder and is usually drunker than the rest. "Tom Pauley is gorgeous!" She holds the last syllable for several seconds and there is audible damage to her vocal cords.

Tom laughs. Alison laughs too. She squeezes his hand and leans into the microphone that Peter Brand has set up on the Old Well. "I second that!"

Alison is enjoying the attention for her husband as much as he is. Her ease with the uproar makes it more of a celebration.

She kisses Tom's cheek then he whispers in her ear, "I'm not universally hot. I'm politician hot. It's a much lower standard."

Tom quiets the crowd with both hands raised as though trying to prove to them that he does have ten fingers. He starts his short prepared speech crediting his Carolina education, thanking his wife and the community, and saying that he plans to hit the ground running once his term starts in January.

Since the earlier interruptions about Tom being gorgeous were met with amusement and not rebuked, the crowd presses to find the limits, the way crowds and toddlers do.

Tom says, "Jobs will be a top priority of my administration. Not only can we rebuild our manufacturing industry here in North Carolina, but we can create more services jobs—banking, technology . . ."

"Hey, Guv!" Tom and Alison both look ninety degrees to the right where the shout came from. There's a row of five guys standing shoulder to shoulder. It feels like a choreographed formation, like part of a coed cheerleading team.

As soon as Tom looks, the five drop down in a squat. Immediately behind each one of them is another crouched guy with a girl sitting on his shoulders. In unison the five guys from the back row pop to a standing position and the girls yank their spaghetti-string tank tops over their heads and wave their breasts from side to side. The guys lower the girls down and all fifteen scatter.

Tom turns back to the center of the crowd. "Possibly some jobs in the entertainment and hospitality field for our friends there."

The crowd laughs but Alison manages only a half smile, which is worse than a disapproving look because it shows she's uncertain.

The event no longer has the gravitas of high office, of hard work and ideas building things that last more than just a lifetime and ought to be housed in the timeless marble structure of a capitol building so that future civilizations will see the bones of the structure still standing and know that it meant something. This now feels like celebrity, to be housed in a thrown-together set of a studio catering to fanciful notions and perverse motivations. Alison hasn't anticipated this part of the job her husband has just won.

Things are changing, she thinks. Tom has the same thought at the same time.

SAMANTHA DAVIS

12

The wrap of yellow plastic police tape makes the poolside cabana look like a piece of installation art. The Delano attempts business as usual despite the spectacle. It's January and they can't afford to close.

Samantha Davis had flown to Miami that morning. Enterprise had given her the choice of a candy apple red or an interstate blue PT Cruiser. Both underpowered. She chose red and drove to the Boulevard Hotel in South Beach. She checked in and walked the mile north to the Delano Hotel.

Two hotel security guards flank either side of the cabana. Samantha walks along the edge of the pool and shows her press credentials to one of the guards. "I'd like to take a look at the scene."

"You can go as far as the yellow tape." The guard seems already out of patience. Since the police allowed the hotel to stay open, the police tape has become an attraction unto itself and good for business.

The cabana has its own patio that faces the Delano pool. There are lounge chairs with thick, white cushions, small tables, and an oversized canvas parasol. The patio is taped off and there's no sign of anything out of place. Samantha looks at the solid white door of the cabana at the back of the patio. It's crossed with more strips of yellow tape like the bars of a jail cell.

"Looks dramatic," she says.

The guard nods without looking at her.

"Is there anything you can tell me about what happened here?" He's not a cop, just hotel security but it's worth trying.

"Lady, I don't know anything about what happened here."

Lady? There's a steady trickle of passersby, like trick-or-treaters, drinking a cocktail with one hand and taking pictures on their phones with the other. "Who found the body?"

"The maid didn't get an answer to the door so she called the manager. He found the body."

"What time was that?"

"I don't know."

"When was the last time anyone saw Meadow Jones?"

The guard turns a bit to look right at her. "Look, lady. I don't know. And I'm not supposed to guess. I'm not supposed to talk about it. Everyone here has been told not to talk about it."

"Sure. Got it." Samantha takes a few photos with her phone to look at later and walks in the direction of the ocean and the outdoor bar. The pool is about a hundred feet long with an infinity edge and is lined with palm trees. The last twenty feet of the pool is given to two-inch-deep water so people can bring in a chair and sit with wet feet.

It's four p.m. so the pool area is in transition from serious sunning and casual drinking to serious drinking and casual flirting. Samantha orders drinks from two different waitresses, mentioning she's a reporter, and is met with no information both times.

She decides to stop introducing herself as a reporter and targets the most handsome of the bartenders.

At the end of the pool is an area of sand with rows of lounge chairs. Beyond that is thick brush and on the other side of the brush is the real beach and the ocean. She walks the trail through the brush where she fixes her hair and reapplies makeup, then walks back to the Delano property.

The outdoor bar has a straw-thatched roof and is by the sand and the corner of the pool. She concentrates on her approach to the bar even though she's certain that the more she tries to look pretty the less she does.

She makes sure to get the bartender's eye as she approaches the bar.

She feels like a twit. He'll either laugh at her or find something interesting, but there's no question there will be an impression of some kind. "Gin and tonic." A more masculine drink will be better to order. Guys love girls who smoke cigars and drink gin and tonics.

"Coming up." He smiles and makes the drink without ever looking at his hands. He keeps his eyes on his audience like a magician. "Tough day at the beach?" He glances at her fingers, confirms no engagement ring, and looks back at her eyes.

He looks about thirty. Old enough that he must be a career bartender and young enough that his tan still looks healthy. A youthful tan is attractive but a tan on old skin makes people think only of wrinkles and cancer. He's almost six feet with lean features and a lean body. "No, I just got here today. Beach day tomorrow."

He slides a gin and tonic across the bar to her still without having looked at it. It's filled right to the rim and he knows this the way a gunslinger knows if there's a round in the chamber by the weight of the gun in his hand. He thinks of himself as a sort of gunslinger. "Here with friends?"

"A girlfriend." This is true. Emily Rosen is the booker UBS assigned to travel with Samantha. Emily's a twenty-four-year-old petite blond scrapper and Samantha likes her.

"Are you staying here?"

"I can barely afford the drinks here, let alone the rooms. We're staying down the road."

"This one's on the house." He raps the bar top with his knuckles.

Samantha takes a sip. "What's all the police tape for?"

"I guess you've been traveling." He puts both palms down on the bar and leans toward Samantha. "You know who Hugh Brooks is?"

"The actor."

"Right. He's dead."

"That's awful." Samantha can feel her own acting but knows everyone's genuine response to this sort of news about a stranger can feel forced. "Isn't he about nineteen?"

"He's twenty-one. He and his costar girlfriend both just turned twenty-one. Meadow Jones. Isn't that a great name? My next go 'round on the planet I want a name like Meadow Jones. Sounds like a superhero with special powers."

Right. "What happened?"

"Two nights ago they were drinking right here. Right where you're sitting and I was pouring them drinks. Except for a few coke trips to the bathroom, they were drinking here 'til we shut the place down. Next thing I hear about it is yesterday afternoon, they pull his body out of that cabana. Dead."

"OD? Suicide?"

He winks at her. "I don't think so."

"Then what?"

"You've seen their movies. They're a couple a vampires."

"So?"

"I'm just saying."

"You're saying they were killed by vampires?" Great, I'm wasting my time.

"I'm saying they took their method acting a little too far."

"What are you talking about? And another gin and tonic." The first one was mostly ice, she tells herself.

He slowly starts to make it. Several other people are waiting to order drinks and the less handsome bartender is struggling to keep up. "I was one of the last people to see them and I was with them most of the night so I got questioned by the cops big-time. I heard a few things and they asked certain things so I put it together."

He's only too happy to tell this story and he does it in the kind of hushed tone that's meant to draw attention. He's probably already told it to anyone who will listen. Hopefully it hasn't been to another reporter. "Exactly what did you put together, Sherlock?" Samantha tries to say this in a flirtatious way as though she doesn't care about the information, she just cares about being entertained.

"I heard there was a lot of blood at the scene. And they asked me if

I saw any unusual markings on either of their necks at any point during the night. They tried to ask it as an afterthought question, like, oh, by the way, but I could tell it was important."

"Wow. Anything else?"

"Nobody saw Meadow Jones leave the hotel. As far as I know. The security cameras must have picked it up, so the cops know. As far as I know they haven't arrested her but they asked her not to leave town so she can quote unquote cooperate with the investigation. She already lawyered up."

"Were they fighting the night at your bar?"

"No. They didn't seem happy or angry or sad. They always act tragically hip like they just smoked too much opium. I told all this to the cops. They wear all black and they hang on each other and kiss each other's neck."

Samantha takes another sip. This is good stuff. "Would you consider doing an interview? Go on TV to talk about this?"

He retreats a step into the bar and holds up his hands like he just found out the guy selling pot is an undercover cop. "Are you a reporter?"

"Yes."

"I'm not supposed to be talking about this."

"They can't arrest you for talking."

"I don't know what the cops can do but the hotel can fire me. Management told everyone to put a gag on it or they'd fire us."

"They're crazy. This'll be great for their business. It'll be a tourist attraction."

"I don't think they want that." He's rattled to find he was on the receiving end of the smooth talk. His gunslinger hubris is gone.

Samantha sees Emily walking alongside the pool toward the bar. She waves. Samantha looks back at the bartender and hands him a business card. "If you change your mind, call this number. You'd look very handsome on TV."

He smiles at this and she stands and walks off to steer Emily to two chairs and a table in the sand.

Emily sits with an exhale. "I'm sorry, Sam. I got bubkes. This hotel's on lockdown."

Samantha leans forward. "I got something. I'm not sure if it's enough to use, but I got something." She leans back. "Have you had a drink yet?"

"No."

Samantha raises her hand for a cocktail waitress and gets another gin and tonic. The first two have worked like caffeine with no edge. Alcohol is a wonderful drug in moderation. Emily orders a mojito.

"The bartender was serving drinks to Hugh Brooks and Meadow Jones the night before Hugh's body was found. They were here until the bar closed. Since the bartender was one of the last to see them, he was questioned by the police. He heard there was a lot of blood on the scene and the police asked him if he saw any strange marks on either of their necks."

"Weird."

"The bartender thinks it's a murder investigation, not an accidental OD or suicide."

"Jesus. This is about to become a huge story."

The drinks come. Emily sips hers and winces.

"What's wrong?"

"It's too sugary. It's like a cup of syrup."

"Get something else." Samantha raises her hand for the waitress.

"No, it's fine."

"Fine? You just said it's syrup."

"It's fine, I'll drink it."

She's twenty-four, thinks Samantha. We're ten years apart but those are a big ten years. "Emily, get something you want. Life's too short to drink twenty-dollar drinks you don't like. There's no sense being a martyr about it."

Emily laughs. She admires Samantha and they like each other. The waitress comes back and Emily orders a bay breeze.

"What do you want me to do?" she asks.

"All we have is a far-fetched vampire story from a not very credible-sounding source. Let's see if we can build on it."

"Okay."

"Bump into as many maids and room service staff as you can. Don't tell them you're with the press, just act like a guest who finds it all amusing. Tell them you already heard there was lots of blood at the scene and that Hugh Brooks had strange wounds on his neck. Get them talking. See if you can get anyone to confirm that, or add anything."

"Okay." Emily stands up. She's excited to be investigating, a little too excited, but that's okay. She'll get the work done. It's always easier to ramp a person down than it is to ramp a person up.

"Emily."

"What?"

"Finish your drink first."

Emily laughs and sits. "This is so exciting."

13

Twenty minutes later Samantha walks along the pool toward the hotel. She's had three gin and tonics and guesses that without another she has about thirty minutes more of feeling great.

She walks up curved steps through flowered landscaping to the outdoor dining area of the hotel restaurant. She passes through a few tables and inside to the massive Delano lobby. It has the feel of stepping through the columns to the inside of a Roman monument. The ceiling is so high you forget it's there. The space is enormous, longer than it is wide and fully open with sparse furniture. The floors are dark wood and everything else is white, including sheer drapes the size of sails on a ship. They sway with the push of the air conditioning and give the room a goddess effect.

Samantha looks to her left where there is a group of guys in their twenties and in linen shirts. They have the energy of the first hours of a bachelor party. She keeps walking, looking for a hotel employee who is higher up the food chain and is alone.

Farther up on the left is the lobby bar. On her right are a few couches and chairs with people glancing at watches, waiting for friends. The Delano is a destination for people whether or not they take a room at the hotel.

At the end of the lobby on the left is a sushi bar. To the side of this and next to a fluttering white drape is a cop in uniform talking to another man. The cop has thinning hair, a mustache and is tall and burly. He looks like the kind of overweight guy who lifts a lot of free weights. Not a runner, but he'd be hell if he ever got his hands on you.

The other man looks the same except his clothes don't look natural to him. He has on a black button-down shirt, black dress pants, and black leather shoes. He's dressed like a younger, skinnier man. They both have the same posture, girth, and wide stance.

With three drinks in, Samantha decides now's the time to try.

"Hello, Officer."

Both men turn to her and like what they see. They're cockier than the hotel security guard and used to having a little fun. "Do we have a concerned citizen here?"

"No, I just love a man in uniform."

"Sure you do. You with the press?"

"That obvious?"

Both men nod.

"Can you tell me anything about what happened?"

"I cannot." The cop smiles.

Samantha braces herself. She tries to work out what will be the most fearless and certain expression. "I have it confirmed there was lots of blood at the scene."

The cop says nothing and gives an expression to show he's not impressed.

"And I have it confirmed there were wounds to the neck of Hugh Brooks."

The cop shakes his head. "Exactly who has confirmed this little tale for you?"

"I can't say. At this time."

"I see." He smiles again. "I tell you what, little lady. I'm going to introduce you to an important man." He sweeps his hand toward the man next to him the way a game show host would gesture to a prize just won. "This is Connor Marks."

"A pleasure," says Samantha, and the two shake hands.

The cop continues. "Connor was a Miami cop. A very good cop who has retired and gone into business for himself. He calls himself a fixer, but as you can see," the cop points up and down at the man's clothing, "he's really what I like to call a fancy boy."

"*Fancy* is such a relative term," says Connor. "There's this mope here, and then a very fancy rest of the world." The two like each other and like giving each other a hard time.

"I'll leave you two alone," says the cop. "I don't want to hear what gets spewed out next." He walks to the other end of the lobby in the direction of the pool and the cabanas.

"What's a fixer?"

Connor seems confident in delivering an impressive answer without his heckler around. "When people with lots of money get in trouble, they pay me lots of money to get them out."

"Like Harvey Keitel in *Pulp Fiction*."

"Not exactly. I'm more of a consultant. I develop strategies for how to handle cops and lawyers. And the press. Most cops can't stand when guys like me get involved, but I'm friendly with the cops around here."

"And why are you at the Delano?"

"I'm on the job." He winks.

"Meadow Jones hired you?"

"Can we talk off the record?"

"I guess so."

"Truly? You take care of me, I'll take care of you. If I have information, I decide which network gets it first. Who are you with?"

"UBS."

"Off the record?"

"Yes."

"Meadow Jones hired me."

"What can you tell me?"

"Let's get a drink. On me. I know how stingy the network expense accounts can be."

Samantha gets her fourth gin and tonic and Connor gets a scotch and soda. "I've seen you before, you know. On TV. Not so easy for a gal like you to go undercover."

"I guess not."

They talk for a drink and a half. Connor is charismatic and she can see he's a natural entrepreneur. He's also not concerned with appearing smart. He's happy to have his intelligence underrated, though Samantha notices he doesn't miss anything.

Connor can see Samantha is smart and looking for a break. "Samantha, here's what I can tell you. I don't think Meadow Jones did this. That's assuming it's a murder and not self-inflicted. Hugh Brooks did die due to blood loss from knife wounds to the neck, not tooth wounds. Cameras have Meadow leaving through the hotel lobby at five a.m. No blood on her anywhere. She confirms this. She says Hugh was asleep and fine at the time she left. She was going to meet friends at a late-night club who were still partying and her friends confirm this. The coroner's estimated range of the time of death can't rule out that Hugh was still alive when Meadow left him."

"Is there any evidence of a forced entry or someone else in the room?"

"They were partying in the cabana all night. Probably a dozen friends plus a dozen strangers who just crashed the party. Probably some damage to the room too. Forensics isn't in yet, but it's going to be a mess."

"And the knife?"

"Missing. The wounds line up with what could be a hotel steak knife that the hotel offers with a few of their entrees and several of these were ordered the night of the incident and not bussed until after the body was found."

"No cameras on the cabana?"

"There are some outdoor cameras of the pool area but none that can conclusively rule out a third party entering the cabana."

"What makes you think she didn't do it? The evidence doesn't rule her out."

Connor leans forward. "This is confidential." He pauses for effect. "She passed a poly."

"When?"

"Last night. It's something I encourage new clients to do when I take them on."

"Who administered the test?"

"It's through my organization. It's legit."

"Jesus. This story is getting crazier all the time." She takes the last sip of her drink. "Will you come on for an interview? Take us through what you know?"

He leans back. He's happy. He's very good at this. "Not now, I can't. Maybe at some point. I'll let you use what you have now, but it's not for attribution. If I see I can trust you, we'll see about more."

"Like what? I'd like to talk to Meadow."

"We'll see."

"I'll be fair."

"Look, I need to give her the right advice, but my feeling is that she should speak out at least one time. It would be an exclusive onetime sit down."

"I want it. Obviously. Connor, I'm here, I'm scrapping for the story. I'm getting the facts before anyone, I'm a lawyer, I know this stuff, I'll be fair."

"Easy, easy. Listen, use what you have for now. A source close to the case. For now. And just like you said, be fair. You be fair, then I'll be fair to you."

She needs to put together her report and call David Mueller and Ken Harper. They exchange mobile numbers and agree to talk the next day.

Two hours later the news division gives her the green light. They send a camera crew over from their local affiliate and bong into the ten p.m. programming on UBS-24 with breaking news from Samantha Davis, live outside the Delano.

"I'm standing outside the Delano Hotel on a beautiful, seventy-degree evening in Miami Beach and what is now the scene of a possible murder investigation. This hotel was restored in the nineties to its original nineteen-thirties art deco feel and has since been one of the iconic hangout spots in South Beach. With the discovery of the dead body of Hugh Brooks two days ago in one of the luxurious poolside cabanas, the hotel has become more of a tourist attraction than ever. At twenty-one years old, Brooks was already a Hollywood legend and bankable star, earning twenty-two million dollars for his last picture. Brooks and his offscreen and onscreen girlfriend Meadow Jones had taken a cabana here at the hotel. Once hotel management found the body, speculation has ranged from suicide to accidental overdose. Multiple sources now tell me another possibility exists. Murder. These sources also say that the scene in the cabana was very bloody and that there were strange wounds to the neck of Hugh Brooks."

Samantha pauses for the anchor to create a dialogue. "My goodness, Samantha. Do they have a suspect? Is Meadow Jones a suspect?"

"Authorities have not communicated that this is a murder investigation yet. A source close to the case confirms this is the direction they are headed. It also appears that Meadow Jones is cooperating with authorities and has complied with their request to remain available."

A crowd is forming around the front of the hotel on Collins Avenue. People are drawn in by the camera and the live shot, then stunned by Samantha's report. People come up from both directions on Collins as well as come out of the hotel in hurried walks. It looks like a nineteenth-century political stump speech.

The UBS-24 program cuts to a few still shots of the cabana lined in yellow police tape. Samantha has one more piece of information that she's been considering whether or not to use. Screw it, she thinks. It's all unconfirmed. "This same source tells us that Meadow Jones may have taken and passed a private polygraph regarding the murder. I emphasize this is an unconfirmed report."

The anchor signs off from Samantha and chaos breaks out. In the next ten minutes, more than 250 airline tickets for Miami are booked by five television news organizations. Every news channel ends its ten p.m. broadcast with a mention of possible new developments from Miami Beach. The AP releases a wire announcing the possibility of foul play in the death of Hugh Brooks.

The Miami chief of police slams down his phone and shouts, "*fuck.*" He calls an immediate press conference and wonders how that good-looking bitch got in front of his investigation. He thinks he should have gone public with more information sooner but he wanted the full forensics report back first to know whether the wounds could be self-inflicted. TV sets around South Beach turn off and people walk out their doors to the Delano to see if they can get a look. Number 1685 Collins Avenue turns into a block party. Many come dressed as vampires as a tribute to Hugh and Meadow.

Samantha heads back to her own hotel to prepare for a wall-to-wall day of reporting. It's the biggest celebrity crime story in years and it's hers. She's a day ahead of the rest of the industry.

14

Samantha has always been able to sleep when afforded the time to do it. This was useful practicing law when she was never afforded much time. She's sound asleep when her mobile phone rings at 5:30 a.m.

"Hello?"

"It's Connor Marks. I wanted to get you before you run off to do the morning show. Your report got a lot of pickup."

"I know."

"The police announced a murder investigation last night."

"I saw that." She's almost all the way awake now.

"I've read only the *Washington Post* and the *New York Times* so far. Both credit you with breaking the story."

"Good, I'll check that out."

"I believe *thank* and *you* are the two words you're looking for. And you're welcome."

She laughs. "Thank you for the scoop."

"You did a nice job and you looked great out there. And you were fair to us."

"I went with what I had. The police are probably a little ticked off with me."

"Screw them. I have another gift for you."

"Oh?"

"Katie Couric would pay us a million bucks for this, you know."

"Meadow Jones made twenty-two million bucks her last picture. She doesn't need the money."

"Exactly. We're giving it to you. Just you and a single cameraman. Four p.m. today, pretape. Undisclosed location, nearby and I'll call you at three p.m. with the address. You should be sitting in your car at three p.m. when I call. I'll see you in person by three thirty and we'll review a few ground rules."

"I'll be ready."

"Samantha."

"Yes."

"You ain't never had a friend like me," he says in a Robin Williams voice.

"It feels like a first."

"See you this afternoon, Sam."

Samantha hangs up and for a moment questions why this gift has come to her but she's a child star and beautiful and smart and she's used to success both earned and unearned. She doesn't question the gift again and she puts a call in to David Mueller to give him the update and make sure she has the resources she needs. The tape will go right to Mueller and be ready for prime time that night. Samantha is already booked on the network morning show, then has a hit at the top of every hour throughout the day on the cable channel. Everyone wants to hear her set the scene, describe the hotel and the change in atmosphere now that it's known to be a murder.

She's the best-informed reporter anywhere on this story and that comes through in her energy and confidence during her broadcast. Every other reporter on the scene projects a silent admission that they're late to the story and merely rebroadcasting another's work.

Samantha finishes her last hit outside the Delano at 2:10 p.m. then takes a short taxi ride back to her hotel to prepare for Connor Marks and Meadow Jones.

Charlie Keating is waiting for her in the lobby, sitting on a green felt couch that has the kind of acceptable mildew smell that comes from twenty years of sea air in a budget hotel lobby. He has two black canvas bags full of camera and lighting equipment. They've never met but he recognizes Samantha and stands to greet her.

"Samantha, I'm Charlie." Charlie's about sixty and has been either deep-sea fishing or working a camera in the Miami bureau for thirty years. His hair is blond and gray and his face is wrinkled and tanned except where his sunglasses usually are. The skin of his body is tan and loose over sinewy muscles.

"Thanks for meeting me, Charlie."

"My pleasure."

"You know the area well?"

"Very. Been here since before Space Shuttle *Challenger*."

When the hell was that? Vague childhood memories. "Okay, good. I'm not sure where we're going yet but it should be less than thirty minutes' drive. Let's get loaded up in the car and ready to go."

They get settled in the PT Cruiser with Charlie behind the wheel and at 2:59 p.m. Samantha's phone rings.

Connor gives an address on Fisher Island. Then he says, "And Samantha, just you and the cameraman and you keep a low profile. Pull your baseball caps down to your eyebrows. You're coming to the house of a friend of mine. There's a garage and the garage door will be open. Don't get out of the car until you're in the garage and we close the door behind you."

"Got it."

"Samantha, you better haul ass. You need to catch a ferry to get here."

"On my way. Bye." She hangs up.

Samantha repeats the address for Charlie. "Fisher Island? Very posh."

"Yeah? Never been."

"Oprah Winfrey has a house there. Julia Roberts too. It's that kind of place and only about two hundred homes. Private."

"I guess it's a good place for Meadow Jones to hide out. Connor Marks is a full-service consultant."

Charlie pulls the PT Cruiser onto Fifth Street. He wants to impress Samantha with manly driving but when he pins the gas pedal the engine pops to a high-pitched whir that feels unconnected to the slow rise of the speedometer needle. "Car's a little underpowered."

Samantha agrees. She likes Charlie and she wishes she knew him a little better so she could mock him.

Fifth becomes MacArthur Causeway, then they turn onto Terminal Island. They're weeks from the shortest daylight of the year and Samantha guesses they have about ninety minutes left of sun. She doesn't have a baseball cap but keeps her forehead rested against an open palm.

They pull up to a terminal dock where a ferry is waiting with two men holding lines and ready to cast off. She wonders if Connor arranged this as well. Charlie steers onto the ferry that has no other cars and the two men cast off the lines.

The ferry looks like a mini aircraft carrier. There's a raised bridge in the back for the captain and the rest is flat area, enough for six car lengths end to end and about four cars wide.

Charlie takes out his wallet and waves to one of the men. "I'll expense this. I think it's about thirty-five bucks for a car."

The man arrives at Charlie's window. "No fee today. It's been taken care of."

A few minutes later they tie up at the dock on Fisher Island. Charlie finds the house and pulls into the open garage. The house is Mediterranean and looks like the houses around it. White stucco on the outside with a red clay tile roof. Samantha looks up as a door from inside the garage opens. Connor Marks steps into the garage and presses a button on the wall. The door closes behind them.

Connor's energy has changed from their last encounter. He's no longer calm and humorous. He's now all business and urgent but still in control. He pulls Samantha into a massive living room with white tile floors and white area rugs. He puts Samantha down on a white sofa and before addressing her, he addresses the cameraman. "Set up there," he says, pointing to a corner of the room. "Samantha will be right here and Meadow in this chair next to her." The room is breezy and getting the last of the dusk light as well as the interior lighting that Connor has already turned on.

Connor gets down on one knee so he's eye level with Samantha. His speech is clipped and fast. "She's not doing well. She's distraught and taking medication to stay calm and keep it together. I don't know if we can pull this off but we'll try it. I'm going to give you ten minutes but if she starts to lose it at any point, I'm going to step in and end it. You get ten minutes, max."

"Alright." Samantha is playing catch-up with the rush of events and his energy. She can't get her thoughts out in front of the moment.

"If this is going to work we don't have much time and we're going to have to start right away. I don't want any talk about murder investigations. She's too fragile for that. Ask her what she remembers happening, ask her how she's holding up. That's it. Got it?"

"Okay."

"Good. Or I'll step in and end it. Right?"

"Okay."

Connor's energy is manic. He makes his point then races on leaving no room for questions or conversation. He turns to Charlie. "How much time do you need to set up?"

"Ten more minutes."

"Okay. We start in ten." He leaves the room without looking at Samantha again.

There are two other men in the room, about thirty years old and dressed business casual. Neither speaks and both stand next to the door Connor just went through. Samantha assumes they're security who work for Connor or Meadow. When Charlie finishes he gives them a thumbs-up and one of them goes through the door.

Five minutes later Connor walks out and is holding hands with Meadow Jones. His energy now is tender and slow and he delivers her to the chair the way a man will deliver a birthday cake so the candles don't blow out.

Meadow has makeup that is already streaked with tears. Her black hair is pulled back in a ponytail so she looks neither messy nor glamorous. She has dainty features and the petite body of Audrey Hepburn that belongs in a gown but now she's in a T-shirt and jeans.

Samantha stands and takes Meadow's hand. "I'm Samantha Davis. I'm sorry you're going through all this." She regrets the apology right away. For all she knows, Meadow is a murderer, but the situation is sympathetic.

Meadow nods her thanks like an ill person who doesn't have the strength for voice.

Connor steps back to the wall out of the camera shot. "You have ten minutes, Sam. Let's get started while we still can."

She looks to Connor then Charlie then back to Meadow. She wants to do a tougher interview but the situation has obliterated any chance of that. "Meadow, I'm going to ask you a couple questions. Do the best you can."

Meadow nods again. Samantha signals Charlie to roll tape.

"We're here for an exclusive interview with Meadow Jones. The investigation into the death of Hugh Brooks is still unfolding and now we have the opportunity to hear directly from Meadow Jones. Meadow, what happened during that night and the early morning hours leading up to Hugh's death?"

Meadow puts her hands to her face and takes a deep breath that makes her shoulders rise and fall. "It was a great day. We were having so much fun, surrounded by friends. We were out by the pool, back in the cabana, out to the beach for a swim in the ocean a few times." She stops because she can't both talk and keep from sobbing at the same time. The way her eyes are shaped, the tears drop from the outside corners of her eyes rather than the inside. She starts again. "Later in the evening we were pretty drunk. You know, we'd been drinking in the sun all day. Not a crazy amount but a few and the sun takes its toll. We went back to the cabana, ordered some food. The crowd with us started to change a little. Some of our friends brought their friends, which was cool. We expected that, but now we didn't know everyone personally. Everyone there was supposed to know someone but there was nobody who could know everyone, so there was no way to make sure a perfect stranger didn't make his way in. Anyone at the hotel could walk right by our cabana." She holds up her hands to show how outrageous she finds this in retrospect.

She moves her hands back to her eyes to wipe tears. "Anyway, we kept partying between the cabana and the pool bar 'til pretty late. I don't know the exact time but somewhere around one a.m. I crashed back at the cabana. I woke up around four thirty a.m. and there was a text from some friends at a club. Hugh was the only one in the cabana that I saw and he was asleep. I shook his shoulder a few times but he was pretty drunk and he didn't wake up but he was fine. He was fine!" The second fine is interrupted by a sob and she drops her head. She shakes it off. "I left for the club. I haven't been back to the cabana since. I haven't seen Hugh since."

Samantha nods. She lets the pause happen. "How are you holding up?"

Meadow starts to answer a few times but instead each time sucks a breath like a diver coming up for air. "Oh, I can't believe he's gone from me. He's really gone. It doesn't seem real to me and I hope it will be just some dream and I'll see him tomorrow." More tears. "Emotionally, I'm a mess. Intellectually, I know he's gone. Hugh's all that matters to me and I can't get him back. I'd like to go home where I can feel supported and in familiar surroundings but if there's anything I can do to help, I want to stay here. Maybe there's something I saw or heard that might mean something to the police. If I can help them solve this I want to do it. I want to do that for Hugh."

Samantha nods. "Has Hugh ever . . ."

"That's all," says Connor and he moves to Charlie to cut off the camera first. The interview is over.

15

The segment gets played in full during the eight, nine, and ten p.m. broadcasts. It gets posted to the Internet and by midnight has more than six millions views. For days journalists have recognized this as Samantha's story. Now the nation does too.

Three days later Samantha boards a flight back to New York. She had flown to Miami in coach and now takes her seat in Delta first class. She had nothing to do with booking the ticket, it's what UBS booked for her. Ken Harper wants to have a meeting.

There's been nothing new in the Hugh Brooks murder investigation. No arrests, no suspects, nobody's talking.

Samantha and Ken have developed a relationship that's different from boss and employee. It's more like coach and player. He's a believer in her talent and has picked her as the one he wants to succeed. He gives her advice and help when he can. In turn, she treats him as a friend but also with the respect an employee should have.

She spends an hour at her desk in New York for the first time in a week and she returns as many personal emails and calls as she can get through. At four p.m. she gets a text message from Ken. She wonders how many of the other on-air talent have a texting relationship with him. It's a good thing for her.

Meet me at Red in one hour. South Street Seaport.

She's never been to Red and only one time in her life has she been to South Street Seaport. She finishes her emails, packs up, and takes the elevator down. On the sidewalk she types back a text.

South Street Seaport?

Her phone beeps with a return text.

No media types and only a few wall street douche bags.

She knows she'll need to be on the east side so she starts walking to Grand Central.

Address? How do I get there?

He returns.

19 fulton. 4/5 train to fulton then walk east. Or pay $20 for a cab you cheap-skate.

She laughs but thinks two fifty is less than twenty and she has a mortgage to keep up. She keeps walking in the direction of Grand Central.

This is a hike. You better not bore me.

Amused by herself she takes the steps down to the train as the phone beeps again.

Trust me.

She climbs the stairs of the Fulton Street stop and walks east toward the river. In front of Red, Fulton Street is cobblestone and is pedestrian only.

In the summer it's more like a city park and the restaurants and bars have outdoor seating, but it's too cold for that now.

It's 4:30 p.m. and a few finance-looking types in suits have come down from their high-rise buildings that loom on the western and southern perimeter and they look ready for drinking.

Samantha walks in. There are fewer than a dozen people in Red and it's early enough that all the furniture is in place like a table setting no one has touched. There's a bar running the length of the wall with a row of high bar stools set at a forty-five-degree angle to the bar. Then there's a single row of two-top tables then a row of booths. She sees Ken sitting in the farthest booth and facing the entrance. He acknowledges her with a closed-lip smile.

"This is very cloak-and-dagger. Why not meet in your office?"

"This is more fun. Besides, I don't want people to think I'm pushing for you or promoting you."

"We can explain your office. If anyone sees us here, that ship has sailed."

"Nobody's going to see us here. People may recognize you but not me. I just don't want Mueller to know we met. I'll explain why."

Samantha nods. She would like to know why.

"The presidential election is a ways off, but we're revamping our politics team and I want to put you in the running for White House correspondent."

"That's great, thank you." This would be the first big step forward.

Ken continues. "Our viewers know you and like you. We just did some polling. A couple times a year we get an outside polling firm to test the likability of our on-air talent. You're near the top."

"Does this mean a raise?"

"Just be glad they like you. You haven't done much politics but you have credibility. People know you're smart. Best of all you're a beautiful woman who doesn't alienate female viewers. We specifically tested that. It's a rare thing."

"Ken, I'm in. I'd love the opportunity. Wherever you can use me."

"The Brooks story is great for you and you should stay on it. I'm going to start working you into more politics. Some sit-down interviews with the GOP candidates as they emerge, work you into the panel on the politics shows. You'll do some substitute anchoring on politics shows. I'll put you on the right track for that position and you need to put yourself on that track as well. Start working that beat."

Samantha doesn't want to say anything because she knows whatever she says will reveal too much, but her silence says enough.

"Your star is already rising." He lifts his beer. "America wants to see more."

"Ken, thank you for believing in me."

"Look, it's not all going to be my decision. It's David's but he likes you and there's no way he isn't already considering this. If I push him, it'll happen but I don't want him to think you and I are in cahoots."

"Okay."

"You'll stay in New York for now. Within a couple months I'll have you move to the DC bureau full-time. You'll need to relocate. You okay with that?"

"Say the word."

16

The following Monday Samantha's back in Delta first class to Miami. The police have nothing new, but two of Meadow's friends who met Meadow at the nightclub the night of the murder have agreed to talk with the media. It's being handled through Connor Marks, who has given Samantha the first interview.

They're set to meet at nine a.m. Tuesday so Samantha spends Monday night at the Delano. Maybe with her increased celebrity on the case, someone new will come forward willing to talk.

From Collins Avenue she walks up the hotel drive to the valet at the entrance. The hotel employees all recognize her and the word of her arrival moves into the hotel faster than she can. She walks past the sushi bar and the white drapes. She decides to find a place to sit that is out of the way so if anyone wants to speak with her, they can do so without being in full view.

She gets as far as the pool table at the end of the lobby and she sees the cop who introduced her to Connor as he's coming in from the pool side of the hotel. When he sees Samantha he scoffs and turns back to go outside. She smiles and waves but only in time to be to his back. As soon as he's out of sight he's there again. He's changed whatever was on his mind and he's walking to her fast and determined.

He's big and unhappy and she can't help herself from taking a step back.

"You got played, little lady." He wags a finger at her. It looks like a crooked banana.

"Excuse me?"

"You got played. I knew he was good, I just didn't know how stupid you are. Any journalistic standards? At all?"

"What are you talking about?"

"Let's see. In your first report Connor got you to say that she's cooperating with authorities. I'd say that's a generous description of her behavior. He even got you to put out the bullshit narrative that she passed a polygraph. Then for your finale, you set up a biased, sympathetic forum for a scripted statement by a Hollywood actress. There aren't any real questions. There's no arrest so there's no prosecutor. There's only one side that can talk about her and that's her. You gave Connor everything he wanted and he didn't even have to pay you."

Samantha's instinct is defensive under this attack but part of her knows he's making sense. She also sees the cop has extra energy behind his anger because he feels his introduction of Samantha and Connor makes him complicit in what eventually embarrassed the police. "If she wanted to talk to the media, she was going to talk to the media whether it was with me or someone else."

"Not like that. UBS isn't a Meadow Jones PR show. It's called journalism, Samantha. With a big *J*." He walks off and straightens his shirt like he just won a street fight.

The crowd around the pool table is staring but Samantha doesn't notice. She's replaying her interview with Meadow Jones. Everything from three p.m. on that day happened in such a rush that it was impossible to get the interview done any other way. Maybe it had nothing to do with Meadow Jones being medicated and fragile. Maybe it was just the media strategy that Connor created. Maybe Katie Couric would never have agreed to the terms Connor demanded. Maybe the polygraph story was bullshit.

17

At eight a.m. Tuesday morning, Samantha and Charlie make the same drive to the house on Fisher Island, this time in Charlie's personal van. It's the real kind of van that house painters and serial killers use. It's more than twenty years old with rust through the floorboards and a dying engine. Charlie doesn't even attempt man-driving. They pull into the garage just as before and Connor appears just as before and he takes Samantha's arm just as before but this time she yanks him back off his balance.

"Charlie, I'll meet you inside. I need to talk to Connor first."

Connor and Charlie exchange looks then Charlie exits. The door to the house closes and Connor says, "Yes?"

"You fucking used me!" It feels good for Samantha to let loose some rage. She's spent so much time trying to be nonconfrontational as a new journalist after a career of confrontation as a lawyer.

"What are you talking about?"

"For starters, the polygraph. Was that bullshit?"

"No."

"Then give it to me. I want to see the results."

"It was a human polygraph. Former CIA interrogators who are skilled at facial pattern recognition. These guys line up with the poly machine almost a hundred percent of the time. They have a consulting company that's real. The test is real."

"Give it to me."

"I'll have to clear if you can report it, but I'll let you look at the report if it makes you feel better."

"I will not be railroaded. I'm not going to be ushered through here like your employee and turn out a PR piece for Meadow. I'll interview your little twits in there but I'll ask whatever questions I want or you can go fuck yourself."

Connor smiles. He's back to the humorous calm he had when they first met. "Hold on a second. Who became America's favorite journalist this past week? Right now your network bosses are figuring out how many millions they need to pay on your next contract to keep you. Have you talked with your agent?"

"You used me. Admit it."

"Of course I did. And you used me."

"Asshole."

Connor likes Samantha. He doesn't like that she's upset but he feels he's in the right and that she's naïve on this point. "Samantha, everything that happened is aboveboard. Not only is everything that we've done legal, but there's nothing we've done that would even interfere with the legal process! If they find evidence to charge her, they'll charge. What I'm offering my client is reputational services. That's all. If she's not guilty, why should she be dragged through the mud in public?"

She notes that he said not guilty rather than innocent but doesn't care about that issue now. "I'm not talking about the legal process, you shit. I'm talking about journalism. You helped me break the story but you set me up to look like a novice in order to do it. That's not how I want to succeed in this business."

Connor sighs. Maybe not naïve. Just overly principled. "Okay. Guilty."

Samantha's shoulders drop a few inches and she feels relief. Nothing's changed other than the fact that he now understands her point.

Connor takes a step back and he squints at her. Then he starts to pace in front of her, looking at his shoes as he walks back and forth. He stops and puts his hands to his hips. "Let me make it up to you."

"Christ, Connor, what now?"

"No, I'm serious. This has nothing to do with Meadow." He's still calm but there's no humor. She thinks he looks angry.

"What is it?"

"I'm going to give you a name. It's the name of a woman who lives in Palm Beach Gardens. She's a retired waitress and I'll give you her address."

"Why would I want to talk with a retired waitress in Palm Beach Gardens?"

"Because she has a story to tell."

"How do you know?"

"It's something I fixed a long time ago." She expects a wink after a remark like that but his demeanor is still angry and flat.

"I need something more if I'm going to go all the way up there."

"No, you don't. Not if you trust me at all." He doesn't give her time to address this. "Tell her you know she's got a story for you. Tell her that her boy is eighteen now and it's time. If you need to do it, tell her you want to hear about Mitch."

"Should I tell her you sent me?"

"Sure. I'm doing this because this is a story she needs to tell for her own sanity. It's right for her and it helps you. I'm the only one who can get screwed. My name can't be near this."

"What's the name?"

"Monica Morris."

18

"Sam, you are kicking ass."

"Robin, if you knew what went on behind the scenes. I'm so pissed."

"Who cares what's going on behind the scenes. The scenes are fantastic and my daughter can't stop talking about you. You're my six-year-old's hero. Heroine."

"Her heroine is getting a crash course in media and PR. I got rope-a-doped." Samantha is carrying the pass card for her hotel room and her cell phone on the way to the hotel gym. It's a dank, claustrophobic gym with old equipment but it has a Lifecycle and no coworkers to check out her ass.

"What do you mean?"

"My reporting was friendlier to Meadow Jones than it should have been."

"Did you get the reporting wrong?"

"Not exactly wrong, but I wouldn't do it over again the same way. One of the things that's good for me about leaving the law is that I do better when I can work without consensus, but it's also going to be one of the risks."

"I'm not going to pretend to understand what you just said."

"I like the independence of this job and I like breaking the story. In this case I could have been more measured. More skeptical."

"Hindsight is twenty-twenty."

"So is foresight if you use it."

"Screw that. You're a commanding fucking presence on that screen.

You're smart and beautiful. I'm so proud of you and America wants more." Robin pauses. "It sounds to me that you're being too hard on yourself, the same way you always are, which is what makes you great. I bet any reporter would give an arm to have broken that story and to do it half as well as you did."

These are all things Samantha wants to hear and never listens to when coming from herself. It's nourishing to talk with someone who believes in you and is rooting for you. "Thanks, Robin."

"How's it going otherwise? Still better than a law firm?"

"Better. There's more Botox here. And more legs with lotion and spray tan. About the same amount of alcohol."

"And happiness?"

"Happier. I'm not sure if people are friendlier or just have more time to be friendly, but this is a happier place."

"What's next for my celebrity friend?"

"I don't know. This has definitely started something. I'm treated a little differently at work, in a good way. I got a text from my dad the other day that I'm trending number one in Yahoo! Search."

"Then there is nothing next. You're already there."

Samantha laughs. "I want to cover politics. I think I have the smarts and the credibility to be a serious reporter. Now I have some name recognition."

"What's holding you back?"

"About a million reporters trying to do the same thing."

"There's nobody like you."

"It's a damn good thing I've kept you around as a friend."

"It's true, Sam. I'm not saying this just because you're a friend. There's a quality about you. You're going to be right in the center of things. I know it."

MITCHELL MASON

19

Two Secret Service agents enter the room and scan from side to side, their eyes focused on something no one else can see, as though examining dust particles in the air.

Mitchell Mason sits in a wide, antique armchair by the lit fire in the living room of Blair House. The two Secret Service agents of his own detail already in the room, one in each of the room corners behind him, nod to the new arrivals who had come up through the cellar.

All four agents seem satisfied and one of the new agents speaks "All clear" into the lapel of his suit jacket signaling that President John Hammermill may enter and join Mitchell Mason by the fire.

Blair House is a pale-yellow, four-story townhouse at 1651 Pennsylvania Avenue, across the street from the White House. The president-elect and incoming First Family stay at Blair House in the days leading up to the inauguration and the the formal move into the White House.

The front of the townhouse has a green awning leading out to Lafayette Plaza. The area can be well protected by the Secret Service, but for tonight's meeting the president uses the tunnel under the plaza to avoid media attention.

Hammermill enters the room. He's wearing a tan cardigan and navy slacks. He's seventy-four and looks older than his years as is the way with most exiting presidents, especially those serving two terms. He is six foot three and was six foot five thirty years ago. He has a slight stoop and looks like the grandfather in an after school special.

Mason is still wearing a charcoal suit for the midnight meeting, which he now regrets wearing. He feels like a dressed-up job seeker who miscalculated the business casual company. He stands to greet Hammermill and they shake hands.

"John, I want to thank you for everything you did for me during the campaign."

"Mitchell, I was happy to do it, though you didn't need much help from me at all." Hammermill doesn't like Mason. He thinks he's overly ambitious and an empty suit, but he was the Democratic nominee and as a matter of ideology they're pretty close, provided Mason sticks to an ideology.

"The election was as much a referendum on the last eight years as it was on me. I wouldn't be here but for your popularity."

"Thank you, Mitchell. Here's hoping you keep it going and we'll have a span of Democrats in the White House that exceeds FDR and Truman." The old man bends noisy joints to get to the chair using both armrests and leaves Mason standing.

Damn, thinks Mason who hurries to catch up and get into his chair. Mason is as good as the sitting president now and wants to start acting like it. Holding this meeting at Blair House is a gesture in this regard on Hammermill's part but Mason still has the feeling it was the sort of kindness an adult would bestow on a minor. Mason adjusts his blue tie to no purpose, then decides he can issue a command by dismissing the Secret Service from the room, which he does.

He had spent a quarter hour picking out the tie he thought would best project authority, only to be outdone by a sweater. Mason is just under six feet with thick dark hair that is the product of a system that uses both his own and others' hair. He started it twenty years ago at the first sign of recession and he's certain he'd be entirely bald now without it. He's always known he'd be president one day. His father knew it too.

Mason went to Yale undergraduate and Harvard Law. His father was a US senator from New York who in later years acted like a talent agent for his only son, calling in favors when needed. Like Joe Kennedy, once Mason's father's personal ambitions for the presidency were unmet, the ambition transferred to the son.

"How are Evelyn and the kids?" asks Hammermill.

"Very well. Excited for tomorrow so I imagine they're upstairs tossing and turning."

"Of course." Hammermill smiles. He has the relaxed pose of a man who has done great things and has wisdom to share. But the pose is in part an act. At seventy-four and now relinquishing power, he has the first doubts that he can still be useful. He wants to be friendly with Mason because he hopes to be called on from time to time. He wants his wisdom to count. "Tomorrow is one of the most important events in modern times. It will mark the forty-sixth peaceful transfer of power as our head of state. No civilization in the history of the world can match that. Perhaps our country's greatest achievement."

Of course Mason knows this but hasn't thought about it in exactly that way. He decides people always think in grander terms when they're at the end of something than when they're at the beginning. "It's remarkable," he says.

Hammermill senses Mason's state of mind and says, "The transfer is always so much more pleasant when it stays within the party. In addition to a social call to wish you well, I hope I can take the liberty of offering some unsolicited practical advice with regard to the office."

"Of course, John. Please." Mason says this out of polite reflex then finds he is happy to sit back and listen a bit. Both political parties regard John Hammermill as brilliant. Mason hasn't taken real advice from anyone since his father died five years earlier.

"The most important thing to get right in the first months is the people around you."

Mason nods.

"You'll have an advantage in this over some presidents since you come in as governor of New York. You've been executive of a big state and you have a big staff to pull from. This was one of Obama's biggest problems. He spent a couple years in the Senate and had nobody around him. Never had a staff so he had to pull from scratch and he screwed it up all over the place."

Hammermill stands and Mason wonders where the hell he's going. He takes a few steps to the coffee table in front of the sofa in the center of the room and picks up a crystal decanter with brandy in it. He looks at Mason who nods yes and he pours two glasses.

Hammermill sits back down. He loves telling stories and this feels more like a story than a speech. "There are three kinds of appointments you'll make. Some have political consequences, some have personal consequences, and some are just gifts. The key appointments with political consequence are State, Justice, and Defense. Above all else, get great people. Here you should sacrifice partisanship, if you have to, to get great people."

Hammermill sips his brandy. Mason is listening but with a look that is challenging Hammermill to show him something of value. "The appointments of personal consequence are your chief of staff, possibly senior White House advisors. This is where you'll have an advantage having run a team for years. These people plan your agenda and run your day-to-day. They're constantly at your hip and do all the blocking and tackling for you. They know all your secrets. Let them do as much of that as possible. That is easy advice to give, harder to take. For these people, talent is nice but what really matters is loyalty."

"Sure." Mason tries to look bored, which he is. He's a little surprised Hammermill is giving him this lecture on the obvious. He was hoping for dirty laundry on some foreign heads of state.

"Now, I understand you've taken a mistress."

Mason's bored look is overtaken by shock. He's as surprised by Hammermill's knowledge of the affair as he is by the man's audacity to bring it up. His instinct is to deny it but recognizes in time that would be pointless so he searches for something clever. "I didn't know you could offer counsel in such matters, John."

"Oh, at seventy-four I don't indulge in such matters but I certainly know how I'd do it if I were a fifty-two-year-old president-elect."

"I see."

"Mitchell, I don't judge this one way or the other. I'm of the belief that it has no bearing on one's ability as a chief executive. I'm merely offering practical advice."

"Of course." Mason glances at the ceiling as though checking on his restless wife upstairs.

"I understand she was your deputy campaign manager."

"That's right. I had a campaign manager and two deputies."

"You plan to continue the affair?"

Mason had never imagined speaking so frankly about it. Certainly not with John Hammermill. He finds he can't put voice to it so he just nods up and down.

"Make her your communications director. It's a role plausibly held by an attractive forty-year-old woman. It's much less public-facing than press secretary so she can be a bit out of the way but still can be directed to travel with you without raising attention. You'll be always on the road and your life is scheduled in fifteen-minute increments. You'll need someone who has a reason to be there. The Secret Service will of course know, and that won't be a problem. They have a one hundred percent track record of covering the sexual indiscretions of presidents."

Mason nods, still refusing to participate audibly for reasons unknown even to himself.

"The gift appointments are Interior, Commerce, HUD, Transportation. You can put any dope in there. Republicans think Labor is a throwaway, but as a Democrat you need to take it more seriously. Agriculture, just make sure you get a real farmer. Treasury and Energy are different. You actually need to get someone good and credible. Health and Human Services, nobody even wants that. Then your other set of gifts are all the ambassadorships. Court of Saint James's is the most plumb. Holy See for a Catholic. You want to return a favor to an Irishman, give him Ireland. That sort of thing."

"Right."

"Don't get too much in the weeds. Get another good loyalist at the Office of Personnel Management and let them do the smaller ones."

Mason just nods again. Hammermill loved stunning him by addressing the affair then switching back to the banal with casualness. He switches back again.

"Listen, Mitchell, your affair is not widely known. As president, I learn things. You'll find that after today, you won't hear much from me unless you want to. There's one good thing you can say about George W. He shut the fuck up when he left office. He showed some class there. Clinton and Obama didn't do that."

Hammermill has met his goal for the meeting. He wanted to let Mason know that he knows about the affair and to do it in a way that is wrapped in helpfulness. Neither of them cares about anything else that was said. It was all just pointless filler.

Hammermill has an excellent piece of leverage and they both know it. Mason decides he'd better keep the old man happy.

20

Mason had joined the Yale Political Union his freshman year. The officers of the club knew his pedigree and called him the first week of school and asked him to join. Six other freshmen joined the nonpartisan club. The six others had an interest in politics but only Mason had lived it.

The freshmen would meet weekly to discuss political news. All seven were either Independents or Democrats which is the way in academia. Reagan was getting criticism for the Iran-Contra Affair and the nation was introduced to Oliver North.

The group of freshmen wanted to discuss the agenda items that would be most advantageous for the Democratic Party to stress in the upcoming election. Biden, Dukakis, and Hart all looked strong.

They went around the room offering their top idea, starting with Jaime Hutton. Mason has since forgotten the name but not the face. Jaime looked young for the class, physically undeveloped and a face that would be handsome in years to come. He was plenty smart but not confident and offered his ideas like apologies.

"I think Democrats should focus on gun control," he apologized. The discussion was designed to force everyone to participate, otherwise he would not have been comfortable making such a declaration. "I think it makes sense given Iran-Contra as a pressure point for Republicans. Senator Rose from Nevada would be a great champion for it and that could launch him into the national conversation."

Mason said, "Ha." It wasn't a laugh, it was the word. Jaime looked at Mason then looked away hoping someone else would jump in with their turn but they were all freshmen and Mason was the only leader in the room. Mason looked five years older than he was. He was athletic and cocky because that's who he thought he had to be around his father. "Do you have any idea what you're talking about?"

Jaime froze except for one more glance at Mason. Jaime thought the answer was no.

Mason said, "Gun control is political suicide. Take a guess who is the number one contributor to Rose." This information was not readily available to the public in those days. Mason knew only by listening in with his father and his father's friends but he traded on the information as though only an idiot wouldn't know. "The NRA."

Everyone in the room nodded up and down just a bit which seemed like the safe thing to do.

Mason went on, "Rose speaks out on gun control and he loses all that support. He's toast. And not just Rose. Half the Democrats get NRA support and therefore they support the NRA. And therefore also support guns. Gun control is an asinine idea."

Mason looked around the room and stopped on Jaime. He was proud of his lecture until he saw that face. Something already frail in Jaime had snapped. Something then broke loose in Mason too.

Mason had been bullied by his own father. He knew how it felt. He didn't want to become his tormentor.

Afterward he went to find Jaime in his dorm room and he apologized. He tried to befriend Jaime with only some success, but he made it clear to everyone that he considered Jaime a friend and he spoke up for Jaime at every opportunity. For his own part, Jaime decided politics was not for him and he treated Mason with cautious kindness, regarding him as a friendly lion.

Jaime never again came to a club meeting. Mason never again defeated a person he considered too weak to fight. Since then he's been a person who fights fair and fights to kill. He's of the warrior class but has found a higher moral plane than his father.

· · ·

Mason hands his tie to his chief of staff. "You do it." He had walked downstairs to the same living room of Blair House in a foul mood and a state of half dress. "And where the hell is Roberts?"

"It's only two minutes after nine."

"He should get here early and wait. I'm the fucking president as of today."

"In a few hours."

"This is deliberate by him. Asshole."

"Mitchell, you should be in a good mood today. Enjoy it." They had agreed Ron Stark would address his boss as Mitchell if just the two of them and Secret Service were in the room. "This evening you'll be sitting in the White House with approval numbers at seventy-nine percent." Stark is struggling to tie a Windsor knot around someone else's neck. He's nose to nose with Mason and he restraightens the two ends of the tie to start again.

"Incredible after the savagery of that campaign. I was a monster to almost half the country four months ago."

"The Republicans' fault. They told twice as many lies as we did."

"Probably even, but damn it, they told the first one. Twisting everything I ever said and going back thirty years. I was right out of college for God's sake."

"As they say, welcome to the national stage." Stark and Mason had been classmates at Yale. Stark went directly from college to an internship on Capitol Hill. He was an Obama staffer just prior to joining Mason as chief of staff for his run for governor in New York. "It's not the only thing you'll find different from Albany. For now, just revel in seventy-nine percent approval. It won't last."

"People are an amazing thing." Mason pauses. "Where the fuck is Roberts?"

Stark finishes the knot. "I'll go look into it." He knows his boss wants loyalty and action with only small doses of friendship. "Relax for a few minutes. I'll take care of it."

Mason had seen the gaffe in 2008 when Chief Justice John Roberts presided over Obama's swearing-in ceremony. He wants to make sure it doesn't happen again today. He knows he comes across as a diva but he doesn't care. Some people come from nothing and through wild circumstances manage to succeed in politics. For these people, once they've made it, the common background turns into an advantage because people think they can relate. This worked for presidents like Truman and Clinton. Other people get into politics with a leg up. Yale and Harvard, a senator for a father, and an eighty-million-dollar net worth. Then they spend their whole career apologizing for the advantages while trying to make the world think they're just regular people. Damn it, a leader doesn't need to be a regular person. He shouldn't be. A leader needs to be a fucking leader. Mason thinks, Kennedy didn't apologize for advantage and I won't either.

Stark and Roberts return to the room. Roberts is already dressed in the robes of Chief Justice and he looks the same as when he was nominated by Bush. Like Dick Clark, he has a period of decades when nothing seems to age. Maybe his bald spot is a little bigger, thinks Mason, making a mental note to circle behind Roberts at some point to have a look.

"Good morning, sir," says Roberts, extending his right hand.

"John," says Mason, taking the hand. Mason notices only that the face looking at him is neutral. Polite, respectful, but there's no way to tell if he likes or dislikes what he sees. Figures, thinks Mason. Probably practices in the damn mirror, has some clerk hold up a picture of Giselle then Rosie O'Donnell and sees if he can hold the line.

"How would you like to do this, sir?"

"Have you got a Bible on you?"

"No."

Stark walks to a shelf behind the sofa and picks up a book without looking at it. He hands it to Mason.

"*For Whom the Bell Tolls*? A bit secular for this, isn't it, Ron?"

Stark shrugs. "It's a dry run."

Roberts takes the book and hands it back to Stark. "Your wife will hold it like this. You put your hand on top like this. Then you repeat after me. I, Mitchell Connors Mason."

Mason repeats.

"Do solemnly swear that I will faithfully execute the office of the President of the United States."

Mason repeats.

"And will to the best of my ability."

Mason repeats.

"Preserve, protect, and defend the Constitution of the United States."

"Okay, got it." He smiles. "You sure you got it, John?" Mason loves the ribbing and Roberts is still neutral, though Stark can tell he's angry and thinks the president is petty and a jerk. Stark knows that the president usually comes across this way and has never minded it much because he knows that the president, except when it comes to his own marriage, is a force for good. Knowing the man is decent beneath the exterior is like being in on a secret. Stark has always admired those who don't mind appearing like a jerk and are actually good people. It's the reverse sort of person that he loathes. He senses that the worst parts of Mason are known to his friends.

Stark also knew Mason's father and knows he was a domineering man who needed to prove he was better than everyone else, a behavior than can normally be laughed at once identified. But when it's directed with particular vigor toward a young son, it's in its most perverse form and stamps indelible insecurities. The way the abused can become an abuser, Mason suffers from this same flaw though he has more self-awareness of it than his father had and he can sometimes control it.

"Are we done here?" asks Roberts.

"We're done."

"See you in a couple hours, sir," says Roberts.

"I'll walk you out, Mr. Chief Justice," says Stark.

21

Mason helps his three daughters into a separate car outside Blair House. Alexandra is twenty-two. She went to Harvard and is now at NYU Law School. Price is nineteen and at Harvard. Madison is sixteen and will remain in boarding school at St. George's in Rhode Island rather than move to DC. "You girls follow behind and we'll see you at the ceremony." The three girls are close friends and almost never fight over clothes or the bathroom or anything at all. They know they're in the same foxhole together for life and they're the only three who can ever be in it and at a young age they understand how important that is.

Mason walks forward to another limousine, helps his wife, Evelyn, inside then sits beside her so they are in the rearmost seats facing forward. The car starts the short and ceremonious drive to pick up the outgoing president and First Lady at the White House.

As Mason's political career has advanced, Evelyn has also grown. Mason's not sure how, but she already seems like a First Lady now, as if she has a unique power source that doesn't rely on his office. She seems more independent than she used to.

"John and Betty have been so gracious through the transition. It will be nice to spend some time with them this afternoon," says Evelyn.

Mason grunts.

"And they make such a handsome couple."

"I'm not going to let this job age me the way it did him. You've seen his skin up close. Looks like he's made out of wax."

"Mitchell, dear, please." He and Evelyn have been romantically distant for years, but they're good partners. Evelyn is satisfied with what she gets out of the arrangement. While Mason isn't in love with her, he likes her just fine and has convinced himself that the duration of this fondness is something close enough to love.

He puts a hand on her knee to be playful. The curmudgeon who's really soft at heart, which is the best reality of him that she can hope for and the one she's decided for herself is true. "Well, it does look a bit that way," he says.

In addition to the two family limousines, six other cars flank them. They drive through the gates and around to a stop at the front of the house, a route almost never used on other occasions. Mitchell and Evelyn Mason step out of the limo and start up the steps of the White House.

John Hammermill opens the door as the Masons approach and he and Betty step outside so the warm greeting can be on view for the world. Mason looks over Hammermill's shoulder and through the open doorway. Later in the day the house will be his.

Mason thinks of this father and how much his father wanted this for himself. Mason makes a long inhale through his nose and lifts his chin. He is happy and what makes him happy is not that his father would have been proud of him but that his father would have been jealous of him.

There are people in DC whose profession is White House transition. These people find other work during the term, but with every new president, they manage the changeover. The Masons' furniture and personal effects are already arranged and waiting to be moved inside today.

Taking a page from Bush 43, Mason asked his wife to design the rug for the Oval Office that each new president brings. She chose a pattern of swirling red, white, and blue that is inspired by a Calder tapestry she had bought years before. Mason can't stand it but says nothing.

"Evelyn, Mitchell, it's wonderful to see you both," says Hammermill from a few steps away, again taking the initiative of the moment. Mason is still smarting from feeling like the junior man in the room with Hammermill the night before.

Mason's eyes move from the interior of the house to Hammermill.

"Good to see you, John. Betty." The couples exchange handshakes and kisses on the cheeks.

"Mitchell, I can't tell you how happy I am to hand over the keys." Hammermill means it. Eight years was enough. "You'll make a fine president." This is imperceptibly less sincere.

"Thank you, John."

"Of course, feel free to call on me at any time."

"I'm certain I'll want to do that." Some urgent matters in Tierra del Fuego.

"Evelyn," says Betty, "if you ever have any questions, or just want to talk, I'm always here."

The wives start a conversation of their own and Mason say to Hammermill, "You did it with class, John."

This is something Hammermill has thought about before and he offers his conclusion. "Mitchell, for most leaders, leaders of any kind, success is the real measure. Every elite coach in sports is a known prick. Steve Jobs was not only a prick, he was a nut. If you're not in public service, all of that stuff is considered part of your genius. Only politicians are expected to succeed with class. The other stuff creates a scandal you need to deal with. It's an inappropriate standard for a political leader to have to do more than just succeed. It's shame you'll have to deal with it."

Mason thinks, He's calling me a prick. Or a nut.

Hammermill goes on. "The public requires a certain amount of class for their consumption. All that really means is that you need to avoid the big scandals and to be an effective leader." Hammermill smiles. "My feeling is that even if you are a prick, we need you on that wall, but the public won't get behind that. So you need to be careful."

"I see you're less careful about that now."

Hammermill appreciates that his point has gotten across. "Expresidents have all the fun."

The conversation is out of the earshot of media and the four of them know this is just an exchange for show. They could lip-sync or recite Shakespeare to the same effect. In unison they determine when enough is enough and as if hearing a silent whistle announcing halftime, they disengage conversation and make a synchronized turn to the car.

The women do the talking during the drive with politely timed laughter from the men. They take twelve minutes for the three-minute drive to the Capitol. The route is lined with gates and onlookers.

Since Reagan in 1981, the ceremony is typically held on the West Front of the Capitol. This location offers more of a stadium effect and looks over the Mall, rather than the East Portico where it used to be held, which overlooks a parking lot.

Mason looks at the crowd from the platform. Hundreds of thousands of people. He doesn't see faces, just a mash of colors and dots like the kind of pictures that if you stare at them long enough are supposed to take the shape of something in your mind. He knows the roofs are lined with snipers and the crowd is mixed with agents undercover. Thousands are on the ground to protect him but he doesn't think about security. Terrorism has been on the wane and the country seems happy and behind him.

Secret Service agents in suits stand at the perimeter of the platform. His wife stands on his left, his three daughters on his right. Mason keeps his feet planted and pointed toward the masses and rotates his shoulders to look at the temporary stands built behind him. He sees the Hammermills seated in the front row like parents at a school play while the country's governing class sits behind them.

He rotates back around and sees Marine One with motionless propellers, waiting on the lawn to lift Hammermill away to Andrews Air Force Base.

His eyes come to rest on Roberts, who approaches and places a closed Bible in Evelyn's hands. Roberts begins the swearing-in and Mason is moved by the moment more than he expected to be. He has never felt like a small thing in the universe. He always feels important within any scale, but at this moment he is distracted by a sense of history, the knowledge that he is a link in a chain connecting history to the future. He thinks of all the lives given in war to deliver this moment and of all the lives he may have to sacrifice to preserve the capacity for this kind of moment.

In this singularly humbling instance of his life, he has a flash of doubt about his abilities, his compass, his resolve to overcome adversity and be great. A moment of buyer's remorse, driving off the lot having spent all his money on the fancy sports car.

". . . preserve, protect, and defend the Constitution of the United States," finishes Mason.

Roberts nods. He shakes Mason's hand. "Congratulations, Mr. President," he says with no smile but not in a rude way either.

"Thank you, John."

Mason steps to the podium and a roaring crowd. He doesn't want to talk yet. He wants to let the noise come to him. He's comforted by the breeze of it as though opening the door of an air-conditioned store from a hot day.

He begins his speech by being gracious to Hammermill, who is enormously popular and of the same party. He needs to set up what will be the major challenges ahead so that it doesn't appear that his chief aim is not to screw up all the good work that was done before him, but he needs to do this in a way that is not critical of Hammermill. Domestically, he picks education reform where US global standing has continued a decades-long slow decline, and green energy which has been slow in coming for decades. With regard to foreign policy, he stresses a need for a stern but diplomatic approach to bring stability to the Middle East. This will eliminate terrorism by eliminating the breeding grounds for terrorists, in the same way one eliminates mosquitoes by eliminating the standing water of swampy areas.

The speech is plain but fine and is met with approval because the moment is met with approval. The country seems headed in a good direction and Mason is in the honeymoon of his relationship with the people.

From his inauguration speech, Mason and his wife are then to attend a luncheon at the Capitol's Statuary Hall hosted by the Democratic Speaker of the House and the Republican Senate majority leader. From there to the parade which leads them to the reviewing stand to watch the festivities. Mitchell had thought Hammermill was planning to attend both events but Hammermill approaches Mitchell on the platform as things are breaking up to offer his thanks and parting words.

"Mitchell, good luck to you. I hope to be of good use to your administration, and remember my advice last night." Hammermill winks, which is a gesture he rarely uses and saves for when he's feeling his most clever.

"Thank you, John. I'll be calling early and often." Fuck you.

Hammermill's detail has clearly known of his plans for some time as his path to Marine One is already charted and secure. The agents assigned to him envelop him and his wife and they start for the helicopter. At the base of the mobile staircase by the side of the helicopter stands a line of about a dozen servicemen from different branches of the military in dress uniform and at attention as Hammermill and his wife pass by and climb the stairs. The crowd cheers him on as he begins his last trip in the equipment of the chief executive.

At the last stair he looks back to the platform and Mason. It's a look that Mason thinks is saying, Communications director.

"Shit," mumbles Mason out loud. He thinks that these days if you don't want a person to know something bad about you, you actually have to be a good person.

"Dear?"

He takes her hand and gives a squeeze. "There goes a good man."

She gives a squeeze back and places her other arm across his chest in a quarter hug. "Takes one to know one, dear."

22

Mason had started the day on the Lifecycle in his bedroom from 7:00 to 7:45 a.m., which is how he starts every day.

He's in the Oval Office, where he's had a new fifty-two-inch TV screen mounted on the wall and is flipping between cable news channels. He's on GEAR when Ron Stark walks into the office.

"Can't anyone stop GEAR? Those bastards are going to be the death of me." He turns down the volume on a report about a quarter of robust job growth in India. "CNN is a snore. 24 says all things I agree with which is wonderful but not interesting. Someone besides GEAR needs to do this in a way that is fucking interesting."

"Sir, you shouldn't bother to watch all this stuff."

"It's the pulse of the nation, Ron. I need to be in touch with what the people are watching."

"Let someone on staff summarize it for you. We can give you a daily report of cable news, by channel. Or five times daily. Whatever you want, but I think it would be a good idea to pull away from it a little." The people who see the president in his office are surprised to find that he keeps the news on low volume at all times. Meetings with him are punctuated by his outbursts in response to reporting. This is particularly unsettling to generals who came to discuss military strategy. The channel is turned to GEAR most of the day, which also generates the most outbursts. Stark and other staffers have tried to dissuade the president from cable news.

"It's not the same, Ron. You know it's not. I can't get it from some report. I need to see what the people are seeing."

"Only a sliver of the population watches cable news."

"Cable sets the tone for the blogs, for print, for every kitchen conversation. It starts here." He points to the TV.

"Sir, you're a news maker, not a news consumer. Let them respond to you, not the other way around." This is as bold as Stark has been on the topic by far, but he's getting fed up and concerned.

Mason ignores the remark. He's seated behind his massive desk in a half recline with a tie and no jacket. His arm is flopped across the desk with fingers loosely around the remote as though offering it to the TV. Stark is at attention in front of the desk in a charcoal suit. Mason flips to UBS-24. "Have you seen this hot new gal on 24? Samantha Davis?"

Stark turns to the TV as though hearing an order he knows is immoral but must be obeyed. He has not seen her before and is impressed right away. Samantha Davis is doing a walk-and-talk interview along the wall of the Vietnam Memorial with Senator Paul Schmidt, who is head of the Foreign Relations Committee. Cam Ranh Bay is in the news again. Schmidt would look like her father except Samantha doesn't project daughter. She projects peer, though she's far more pleasing to look at than the old senator. "That should help their ratings."

"Absolutely."

"Don't even think about it, Mitchell." He still uses the name when they're alone and especially when they're alone talking about women.

"I wasn't thinking about it."

"Yes, you were."

"Not in a practical sense," Mitchell says, sounding disappointed in himself.

"Good."

"Ron, on that score"—he mutes the TV—"we need to keep things just to Susan." Susan Fitzgerald had been appointed communications director just after Mitchell's inauguration the month prior. "Anything more is too risky so I want you to keep women away. Just keep the young women away, I mean. You need to protect me." He looks hard at Ron.

"I'm serious. I don't want to have to deal with the temptation. Don't let any young, attractive women near me. Except Susan."

"I think that's a good idea, sir," says Ron, feeling like he's had the first bit of good news in a month. "I'll see to it."

Ron steps forward and places a binder on the president's desk. It contains about fifty pages. The first two are an agenda for the day, broken into quarter-hour increments. The rest of the pages are summary information and copies of press clippings to inform the president on each of his meetings. Sometimes the president skims the binder the night before, sometimes he doesn't get around to it.

The first meeting each day is at 8:30 a.m. and is with "staff," which typically includes Chief of Staff Ron Stark, White House Press Secretary Ted Knowles, Senior White House Advisor Armando Gomez, and Communications Director Susan Fitzgerald.

Ted Knowles is five eight and skinny with glasses and is just as smart and geeky as he looks. He always stands to his full height with a rigid back the way tall people never do. But he's the sort of geek who embraces his geekiness with good humor and so is liked by both geeks and non-geeks. He had been a politics beat journalist for the *Washington Post*, where he won the Gerald R. Ford Prize for Distinguished Reporting on the Presidency during the Hammermill administration. He has a wife, no kids, and is devoted to politics. Many, including Ted himself, anticipated he would rise to be editor of the paper but for reasons unknown to him, his upward climb stalled. He leveled off at politics beat journalist, though an award-winning and well-liked one.

Presidents tend to choose their press secretary from the press. Mason thought Ted's nonthreatening manner and likability would play well. Mason had also heard from Stark that the little geek had managed a number of affairs with younger women and both Stark and Mason felt it was safer to take a person like that in as an intimate.

Armando Gomez, prior to the call from Mason, was CFO for Goldman Sachs and has a net worth of two hundred million dollars, making Mason the second-richest man in the room. Gomez was raised in Brooklyn with very little money and managed scholarships for most of his education, then worked his way up at Goldman as an investment banker. He's fifty-two with young-looking skin and hair as black as ink. He's six feet and trim and feels that suits off the rack cannot flatter his trimness well enough, so all shirts and suits are made by Saint Laurie Merchant Tailors on Thirty-Second Street in Manhattan, where he's gone since before he could afford to. He's the kind of man that both Democrats and Republicans want to claim can be the product of their policy. For Mason, he checks two boxes. First, he's Hispanic. Second, he's a Democrat capitalist success story, which undermines the critics of liberal economic policy.

Despite the fancier clothes, Gomez is only a few decades removed from the younger Armando Gomez who fought on Brooklyn street corners, broke into restaurants overnight to steal food, and dealt marijuana and cocaine his last two years of high school, right up to the day his scholarship letter from Columbia arrived in the mail.

He's tough and opinionated. His background made him what he is without making him angry. Mason, he could take or leave. He accepted the position because the office of the president called upon him and he knows America is the only country where he could have gone from dealing on the street to two hundred million in personal assets as the CFO of the most prestigious bank in the world. His advice is good and unafraid, but he's not treated as an intimate.

Susan Fitzgerald is thirty-eight with blond hair and green eyes. She's not beautiful but is nice-looking and can make herself up to look close to beautiful and so she seeks affirmations of beauty from others by dressing in a seductive way and then is just good-looking enough to attract attention from the wrong sort. A man like Mitchell Mason, who has affairs.

She was a theater major at Vassar. After one year serving coffee in the West Village and failing auditions all over Manhattan, she took a job with a PR firm. She is five ten, which always made her feel awkward until she was thirty-four and met Mason for the first time in his office in Albany. He loved her height and coaxed an assuredness from her that theater directors had failed to do. She has a husband she likes and a five-year-old daughter she loves.

The affair with Mason gives her power beyond Evelyn and puts her second only to Mason himself. She has full knowledge of this power which gives her a strength that she carries around the White House like a badge. Those who know of the affair are slightly less intimidated than those who only suspect. Those who know feel that as a matter of survival they have some leverage in the knowledge they could use to defend themselves. Those who suspect are left to fear a force of unknown strength.

Stark opens the side door and the staff walk in to their seats. Mason comes around from his desk to sit in a cushioned chair at the head of a pod of furniture around a square coffee table. Across from Mason is a sofa where Ted Knowles and Armando Gomez sit. To Mason's right, Ron Stark sits in a chair. To Mason's left, Susan Fitzgerald sits in a chair.

Stark runs the meeting. "Sir, you're in the White House all day. No travel."

"I see that," says Mason reviewing the binder. "Looks like a lot of glad-handing and Boy Scout visits today."

"You have Edmund Tasker at two p.m." Tasker is the billionaire chief executive of a luxury hotel empire founded by his father. He's been an acquaintance of Mason for decades and was a large campaign donor.

"Right. Remind me. He wants France or Italy?"

"I suspect he'll settle for ambassadorship of either one. He opened hotels in Paris and Rome in the last three years. It's in your binder."

"I met Tasker about a month ago," says Gomez, "at a dinner party in Rye. You know he drives a Volvo? About a twelve-year-old Volvo."

"Isn't he worth a billion?" asks Ted Knowles.

"Five billion," says Gomez. "I like it. Shows a guy doesn't have to surround himself with toys. He can still be down to earth."

"Down to earth?" shouts Mason. "You think it's down to earth of him to drive a beat-up Volvo? A rich guy should drive a nice car. It's ostentatious for him to think he's great enough to permit himself that crappy car. He's making a statement just as much as if he were driving a Lamborghini. It's something in the extreme." The president smiles. "You have a lot to learn about snobs, Armando. I know about them, I come from a long line of snobs."

Coming from the streets of Brooklyn, Gomez is uncertain about snobs. He smiles while deciding and Stark gets them back on agenda.

"Italy and France are equally available. Both would require recalling one of Hammermill's men. Both have been in for about eight years and did little for your campaign. Easy transitions."

"Fine. I'll flip a coin," says Mason. Susan Fitzgerald laughs, finding the casualness with such power to be amusing.

"Otherwise, a light day, sir," says Stark.

"Good."

"Latest poll numbers have you at seventy-one percent approval," Stark adds, no longer waiting for Mason to ask. "That's a great number."

"It's down eight points from inauguration."

"That's typical as the honeymoon period ends. We can lose another ten and you're still doing great."

"We're not going to lose another ten damn points."

"Obviously that's not the plan, sir. I'm only saying an approval in the low sixties is historically a good number."

"Ron, don't underestimate the momentum of reputation." Mason takes the tone of a teacher barely keeping his patience as he tries multiple ways to explain a thing to a kid who just won't get it. He always takes this tone in meetings though, the same way he takes the chair at the head of the table to show who's the senior man in the room. "A man is never as good as his good reputation and never as bad as his bad reputation. Momentum carries it farther in either given direction."

Nobody in the room cares for this lecture, but they have to endure it. Only Stark could stop it by claiming a time constraint but this isn't the battle he wants to choose this morning.

Mason continues, "Take Lincoln. Revered now and beyond reproach. The Emancipator. Did he believe throughout his career that to free the slaves was a moral imperative and did he make that the keystone of his policy at great peril? No. Did he think it was a good thing? Sure. Was his timing expedient? Of course." Mason turns his head in a half circle, making eye contact with Stark, Knowles, Gomez, and finally Fitzgerald. "Lincoln's presidency is as old as the founding of the Mormon church. In the same way, his presidency has developed a myth and mystery so that people can't penetrate to the raw facts, nor do they want to. People want religion."

Mason's body language signals he's done and that he feels he's shared excellent wisdom. The staff is uncomfortable breaking the silence because they're so far off the agenda it seems impossible to speak without acknowledging the distance.

It's up to Stark, who actually forgives his boss and friend these moments. Mason's day is so jammed full of business with strangers that he needs these respites with his team to bullshit around a little. "Sir, momentum aside, we should accept now that this administration will see numbers in the sixties and fifties. And probably forties."

"We don't have to accept anything, Ron. Steve Jobs didn't accept that the iPhone had to be the size of a shoebox. It's time to get on the move." Mason also stands up. He steps behind Susan's chair then circles the staffers and goes back behind his desk and looks out the window with his hands on his hips. It's a pose that reminds him of a photograph of Kennedy during the Cuban Missile Crisis and he likes to stand that way. "Susan and I have discussed an overseas tour." He says her name while looking out the window so any eye contact with anyone is impossible. "I'm a month in office now and it's time. A two-week trip, starting in London. We'll make stops through Western Europe." He turns from the window to the group. "And I want to make a stop in Pakistan. The American people need to see me there."

It's a good plan, though the mention of Susan Fitzgerald felt gratuitous to everyone. Stark of course knows of the affair. Knowles has never been told but is certain of it. Gomez has sensed a flirtation but is still of the mind that there is no affair.

Susan takes this as a cue. She opens a folder on her lap and suggests to the team a two-week period to block out and a list of countries to visit and in what order, and that details will be forthcoming.

"Thank you, Susan." Mason gives a job-well-done smile. He's looking forward to two weeks in hotels with her and the lingerie he's already requested. Evelyn will not be making this trip.

23

All that day Mason is looking forward to his 3:30 p.m. meeting with Susan Fitzgerald to review the plan for the overseas trip. Mason has instructed Stark to schedule a few one-on-one meetings with Fitzgerald each week. Not enough to satisfy him and not enough to draw too much attention.

Mason has a 3:15 p.m. meeting with the ambassador from Spain which he ends five minutes early by blurting out his thanks to the ambassador for stopping by. Stark shows the ambassador out and knows Mason will want to be left alone. This also gives Stark the time he needs to make sure the security cameras in the Oval Office are temporarily turned off.

For his part, Stark would prefer that the president didn't have this distraction and vulnerability, but Stark is a realist. He knows Mason can't be more than human. With that much power comes sexual entitlement and if he wants one extra girl on the side, so be it. At least he's discreet and measured. He was an effective governor for New York and he can be an effective chief executive for the nation. He's certainly doing great things for Stark's career.

Fitzgerald enters the office from the main door, passing the three secretaries. Nothing clandestine. Her arms are crossed and full of binders and she looks very important. The head secretary closes the door behind Fitzgerald who walks forward and drops the binders in the chair where she had sat during the morning staff meeting.

She lifts her right heel out of her pump so that the shoe dangles from her toes and she kicks it over the president's desk at Mason, then does the same with the left. She steps up on the square coffee table in stockinged feet and turns her back to Mason. With her feet in place she swings her hips side to side while she lifts her black skirt over her waist to show off a red thong. "I'm here for my three thirty, Mr. President." Susan does this routine as much for herself as for Mason. Every woman should know what it feels like to do a striptease in the Oval Office, she thinks.

"We have only fifteen minutes, darlin'. Come on over here and don't adjust that skirt on your way."

She steps off the table in the direction of his desk. She feels like a cat. Her walk is more exaggerated than just foot over foot, and with the placement of each step her foot crosses her center line which gives a pleasant motion to her ass.

She comes around behind the desk and rolls Mason's chair back by pushing on the armrests. She sits her ass, which is bare but for the thong so it's only ass touching anything, where a pad of paper might go.

Mason rolls forward. She's above him and he reaches to grab the flesh of her behind and rests his face against the cashmere sweater covering her breasts. She embraces his head and massages his neck, careful not to mess his hair beyond what can be fixed by 3:45 p.m. The intensity of their hasty fondling increases until they're like teens at a drive-in.

Stark stands in the hallway outside the office next to two Secret Service agents, which is where he'll spend the full fifteen minutes. All three know exactly what's happening. It feels like a sad moment. Stark hopes the other two also feel this is a small price to pay.

24

Mitchell sits behind his desk in the Oval Office feeling very comfortable. He's already learned how to make the most of his home court advantage. He doesn't overplay his hand by looking cocky or too relaxed. He just looks in control.

Across from him sit Ron Stark and Jason Warren, the Senate majority leader and a Republican. Mason remembers Obama didn't invite the opposition party leaders in for a meeting until a year and a half into his administration. He was supposed to be the postpartisan president but this was a snub to Republicans and the press hit him for it. Mason isn't going to give something like that to the media or to any loudmouths in the Republican Party.

Mason is six weeks into his term and it was his idea to extend the invitation. Stark agrees it's a smart move. Mason is a damn good politician, thinks Stark. Mason and his team are set to leave for their overseas trip the following day, which has the president in an excellent mood.

"Jason, thank you for coming." Mason doesn't know Jason Warren well at all but knows that he and Hammermill had a good relationship. Hammermill governed as a moderate Democrat, even managing some entitlement reform including raising the social security retirement age to sixty-eight. The final two years of his administration had balanced budgets, something not achieved since Clinton, so the political frenzy around deficits and debt ceilings has abated. The last balanced budgets in decades were both under Democratic presidents, an effective sound bite for public consumption when Democrats paint Republicans as ridiculous for their key tenet of fiscal responsibility. Mason and Warren know it's more complicated.

"Thank you for inviting me, Mr. President. We look forward to continuing a close relationship with the White House."

"Of course, and I hope this meeting will set the tone for that."

"I hope so too." Warren is pleasant but cautious. He's heard the new president is a politician through and through, which could be made to be a good thing. Warren is a sixty-one-year-old senator from Arizona. The hair he has left is only around the sides and is gray. He's average height, average build, and he always wears a black suit, white shirt, and red tie. He's a conservative and proper man that nobody in the Senate dislikes.

Mason recognizes this as a sort of dance but as the leader of the world decides he doesn't need to play along so he charges in. "Jason, I want achievements in my first year. I'd like to do it with your support and deliver it to the American people wrapped in a bow. Now, I've called my shots and they're easy ones for you to get behind. I've chosen these issues in part for that reason. I want additional funding for green energy jobs and I want to cut back on tax breaks for oil. Oil companies are doing fine and we can present this as a package that will be cash flow neutral to the budget."

Warren shifts in his chair.

"Second is an increase in budget for the Department of Education with a mandate to improve urban public schools. We'll think of a name more clever than No Child Left Behind and roll it out."

"Well, it's in the details, sir. Education certainly needs help and I think people would certainly send more money in that direction provided they feel the money is spent efficiently. The Department of Education is seriously mismanaged. Any additional funding would have to be coupled with reform."

"We'll work in some reform. We'll appoint a bipartisan committee. You and I will choose the members. Don't put any of your hard-asses on it. Let's both pick people who can play ball. I want legislation passed in these two areas in year one, Jason. Just these two areas. I need that for my base. And I'll reciprocate support for your hot-button area. I can make some moves with regard to illegal immigration." Mason knows this would play well with Warren in Arizona.

Warren is a powerful man but Mason knows congressional leaders can't pull their party together in a block the way they used to. People at home watch Kevin Spacey play the House majority whip on TV and he uses leverage to intimidate congressmen to vote the way party leadership wants. People at home think that's how it really works but it hasn't worked that way in years.

The Supreme Court ruling on Citizens United let corporations give unlimited amounts to campaigns. For better or worse, that means party leadership can't pull their caucus together because congressmen don't owe the party, they owe whichever group gives them the money to win elections. The whip doesn't have a whip anymore.

When Senator Warren and others from Congress come to the Oval Office, they don't have the power they had a decade ago. It's a relative advantage to Mason. Congress isn't what it used to be. Most congressmen serve a few terms hoping they can turn that into a job in cable news.

"Again, it'll be in the details," says Warren.

"Of course. Let's set a bipartisan committee and you be the chair of it. Come up with a set of recommendations and brief Homeland Security two months from now."

"Okay. It'll be done." The new chief executive is much more prone to delegation that Hammermill was, thinks Warren. Hammermill was deep in the details. He loved it. That wasn't always for the best but he knew the issues as well as any of the lawmakers. Maybe Mason's methods are better. Mason was a governor and Hammermill a senator, so maybe that accounts for the different style.

"Very good. I think we have an understanding, Jason."

Cuts to oil company tax incentives have not been discussed. Warren knows that's a tough issue. It's been on the table for years and never gets resolved. Maybe he can get something very small. A token that's at least directionally correct. "As far as the big picture goes, sir, I think we do have an understanding. Let's see what we turn up."

The president's goal is to push his two issue areas and to keep it friendly. He knows detail will interrupt the friendliness. "You're a golfer, aren't you Jason?"

"I'm from Arizona."

"Of course. We'll get a round on the schedule. Maybe after your Homeland Security briefing."

"Certainly. I'd like that."

Mitchell knows Warren is sizing him up and decides to be active rather than passive in the process. "I'm a different man from Hammermill. People describe him as a collector of friends. They say that as a compliment. I think that's a bullshit way of being a friend and I never trust a man who is a collector of friends, a person who would acquire friendships like baseball cards on a shelf. That may make for good politics but it's shallow and it's bullshit. I'm the opposite. If someone is a friend of mine, they've likely put up with a hell of a lot of crap over the years. So we'll see how things work out for you and me."

Stark knows his cue and helps wrap things. He shows Warren out then returns to his chair by Mason. "What did you think, Mitchell?"

The president leans back with his hands in prayer position under his chin. Mason doesn't like dealing with congressmen because he doesn't respect them, especially those in the House. Congressmen think the people hate them and that's true. They think they accomplish nothing and that's also true. With the crackdown on earmarks, they can't even swindle money home for their constituents. They have no individual power but are around power all the time and when they meet with a powerful person they scramble around for the second-most-important chair in the room, or in the Suburban, thinking that the chair will bring them some respect if they get it. DC is a hierarchical town. "Nice enough. Very civil. This wasn't a meeting about commitments, but he seems like a noncommittal bastard."

"He's got his own base to look out for. There's enough common ground that we'll get something done, even if it's small. Then each side will start the spin on why it was a win and real progress for their own party."

"Exactly. And I have the bigger podium." Mason never would have run for Congress. It was the governor's mansion then the White House. He's a natural executive. He finishes that thought and is on to another. "He looks awfully stressed out for a guy from Arizona."

"The baldness doesn't help. He looks healthy enough for sixty-one."

Warren stops just outside the door to the Oval Office, trying to burn in his memory of the meeting with Mason for further review later. Little things in his subconscious will eventually surface to shape his opinion of the president. At the moment, he has no read of the man. He can't decide if he likes him or not, though there's no question he's very different from Hammermill. Things are changing here, he thinks.

After the meeting with Senator Warren, Mason needs to get to a Washington, DC, school where he is doing a reading with a kindergarten class. He and Stark leave the Oval Office for the motorcade.

Just outside the Oval Office are the three secretaries, seated at desks with their backs to the Rose Garden. Marianne Aidala is seated at the desk closest to the office door and when Mason steps out he sees her hand rush to her face to wipe tears. His pace never changes but he makes a ninety-degree turn to her desk as though he has planned to do it.

"Marianne, what's the matter?"

"I'm sorry, sir."

"What is it? Tell me." In a soft voice.

She looks at him without squaring her shoulders to him. "It's nothing, sir. I'm fine, thank you."

Mason is standing straight up in front of her desk, trying not to invade her personal space. He turns to Stark. "Ron, back in my office."

Mason and Ron Stark return to the Oval Office and close the door. The entourage that was on the way to the motorcade waits outside by the secretaries. "Ron, what's that all about? It's not the first time she's looked upset about something."

"I think that she and Regis Child are working through some issues." Regis Child is the president's personal aide. He's responsible for making sure the president stays on schedule, knows the dress code for events, and anticipates any and all needs. He also manages the secretaries and sits in a small room across from their desks.

"What are the issues?"

"Regis has had a problem with her commitment. The hours she works."

"She's in here at six a.m. every day, at least two hours before I am."

"And she leaves at four."

"Exactly. It's a ten-hour day. She has two kids she picks up from school. We went through all this when she started and we agreed to this schedule. Regis agreed to it."

"Regis works a lot more than ten hours and he thinks that from time to time, if certain days require it, she should stay late and find an accommodation for the kids."

"What does 'working through issues' mean? How has Regis been handling this?"

"He's been a little hard on her lately. He's working hard, under pressure. I guess it bothers him to see a regular ten-hour day."

"We agreed on a ten-hour day with her." Mason rubs his chin. "Damn."

"Sir?"

"Regis is good and he does a hell of a lot for me. But I won't have this. Fire him."

"Sir?"

"Marianne's a tough lady and he has her in tears for Christ's sake. Fire him."

"Are you sure?"

"Ron, number one, I won't have any bullies around here. I have no tolerance for that. Number two, I'm not going to lose talented people, especially young women, because they need to balance work with family commitments. The woman needs to be with her children, we told her that would be fine, and I'll be goddamned if we're going to give her a hard time about it."

"Yes, sir."

"Tell Regis he serves at the pleasure of the president and it is no longer my pleasure that he serve. If anyone asks why you let him go, you tell them exactly."

They walk back out of the Oval Office to the secretaries' desks. Mason walks back to Marianne's desk and this time puts his palms down on her desk and leans into her space.

"Marianne, I value the work you do here. Very much."

This triggers a response in Marianne right away. She's not recovered but is recovering quickly. Small praise from the president is powerful. "Thank you, sir."

Mason straightens back up and the entourage moves on without another word.

Stark is smiling. He likes Regis and isn't looking forward to firing him, but watching Mason make this decision is one of the occasional reminders he likes to have of why he loves the man.

25

About three times per week Mason and Evelyn have dinner together in the private dining room of the upstairs residence in the White House. The marriage is not typical but they are connected and these dinners fuel the connection.

The waiter, butler, and chef come with the job. The Masons pay for the grocery bill. Evelyn agrees on the menu with the chef at the beginning of the week. Mason is easy to please and when at home he likes simple meals because the rest of the time he eats at places that have many courses of small portions and sauces that are a chef's experiment.

Mason takes off his tie, changes his suit pants for jeans then walks the hall from his bedroom to the private dining room. The hallway is empty because they like to keep the Secret Service away when they're home together.

He turns right into the dining room and Evelyn is at the table reading *Harper's Bazaar*. Newspapers may die off but magazines with big, glossy fashion photos will be as tough as rats. "Hello, dear."

"Hello, wife."

"Spaghetti with meatballs."

"Thank God." Mason wonders if it would be better or worse for him if the public could see how normal he and Evelyn can be sometimes.

They had brought the Chippendale table and formal dining chairs from their home in New York because they wanted this room to feel familiar.

Mason sits under the Caio Fonseca painting which he bought when he was single because the painting seemed musical and made him feel good, which is the only reason to buy anything. He can't understand why anyone would have another person buy his art.

Evelyn is across the table and behind her on the console are busts of each of their children made by Bob Clyatt, an artist from home in Westchester.

Mason likes to think that the busts are there to remind him of why he does the hard work, that it is all for his daughters and the next generations. He is only semiconscious of the truth, though. The truth is that while he is mired in his imperfections, he has done the perfect things before that are represented in the busts, and that he can be a force for good. When the girls eat with them, they cover the busts with napkins.

"You're looking very handsome this evening."

"And you look ravishing as well." And she is a pretty woman. Mason says, "I saw a clip on the news from your speech at Georgetown Law School today. You were terrific."

"Thank you, dear."

The waiter enters in a tuxedo and white gloves and places salads of mixed greens in front of them.

There is kindness and warmth between Mason and Evelyn but in a Hallmark way. Each would spend twenty minutes picking out a card for the other with just the right sentiment, which is a thoughtful thing to do, but it would be better to write something on a blank page.

Both are a bit this way and both are capable of more but needed someone different to realize that potential in them. With each other, they have defaulted to what is emotionally easy and safe. But they have helped to realize the potential of other gifts in each other: efficiency, determination, and a desire to make the world better and to leave their mark on it.

A week ago, Ron Stark had shared news with Mason that had been less surprising to Stark the more he thought about it.

Stark had said, "Sir, I'm sorry to do it but I need to speak with you on a personal matter. It's about Evelyn." Stark had strained to keep eye contact and managed to do so right up to the word *lesbian*, when his eyes dropped to the floor then came back up for the next sentence. "Nothing's certain, just rumors going around, but you should know, sir, while the rumors are still well contained."

What the fuck? A lesbian?

"How is the State of the Union Address coming along?"

The president always begins major speeches with an outline of his own that he sends to speechwriters, then back to the president for changes, then back to the writers. "I'll finish a draft tonight. I'd like to read the opening to you after dinner."

"Of course."

Evelyn can always tell when the words are something Mason can make to sound authentic and in his own voice.

He looks at her and wonders if she's been with another woman. Recently. There's nothing off-putting about the concept itself. He knows he's worked with plenty of lesbians. It's the not knowing that is so fascinating to him. He hears rumors that his wife is a lesbian and he doesn't know her well enough to have an opinion on the rumor, and he doesn't connect with her well enough to ask.

It's not that he doesn't know her well at all. He has plenty of intellectual knowledge of her but very little emotional knowledge of her.

Mason thinks how this captures the dysfunction and the greatness. Their senses are deadened in one area and heightened in another.

He thinks he could come out and ask her about it, but where to start? So, dear, I hear you like girls. Do tell.

Evelyn looks into her husband's eyes and knows he'll look away first. She can always hold eye contact longer. It's a game she plays sometimes though he knows nothing of it. Tonight he's holding his gaze with her longer than normal and he's much more present tonight, she thinks.

Evelyn hasn't given thought to labeling herself though she's had a female lover for six years.

Helen Bly was on Mason's staff in Albany. Professional, respected, and as appearances go would be the less feminine half of a lesbian couple. Her hair is brown and short enough to cut with clippers except for the bangs. Her body has the hard lines of a fifty-year-old woman in great shape.

Helen and Evelyn were friendly from the start and without any sexual undercurrent. Helen was openly gay and comfortable and Evelyn once made a joke about a sexual connection between them. It was only a joke and in innocent conversation but in a subconscious way had identified a possibility.

Soon in a conscious way, Evelyn would come back to the theme. Helen, it would all be so much easier if you and I were just lovers.

Helen would laugh and agree and arrange the governor's schedule so that she could be near the governor's wife as often as possible. It was self-inflicted tease and denial but she'd known many women exploring the borders of their sexuality and she recognized something in Evelyn that suggested a relationship was no longer impossible.

At a fund-raiser for Mason in a private home in Bronxville, Helen and Evelyn walked together into the study that served as a coatroom for the evening. Evelyn doesn't remember who closed the door behind them because her heart rate blurred her recollection.

They both had been drinking wine. Before they could sort through the coats, Helen walked to the front of Evelyn and slowly closed the distance while they stared at each other on a dare, trying to find the courage between them. Helen stopped in front of Evelyn, too far to kiss and too close to talk.

Evelyn was in the position of authority and is on paper the nonlesbian. Helen has done all she can do and so they stare at each other with frightened smiles.

What Helen said next, Evelyn captured as a memory in the chaos of emotions and has savored it. "You have to be the one to do it."

It was infectious courage. Evelyn loved that Helen said it and so she kissed Helen there in the coatroom.

Sex with Helen is slower, more knowledgeable, and more effective than sex before. It happens in utter secrecy and about once per month, which is enough because Helen works in the East Wing now and she sees Helen every day and that gives life to something in her that Mason thinks is dead.

What lives between her and Mason she also loves, even if she doesn't love the man. She likes him and respects him, and the relationship allows her to do work she thinks is important. She believes in Mason and when his time as president is done maybe she'll leave him for Helen, though she thinks probably not.

Probably she'll just be honest with him about Helen and then maybe he'll be honest with her about the affairs she knows he's had. The openness would solidify the partnership and make them stronger.

Until then she has a role to play that comes from only a part of her. To be tough and smart for him and to be tough and smart for herself. On the whole, she likes life in the White House very much.

26

The Secret Service is not only discreet about what they witness, they won't let others see them witness the indiscretions. It's very considerate behavior.

Susan Fitzgerald walks into Mitchell Mason's room at the Fairmont San Francisco at one a.m. They're in town for a fund-raiser dinner, then another the next night in L.A. Mason's wearing a puffy white hotel-issue bathrobe and sitting in a chair with his feet up on the ottoman.

Susan waves hello and walks to the bathroom where she drops her black cocktail dress to the floor and puts on the other hotel robe. She doesn't tie the belt and walks back out to Mason with the front of the robe open as far apart as her nipples.

She straddles the ottoman in front of Mason and it all feels more erotic in silence. She massages the tops of his legs and parts his robe.

"Finally," she says. "That was a long night."

"Jesus, I know." He pulls his legs back and puts his feet on the floor. He leans in and kisses her forehead, then holds her shoulders and guides her into his lap so they can both lean into the chair. They're too tired for sex and prefer to enjoy a safe and comfortable moment.

Susan's cheek is on his chest and the top of her head touches the underside of his jaw. They both look out over the room and not at each other.

The most thoughtful and honest conversations between lovers happen without eye contact. When one of the couple is driving the car or preparing a meal or staring at nothing in the hotel room. Sustained eye contact is too dominant a force for dialogue.

"Thank God for this time with you, Susan," says Mason. "I need you."

"That's nice to hear."

"It's true. I need you and I need this time with you. It does so much for me. There's nowhere I can sneak away."

Susan swallows. This is less nice to hear. It sounds more like appreciation for a massage with a happy ending than for a spiritual connection. This thought comes to her now because it has come to her before. "Nowhere but here," she says.

"I'm trapped in my life. For the rest of my time on earth, I'm an historical figure. That's a claustrophobic idea."

"A lot of men would be happy to be trapped in your life."

"Even though I have no real friends, no real relationships? Do you realize you're the only relationship I have that's not shrouded in deception? How's that for irony? I deceive my wife. For Christ's sake, I don't even tell Ron Stark the whole truth of things, let alone anyone in Congress. They're all adversaries with respect to one thing or another. You're the only one. I trust you completely. There's nobody else I can really talk to, but look at us. We're a couple of cheaters."

Susan doesn't say anything for a few minutes. She always tries to dress up the truth in something better but Mason has said it too plainly. She says, "This affair makes me happy and so unhappy. I don't even remember a conscious decision about starting it. It somehow just started and seemed like the thing to do."

Mason does remember a conscious decision to get Susan into bed. "Well, it works for us."

"It's amazing what works for us. No little girl dreams of growing up to have an affair, even with the president. But I'm doing it anyway."

"You know how to sweet-talk a guy."

"People see me as a power-hungry, or at least power-enthralled, soulless slut. Don't you know that ninety-nine percent of the time I see myself the same way as they see me? The only one percent of the time that's any good is when we're together."

"Jesus, Susan, let the good times roll."

"I'm sorry. It's just that sometimes I think about my husband, or when I hold my daughter I think, What am I doing?"

"You're doing what you need to do to take care of yourself, to give yourself what you need. And so am I." He smooths her hair with his hand. "That's what this is for both of us. It's time away that we need. It's an adventure outside our obligations, not just away from marriage but from the office and everything else. This is a secret place to go where we can be ourselves and there's nobody to judge us or scrutinize us. It's a chance to be someone else for a moment. That's what this affair is. It's not cheating on our spouse, it's cheating on who we have set ourselves up to be."

Mason is happy with the analysis.

It makes Susan feel better because she needs it to.

PART TWO

He has all the virtues I dislike and none of the vices I admire.

—Winston Churchill, 1874–1965

SAMANTHA DAVIS

27

Samantha drives alone to the address in Palm Beach Gardens that Connor Marks gave her. She takes the Florida Turnpike to Military Trail then all the street names become words from golf. She turns on Fairway Drive to a traffic circle past the offices for PGA National. Roads with thirty-mile-an-hour speed limits and little bridges that exist only to make an underpass for golf carts run the perimeter of an eighteen-hole course. On either side she sees water hazards with fountains in the middle that cause the sun to glitter off the ripples that keep the mosquitoes from breeding.

Before she gets all the way to the PGA National Resort she turns right and into a gated community. It's the kind of security gate that's mostly for show because the condominiums behind the gate are almost all rentals to golfers and hardly anyone can produce identification with an address for the community. Samantha says she's here to visit Monica Morris. The guard looks dazed from too much sunshine and waves her through and as an afterthought presses a button to lift the wooden beam of the gate. The road winds around as before except there is a series of six-unit condo buildings nestled into palm trees on either side. Each is two floors with three units per floor. It's January, when most of the country's golf is happening in Florida and Arizona, so the units look full.

Samantha finds a spot in front of Monica's building. She's unannounced but it's 8:30 a.m. so she hopes to find her in. The hedges and grass are kept up well and it's a pretty high-end place for a retired waitress. Samantha's still not sure what she's doing here.

She rings the doorbell and takes two steps back so she doesn't seem confrontational. In seconds a chain latch slides and the door opens. A woman in a nightgown stands in the doorway looking friendly. She's early fifties and about five foot five with hair colored blond. She's had too much sun in her life, like everyone who lived in Florida in the seventies when they used baby oil instead of sunblock, but she's very attractive for her age except for the onset of sun damage. "Hello? Can I help you?"

"Hello. I'm Samantha Davis."

"Hello, Samantha." Samantha is getting good at picking up on when people recognize her without acknowledging it. It's just a flicker. Monica does not recognize her.

"I'd like to ask you a few questions."

Monica is pulled in opposing directions by loneliness and suspicion. "What kind of questions?" She holds the frame of the door.

"It goes back a few years. It might take only a few minutes of your time."

Monica opens the door all the way and takes a step back into the apartment but doesn't clear the entrance. It's progress and Samantha takes it. She moves two steps forward. "I know you have a story to tell. A big one, from your past."

Monica's eyes go wide but it's not the kind of fear that freezes a person. It's more. Monica can no longer make eye contact. It's fear and shame. "Who are you? Who are you with?"

"I'm a reporter."

"What do you want?"

"I want to know what happened."

"There's nothing to tell. What happened with what?" Monica's shifting her weight between her feet. Samantha knows she's about to get kicked out.

"Monica, your boy is eighteen now. It's time."

This stops the transfer of her weight. Monica plants her feet and meets Samantha's eyes. Questions are running through her mind but she doesn't ask any of them. "You need to leave, please."

"I'm sorry. I didn't mean to upset you." Samantha takes a step backward. She tries Connor's trigger. "Connor Marks sent me. I'd like to hear about Mitch."

This changes everything for Monica, as though the evil mask is removed to reveal a friend playing a goof the whole time. "Connor sent you?" She smiles a real smile and looks even prettier. "How is he? Oh my gosh. Come in, come in." She takes Samantha by the back of the arm, which she had wanted to do from the beginning. "Can I get you some coffee?"

"Coffee would be great, thank you. Black."

"Come sit down." It looks like a two-bedroom condo with an open floor plan for the living room, dining room, and kitchen. There's a round breakfast table with four chairs that must also be the dining table. Monica doesn't entertain much.

"Thank you."

"How is Connor?"

"He's doing well. His business is doing well. Lots of celebrity clients."

"Of course he's doing well. He's such a kind man and a smart man. He'll do well because people love him and he deserves to be loved." Monica has the energy of a person who is so excited to have company and so out of practice with it that she hardly knows what to do with herself. She gets out cream and sugar then remembers Samantha said black. Samantha watches and says nothing.

Monica brings the coffee and sits next to Samantha. She looks right at Samantha and holds the gaze while forcing her energy to level. "Connor wants you to speak with me about Mitch." It's not a question.

Samantha nods. She doesn't need to ask for it now. It's coming.

"I've wanted to for years, you know. I wanted to right away, on the spot. Sean was only six at the time. He's a freshman at Florida State." She smiles to say, How 'bout that. "That's when I met Connor. Twelve years ago. He told me to tuck it away, and God knows I've tried. Of course I would go to jail and I should but he told me Sean's only six so I couldn't be his mom. Someone else has to be mother to a six-year-old if a mother has to go to jail." She pauses. "Now he's eighteen and an adult, so I guess I can be mother from a jail cell. Connor might still be a father figure. He's looked after me these years and always looked after Sean. Takes him to a Miami Dolphins game every year. And they always do preseason baseball. I wonder how long I'd go to jail for. I guess it is what it is."

"Why would you go to jail?"

"Oh, he died, Samantha."

Samantha doesn't want to disrupt things by revealing ignorance. "Can you take me through what happened in your own words?"

Monica takes a breath and a sip of coffee. "Well, we had a lovely dinner on Palm Beach Island. Brazilian Court. It was a beautiful night; we sat outside in the courtyard. We had too much wine, I suppose, obviously. He was staying at a house in Jupiter, a friend's house. He had meetings in Stuart the next day. We were driving north on US One from dinner. We hit a man on a bicycle. I hit him. I was driving. He went flying and I pulled off and we saw him all mangled up. It was awful. I started to get out of the car but he held my wrist and stopped me. Told me to go on to Jupiter, that there was nothing we could do." Monica looks smaller and older than she did a few minutes ago. Her eyes fill with tears but don't release any. "Of course I knew that was wrong but he persuaded me." She says more firmly, "I let him persuade me. We were both so damned drunk. Anyway, we went to the house in Jupiter and we stayed around the house all the next day, both of us wrecks. Especially when we heard the news that the man on the bicycle died. That's when I met Connor."

Samantha nods. This poor woman has been wracked with guilt and the fear of losing her son for twelve years. Samantha would like to take notes of the interview but doesn't want to spook Monica. And anyway, even though it's an interesting human interest story, it's not the kind of thing she's likely to cover. More for local news. "So, Connor wasn't your dinner partner. You met Connor the day following the incident?"

"Yes."

"Well, who was in the car with you?"

Monica frowns. "Mitchell Mason, dear. The president of the United States."

TOM PAULEY

28

"Selling is at least half of what I do. For the first time I see the appropriateness of the election process. It's the best preparation there is for this crazy job." Tom Pauley sounds embattled but it's the brawny talk of a man who's winning.

"You're selling well," says Peter Brand, who stayed on as Tom's chief of staff after the election.

"I've been selling for a lot of years. If you're a trial attorney you need to sell the jury on your presentation of the facts. This is about the same thing, I just didn't realize I'd be doing so much of it. You know, the big difference is that when I was trying cases, I'd make a hundred decisions a day about the case on all sorts of matters big and small. Now the staff handles anything small. I set a policy and they do all the blocking and tackling. Instead of a hundred decisions a day, I make about three decisions a month. But they're big and I need to get them right."

Peter Brand nods. He's come to know Tom and knows this kind of ruminating means he's decided on a course for something. "What's on your mind?"

"The Republican base is firmly for what we're doing. So we're selling our plan to independents. That's our target, but we need to expand that. I want to go talk to the core of the left."

"You want to speak in front of a teachers union meeting?"

Tom nods. "Annual meetings are coming up. I may not win them over but maybe I can get them to view me as not evil. Maybe I can soften them. I know I just got in here, but maybe they'll be less motivated to vote against me next time even if they don't vote for me."

"They're going to view you as evil no matter what. Your policy is to make them fireable and pinch their pensions. There'll be some very bad TV footage—you getting booed and shouted down, possibly you getting some crap thrown at you."

"Who cares? If they treat me rough, that'll just fire up Republicans and it may offend some independents enough to come my way. I have thick skin."

Brand thinks this over. Tom comes across as such a nice guy. He is a nice guy. "It could work. You want me to set something up?"

"Show me a few options where we can do this. I'd like to do it in the next few weeks."

29

Tom is only four months into his administration. Fixing the public school systems was always a top agenda item through the campaign and a month earlier he was delivered the crisis he needed to make bold moves.

Three public schools in the Cumberland County system were exposed for cheating on standardized tests. Teachers had walked up and down the rows of students while giving the exam and announced that the answer to question number two was B, question number three was D. This was filmed by a student on an iPhone. The teachers released just enough answers to get a pass for the school without attracting unwanted attention.

The teachers in Cumberland don't feel guilt given the impossible task they have. The kids rarely show for class and when they do are either sedated by marijuana or are violent. A teacher doesn't have the opportunity to teach so all is fair in love, war, and insurmountable problems.

The states usually don't police this problem heavily. If the schools fail the tests or get caught cheating trying to pass, the state can lose the No Child Left Behind federal funding. If the state loses federal dollars, they need to raise the money somewhere else, usually by increasing property taxes. Nobody in North Carolina wants that.

When the Cumberland scandal broke, Tom knew he had what he needed. Fix the problem or everyone in the state is going to get a bigger tax bill because North Carolina might lose its federal funding.

Peter Brand enters Tom's office. "Okay, I have options and a recommendation. There's an American Federation of Teachers meeting in two months. I can get you on the speaker list for the AFT. But if you really want to go behind enemy lines, we should see the National Education Association next month. The AFT is teachers only. The NEA is more than teachers. It's school bus drivers, janitors, administrators. They don't care about the classroom so much, they just care about benefits, time off, work conditions for all the people paying them dues. They fight consolidation of schools even when it makes sense because that means fewer jobs for janitors and administrators. The NEA state chapter has an annual meeting in Raleigh next month. I called. They'll put you on the speaker list."

"Do it."

"Good. Consider it done." Brand writes a note and while still looking down says, "How are you going to address them?" It's a question that is meant to lead to the opportunity to give his own opinion of the matter.

"These kids need a fair start. They need the fundamentals, and once you get that, then all the bigger stuff happens after school. I had plenty of time in school and it doesn't compare to getting out there and doing. I loved law school but I learned more in the first six months of practicing law."

"You just touched on why universities are so liberal. It's the jaded professors. They think they're smarter and more valuable to society than lawyers, doctors, and forget about the bond traders. But we live in a society that thinks the best classroom is the real world so the guys out there doing it are making the most money and the professors are so poor they have to wear tweed jackets with holes at the elbow. They think we should live in a socialist society where the government determines that a bond trader makes a pauper's wage and that a university professor is our most distinguished position and is pegged at the highest wage."

"They'd still wear the tweed jackets."

"Designer tweed with fake holes."

Tom leans back, interlocks his fingers, and rests them on his stomach while he looks up at the ceiling. "I don't want a fight with the unions. I want to connect with them. There's no question the schools have a problem; that's an objective fact. I just want to accomplish two things. Without getting into ideology or methods, I want everyone to agree there's a problem to be solved and to feel motivated to solve it."

"No policy talk?"

"I'm going to talk problem first, then inspiration."

"Inspiration? You want them to start believing in excellence?"

"I know. Utopian. Look, I'm relatively new to this, much newer than you, but it seems to me that in the business of politics, ideology doesn't matter that much. We're basically the same animals; ideology is just how we arrange ourselves. It depends on what kind of house you grew up in, were you a young R or a young D."

Brand is a conservative thinker and he leans forward in disagreement. "Tom, I'll give it to you straight because that's the only thing I'm here to do. If you think we're all basically the same, you're way off the reservation. The differences are fundamental. A liberal thinks government is the best custodian of wealth. A conservative thinks it's private enterprise. With few exceptions, a liberal is a person who has either given up on being rich or has decided he's already rich enough. A conservative is trying to amass wealth."

"That's fine, but I can't say any of that. These people may fit your category but they don't see it as the insult that you do. They won't be millionaires but they'll make fifty grand a year while teaching and fifty grand a year for life once they retire. That's the plan they signed on for and they don't want it threatened. They're not thinking in terms of rich or not rich or free enterprise. They're thinking in terms of security." Tom's still looking at the ceiling. He likes these talks with Peter. They see things differently enough that it makes for good conversation. "There are ways to preserve a lot of that security. Especially for the good teachers. Hell, the good ones should be rewarded with much more. I need to inspire them to want greatness. Just a percentage of them. They can start to break the ranks that way."

30

"You ready?" asks Brand. Tom's set for nine a.m. as the first speaker of the day, the union hoping for lower attendance at that time.

"I am. Without saying the word *competition*, I want to remind them that it's human nature to believe in competition." Tom looks like a man on vacation about to walk to the beach for a swim. "We're going to do something important here today." Tom knows Peter is angry that he wasn't involved in the speech writing and angrier still that he hasn't even been allowed to read the speech. "Peter, I value you. I also know where you stand on policy. This isn't a policy speech. It's a human speech and it needs to come from only me."

Tom doesn't ask for absolution and Peter doesn't give it. Peter nods and they have a tense parting.

The Raleigh Convention Center opened in 2008. It's three levels, 150,000 square feet, and has a 32,000-square-foot ballroom where the NEA has three thousand chairs set up theater style and all the chairs are full at nine a.m. for the governor.

Tom takes the podium to zero applause. He puts his hands on the podium and smiles as though this is exactly the greeting he enjoys. "Thank you for the warm welcome." This gets a few laughs.

His voice is calm and slow. "Y'all ever read any Vince Lombardi quotes? Whether you like football or not, and I know many of you do, they're just the best things going. 'Winning is not everything, but wanting to win is. Winning is a habit, and unfortunately so is losing.'"

Tom takes a long pause to look around the room and connect with as many eyes as he can. His accent is extra folksy and Southern. He sounds like any man in the room. He continues, but in a voice that is faster and more harsh, "We are not winning. Our schools are not winning. Our children are not winning. North Carolina schools rank forty-six of the fifty states, this in a nation that has dropped to thirty-three in the world. Ladies and gentlemen, you are the custodians of a state education system that is the equivalent of a third world, underdeveloped country."

Tom lets the insult set and looks around the silent room. "I'm not talking about Republicans or Democrats, liberals or conservatives. These are just the plain facts. We have a major problem on our hands and are now under the threat of losing federal dollars." He points to the audience in cadence with these last three words. He takes a breath and slows his voice back down. "Let me go back to Vince Lombardi. 'Leaders are not born, they are made. Like anything else they are made through hard work, and that's the price we have to pay to achieve any goal.' 'The difference between a successful person and the others is not a lack of strength, not a lack of knowledge, but a lack of will.' 'The measure of who we are is what we do with what we have.'"

Tom takes another break. He wants this talk to come in simple, digestible bites. "Lombardi has a million of these but none of them is the best. The best one of all belongs to my daddy. When I was a boy he gave me some advice. He said, 'Son, it's not good to be a cocky person, but it's good to be cocky about one or two things.'" The crowd is silent. "He was right." So far there's been no policy to boo about. "Now I was a pretty damn good lawyer, and I'm a damn good governor." A few boos from the back of the room but few enough that individual voices are discernible. "Raise your hand if you feel cocky about our schools in North Carolina. Do you feel cocky about our standardized test scores?"

No hands are raised. Tom waits an extra long time with all hands in laps to drive the point. This is a rebuke and the rebuke has been acknowledged and accepted. "I didn't think so." Tom has been getting a sense of the energy of the crowd. Some seemed to like the Lombardi stuff and he thinks now is the time. "Raise your hand if you want to feel cocky about our schools. If you think we can do better!"

A few hands go up, which spring a few more, and for a moment momentum builds, then levels off at about thirty percent of hands. Many more would raise their hand but are not willing to show support for this governor.

"You brave ones are the start of something great. We need to do better, people. We must. Today we are robbing the future of our children and that must stop. We need to reward our great teachers and we need to remove those that would cheat and throw our state into scandal. We must fix a system that is clearly broken and I am here to ask you to help do it now!"

A few cheers start to go up from younger people in the crowd, people who were touched by Lombardi and have had their coffee. The cheers are then countered by boos, concentrated in the front left corner of the theater-style seating where the union leadership sits. Several stream an open-mouthed boo while pumping their arms with palms to the ceiling to say to others, Get up and boo.

Tom waits while the sounds intermingle. This is the result he wanted. When it quiets he says, "We're letting our children down. Doing better starts right here, here in this room with all of you. Muhammad Ali said, 'I will show you how great I am.'" Tom looks around. "Show me." He pauses, then says louder, "Show me." Then in his loudest voice, "Show me how great you are!" Tom hadn't been sure about using this part. On paper it felt overdone, but here it's working.

There's some clapping and more booing. "The fault of these test scores does not lie with our children. You know where it lies. We cannot sit by for this." Tom looks to the leadership of the union which is the source of the boos in the corner. He's made the ground he wanted to make and he wants to end with a challenge. He makes eye contact with Terry Stanton who is the president of the North Carolina chapter of the NEA. "I leave you with one last Lombardi. 'Show me a good loser and I'll show you a loser.'"

Tom keeps eye contact with Stanton an unnaturally long time then walks off the stage and the crowd is as silent as when he entered. He gets backstage where his nervous security detail flanks him and Peter Brand walks over to shake his hand. "Nice speech."

"Thanks."

"Interesting strategy."

"I realized five minutes into drafting it that a Republican governor can't inspire them. I had to create a third person in the conversation that they can trust and believe in. And who can get away with insulting them. Who better than Lombardi?"

"I actually like the one from your dad the best. Really your dad?"

"No, that's actually me, but it sounded better from my dad. I need to be only a messenger today."

"You're becoming a real politician. In the best way." Brand smiles. "And Ali. That was nice."

"I'm a Frazier fan myself, but that was a hell of a thing to say."

31

It takes two days for Tom's speech to the NEA to make national waves. At first it was covered by local media. Once the video footage got pickup on the Internet the national cable channels used it and it dominated the conversation through the Sunday morning political shows.

Never before had anyone stood in front of a union meeting and told them they were robbing the future of our children. Never had anyone stood toe to toe with the union and laid the fault for the failure to educate at their feet. Never had anyone looked Terry Stanton in the eye and said show me a good loser and I'll show you a loser.

Tom is back in the national spotlight. The unions fund a television ad campaign painting Tom as a wealthy and immoral plaintiff's attorney. The RNC funds a counter campaign praising Tom's legal career, his pro bono and successful defense of the Darby brothers, and his commitment to a better North Carolina public school system. The Cumberland County cheating scandal is discussed in the RNC ad by a deep and scary voice, followed by a child's voice asking for an opportunity to learn.

The nastier the fight gets, the more the RNC digs in to support Tom and the more he is a national figure. The RNC conducts a poll finding Tom's approval rating at sixty-six percent, one of the highest of any governor in the nation, and in a state that's been trending Democrat. The RNC publicizes the results at every opportunity as a way of declaring de facto victory for Tom's positions.

Three months later Tom has a scheduled visit at the governor's mansion from Benson Hill, the man who first vetted him at the Washington Duke. It's a private meeting between the two of them. "Boy, did we back the right horse."

Tom nods. It's a compliment but he doesn't like to be made to feel like a puppet on Benson's string.

Benson lacks any ability to pick up on subtle responses. He's like a one-way radio that can only send and not receive. He blazes on. "You've come a hell of a long way since our meeting at the Washington Duke. A hell of a long way." Benson pats his belly with one hand the way he might after a good meal. "I can tell you that people are very pleased. Very pleased."

"Good, thank you." No agenda was set for the twenty-minute meeting and Tom would rather not spend the time enduring condescending praise.

"So pleased that I have something to discuss with you."

Thank God. "Do tell."

"How do you feel about running for the big job?"

"It was a pain in the ass. This is great but I don't know if I'm going to run again. It's way too soon."

"I don't mean reelection. I mean election. To the big job. The White House."

Tom smiles, not taking him seriously. This time Benson does pick up on the sentiment.

"It's not me asking, Tom. It's the well-heeled powers that be around the RNC. They asked me to set up a meeting between you and Walter Shepard. He's the most well heeled of the behind-the-scenes guys. No GOP candidate is going very far without him, and he seems to like you."

"When?"

"ASAP. This week. Off the calendars, secret meeting, just you two, maybe me."

"Jesus, I've been here less than a year."

"Obama was in the Senate less than two. That's how it works, these are early talks. Exploratory, just like when you and I first met. If you want to make a run on this level, things start now."

Tom spins his chair so he's not facing Benson and he can concentrate. He'd prefer to leave the room but needs to finish the conversation. "Benson, I can't begin to weigh this. They can't possibly think I'm ready, or that I'd be ready in three years."

"The last person to run for president right out of his first term as governor and win was Jimmy Carter." He holds up a hand to say, Bad example. "My point is that it's happened. It can be done."

Tom is silent. He's not processing the information.

"Look, Tom, you're good on the issues for the most part. You have plenty of chops on domestic policy. They'll bring in foreign policy experts to get you up to speed on the other stuff. You'll be well versed by the time you need to be."

"There have to be better choices than me. The president's reelection team will call me inexperienced and they'll be right. They'll kill me on that."

Benson takes a breath. "Tom, you're a great choice. I like you. Personally I like you, so I'm going to just tell you flat out. Beating Mason will be tough. Unseating an incumbent president is always tough and right now Mason's approval numbers are strong. There are some quality GOP contenders who may sit it out four more years."

"So I'm a lamb being led to slaughter?"

"Hell, no! Anything can happen. Especially three years from now. Look at what's going on here in your state. This is the kind of thing that can spark national momentum and things turn in your favor." Benson leans forward and talks in his quieter, confidential voice. "And a national run wouldn't hurt you a bit. You remember you ran for governor thinking even if you lost, it would benefit your law practice. Imagine a national run for president. Even if you just kick it around in the early days. Put your toe in the water. You'll be a goddamned household name, Tom."

Tom spins back to face Benson but is looking through him. Once again, the guy makes some sense. Tom starts searching through a lifetime of memories for embarrassing moments. What would the national media dig up on him?

"Take the meeting, Tom."

Tom nods.

"I'll set it up. One hundred percent secret."

Tom nods again.

32

Tom can't go to a restaurant, café, or grocery store without being recognized. In addition to the regular public appearances of a governor, most people have seen an ad with his face, paid for either by the RNC or the unions.

Kenny Landers owns a private security business employing mainly army and marine veterans. He's one of the largest GOP donors in North Carolina, has a net worth around six hundred million and has a mansion outside Raleigh that makes a good location for Tom Pauley and Walter Shepard to have a private meeting.

"It's a pleasure to meet you, Tom."

"Nice to meet you, Walter. I appreciate the RNC funds defending me on the air waves."

"Of course. Defending you and the position. It's an important debate."

Kenny Landers is not present. A butler in uniform answered the door for both men and led them to a study where he took a drink order. Walter arrived first and got a scotch. Tom was five minutes later and got a gin and tonic. Neither man sat in the chair behind the desk of the study. They each picked a wooden armchair set in the area before the desk.

"I know Benson spoke to you. I'm here to reinforce to you our conviction that you're a strong candidate."

Tom has a lot of questions. He doesn't want to get interviewed by Walter. He wants to interview Walter. "What do you see as the downside of me getting in the race?"

"Well," Walter opens a palm in a here-you-go gesture, "conventional wisdom is that a sitting elected official who makes a run can face the risk of being viewed as abandoning his post. I think that's mitigated here because the central issue of your administration is a national issue. The people in North Carolina who don't support you will continue not to, either way. The people who do support you will want to see you carry forward with the issue on a national level, which of course includes North Carolina. They'll continue to support you."

Decent answer, thinks Tom. "Okay, what else?"

"Scrutiny. Like you haven't seen yet. Anything I need to be worried about?"

"I'm a plaintiff's attorney."

Walter laughs. "We can work around that. Anything else?"

Tom spins the ice in his glass. "I'm a pretty boring guy. Not much to talk about."

"I'm serious, Tom. Millions of dollars will be spent in pursuit of something to talk about."

Tom takes a sip. "There's nothing, Walter. I'm human, but I pay my taxes and have never had a run-in with the law."

"Drugs?"

"Pot in college and not since. And nothing other than pot and alcohol."

"Hookers?"

"Nope."

"Girlfriends?"

"Nothing very serious."

"Gay?"

"Are you vetting or propositioning?"

Walter smiles an impatient smile rather than ask again.

"No, and never dabbled either. Look, aren't you guys going to investigate all this?"

"We have already, a little. We're just talking now, but we'll spend a lot of money looking into you. I hope you don't mind." Walter smiles. "It's just the process. It's better this way. If we find it now, it doesn't go anywhere and you don't run. If they find it later, you're screwed."

"Fine. Hey, what the hell."

They're both silent for a moment and a drink.

"What's the upside, Walter?"

"You're a national name. You get paid fifty to a hundred grand to make a speech. You'll wind up getting tapped for something plum with a nice salary. That's if you lose. You're a hell of a candidate, Tom. You could pull this off."

"Why are better candidates sitting this out?"

Walter stands and puts his scotch on the desk. He turns to Tom and points a finger, not at Tom but up, like a lecturer. "I don't think there is a better candidate, Tom. For a candidate to come from out of the pack to win an election, he needs two crises. Carter had the Vietnam War and Watergate. The DNC had a total meltdown coming out of the Vietnam War and Carter fell into the primary win. Watergate gave him the White House. Obama had the Iraq War and the 2008 financial crisis. Hillary Clinton had voted to authorize the use of force in Iraq and in the Democratic primary Obama used that to club her like a harp seal. In the general, just as McCain is tightening with Obama, the economy collapses under Bush and any Republican is toast."

Walter turns back to the desk, takes a sip of scotch and puts it back down. He turns to Tom and now he points right at him. "You already have one crisis. Cumberland County is going to win you the primary. Then you're one crisis away. Just a flap of a butterfly's wings from around the world that shows up here a couple years later."

Tom is silent, replaying the words in his head. He knows Walter is here to sell him, but despite the skepticism that comes with that awareness, he feels himself being sold. "I have no organization."

"Bullshit. You have the governor's staff of a good-sized state. You're fresh out of an election so you're tuned up. You'd have the unofficial support of me and most every large GOP donor, and things would start developing behind the scenes in very official-looking ways."

Tom finishes his drink. "I need to talk to my wife."

33

After promising to wait twenty-four hours before answering her husband, Alison says she wants Tom to run. She says we get one chance to live this life and this is too big to sit out. They discussed the risks that Walter raised with Tom, but they do so only halfheartedly. Alison's instinct was to say yes from the start.

Tom calls Benson Hill and says he's willing to take the next steps with Walter and that they should continue what Tom calls a mutual feeling-out process.

Benson is happy with the call. He tells Tom it's the right move for the party and for the country and Tom can count on Benson's full support and lots of money.

Within two weeks Tom starts to get phone calls from people he knows but has never met. Republican governors from three states call and tell him how important it is that he run, that he's the man for the job, and that he can count on their support. Senate Majority Leader Jason Warren calls to say that he's a long way from endorsing anyone but thinks it's the right thing for Tom to get in the primary and that, at the moment, he thinks Tom is the most promising candidate. He goes on to advise with a laugh that while he loved the NEA speech, when Tom gets to the national stage he should tone down the talk of losers and idiots, but then he adds that maybe he's just gotten too old and careful.

Two weeks after that, Walter calls again. He wants to set a dinner with Tom, the Koch brothers, Kenneth Langone, Stanley Druckenmiller, and Foster Freiss. They want to take the measure of the man, in person. If the dinner goes well, Tom can count on a decent amount of early money to get an organization built. As the field narrows and if Tom is still standing, he can count on much more money.

Tom starts spending an increased amount of time meeting with potential donors, watching the polls on the president's approval rating, and watching cable news. None of these activities is specific to North Carolina, and word of Tom's possible candidacy for the GOP ticket is already in the media and his lieutenant governor is already picking up additional responsibility.

Six months later, Tom publicly announces his intention to run and starts holding fund-raisers.

34

The Lincoln Town Car takes Montgomery Avenue past the Merion Cricket Club to Bryn Mawr. Peter Brand turns pages on a clipboard while Tom looks out the window. Peter's goal is to keep Tom rested, happy, and informed going into these events.

"There'll be two quick intro speeches, then you give the twenty-minute version of your talk, then Natalie Richards is going to do four songs. Then drinks for thirty minutes followed by a sit-down dinner, ninety minutes for that. Should be out of here by nine thirty."

"How'd you get Natalie Richards for this?"

"She's Republican and she's decided you're her man. She went to high school here and she was visiting home for the holidays, so it worked out."

"A country music star from the Main Line?"

"They don't have to grow up in Nashville, they just have to move there."

"Hmm."

"We actually had to clear it with her as well as this production company she's in the middle of a messy breakup with. J. K. Livin. Run by Matthew McConaughey."

"Jay Kay Livin'?"

"J. K. stands for 'just keep.'"

"Just Keep Livin."

"Right. I know. He sounds like a dork out of *Fast Times*."

"Jesus. That's a sign of a person who surrounds himself with people who do nothing but kiss his ass. Don't ever let me do something that absurd."

Peter reviews the names of people Tom needs to remember as the car pulls up to the stoplight before the Baldwin School. They're an hour early to the event which gives Tom the opportunity to meet with Senator Carol Chance before any guests arrive.

The Town Car turns off Montgomery Avenue through the iron and stone gates that date back to the 1800s when the private girls' school was a private home and hotel. They drive a winding approach through the willow trees in winter, which look translucent and ghost-like. The historic schoolhouse is a mix of red brick and gray stone with a half dozen chimneys and looks like a French château for a prince. They drive past the schoolhouse to the new athletic center that was built in 2008.

"I think we're in the right place to raise some money," says Brand.

They pull their wool trench coats over their suits and step out of the car. Tom doesn't wear a hat because it will be an evening of photographs and he needs his hair to stay in place. The twenty-degree weather makes his ears sting and turn red.

The event is staffed by volunteers from the Pennsylvania Republican Party, and a twenty-five-year-old handler greets them and brings them in the building. He's wearing a suit that hasn't been dry-cleaned in many wears and the creases are all flat.

The handler takes them into the high school gymnasium, which is in the last stages of transformation. The basketball nets have been raised so that the backboards are parallel to the ceiling. Streamers and banners with Pauley for President line the walls and bleachers. Red Chinese lanterns hang from the ceiling.

"I'd like to introduce you to Dorothy Pierre who has organized the event preparations." The handler walks in front taking short, fast steps and keeps looking back at his guests and forward again in a jerky motion as if he expects them to disappear at any moment. Tom and Peter follow with long, even strides. The handler never introduces himself and seems to think his name is too inconsequential to mention.

They approach a tall woman in her fifties whose body is all sharp angles. She has a black evening gown with a pearl necklace and pearl earrings. Her hair is dyed blond and she wears it up. Tom notices she's had some facial work done. He imagines she had a nice eye lift in her thirties that was too soon, and now in her fifties when she needs it, the second one can't look natural.

She doesn't see them coming and is hollering at a vendor and pointing at ostrich feathers that are part of the centerpiece of each of the round, ten-person banquet tables.

"These won't do. They're too short."

The vendor is speechless. The handler leans into her line of sight. "Ms. Pierre?"

She turns. "Governor Pauley! How wonderful to meet you!" she says in a practiced way. "One moment." She turns back to the vendor before Tom can respond. "I said these are too short. We'll need longer feathers."

"Ma'am, they're ostrich feathers."

"I know that. We need longer ones."

The man answers like a subordinate who knows he's on the firmer ground. "They come in one size. That's how God made them."

She smiles. "Honey, we can always improve on what God did."

Tom looks at her face and thinks, Not in the long run.

"What should I do?" asks the man.

"Find a black stick that's a foot long and the same width as the feather stem and attach it. Give it some lift out of the vase. Break into the arts and crafts classroom if you have to." She turns back to Tom. "Governor, Governor."

She opens the space between her body and right elbow the way a lady can be taken by a gentleman, then with her off hand she takes Tom's arm and threads it through so they can do a lap of the gym floor arm in arm. Tom thanks her for all the hard work and has the opportunity to say almost nothing else before he is shown to a table with Natalie Richards.

She has tan skin under faded denim. Her body is incredible and she presents it in the way that female athletes do. Physique isn't the goal, it's just what happens. She works out for the job, not to be pretty. She's part tomboy, part sexy, and even her blond hair is simple and straight to the shoulder and couldn't look better. Tom guesses she's thirty.

"Governor Pauley, it's a pleasure to meet you."

"Call me Tom and thank you for coming. Your star power is out of proportion with our little event here."

"I'm happy to do it. I'm a big supporter of yours, ever since I saw your speech to the NEA. Anything I can do to help you is helping our country." She's picked up some of the Southern accent, especially with the word *country*.

"I understand you went to high school at Baldwin."

"I played point guard on this hardwood under your feet."

"I bet you were good."

"I still am!" She slaps the table like a girl who takes charge of her flirting. "Don't eat too much tonight. I know where they still keep the basketballs around here. After dinner we'll lower the nets and I'll take you in one on one."

"I don't like my chances."

Peter Brand walks to the table and leans over Tom's shoulder. "The senator is running late. She'll be here in time for the introductions and we can have a private meeting with her after the event. She sends apologies."

"Fine," says Tom. Peter walks away to direct staffers and Tom turns back to Natalie. "I had no idea you're political."

"Then you must not follow me on Twitter."

"That's true."

"Most people who like country music don't live near either coast. And most of those people like smaller government and a strong military." She's drinking beer from a glass and takes a sip. She smiles and says, "No bourbon before the show."

"Of course not."

"You, on the other hand, need a drink."

A waiter has been standing a respectful ten feet from the table with his hands in the fig leaf position. Natalie waves and he comes forward with a bow.

"Gin and tonic," says Tom.

"Right away, sir. For you, ma'am?"

"Maker's on the rocks." She looks at Tom. "What the hell. How often does a girl get to play for the next president?"

Tom laughs. "As often as you like." He says this just in time for it still to be a joking response to her joke, rather than an awkward and seriously considered answer.

The waiter walks to the bar set up on a long folding table in the corner of the gym and is back with the drinks.

"You like music, Governor?"

"Most boys from North Carolina grow up with Southern rock."

"Lynyrd Skynyrd."

"Exactly."

"Do you play guitar?" she asks.

"Terribly."

"I'll be the judge. Follow me, Guv." She smiles. The smile is not a reflex to happiness. It's deliberate and very appealing. A person knows when he's flirting and being flirted with. The level of attentiveness increased above what's required for normal conversation, which is why Bill Clinton was so effective. He flirted with everyone, even the ones he wasn't trying to sleep with.

"Lead on."

"Bring your gin." She stands and starts ahead of him. Her jeans are thin with no back pockets and made from a stretchy material that grabs her ass. Tom can see the muscles quiver up her leg with her footfalls. He stands and catches up with her and he knows he would have been better off if he hadn't seen that.

They both walk and understand that it's better not to look to see if anyone is watching. They walk with purpose, projecting innocence. An elevated stage is set up in the corner of the gym opposite the bar. The stage is about three feet high and eight feet square. Natalie will be playing solo and acoustic so there is only one chair. There are two guitars set in stands on the stage.

She leaps up on the stage in front of Tom. From knees to navel she's very much on display to him.

"You're in great shape," he says. He's keeping track internally and knows this is a line crossed and he disapproves of himself.

"All part of the show."

Tom steps up onstage using his hands for support. Still neither of them has dared to check what sort of interest they are creating in the gym. Tom knows this is self-defeating behavior but people who have been on the road have pent-up demand for human connection. There is a physical craving for a spark and a rise in heart rate.

"I'm going to see what you can do on my Gibson." She hands him the guitar with "Natalie Richards" written up the neck in mother-of-pearl. "Have a seat."

Tom sits and strums chords. "There'll be no singing."

"Fair enough."

After the warm-up, Tom starts to play "I Won't Back Down" by Tom Petty, and Natalie recognizes it. "Pretty good," she says.

A few cameras flash and Tom keeps playing. "Thank you."

"Your G could be a little tighter," she says and walks behind his chair. She wraps herself over his shoulders and reaches her left hand down to the neck of the guitar and pushes his left hand aside. "Try positioning your hand like this."

Tom can feel her breasts against his back and the skin of her arm on the back of his hand and he prays for no more camera flashes.

"That's better," he says.

She straightens up. It's a moment that leads to sex for people who don't respect the lives they're in.

"How about a duet tonight?"

"I don't think that would help the campaign."

She laughs. "Then how about another drink?"

They step back to ground level and find Peter Brand nearby. Tom thanks Natalie then tells Peter he needs to make a quick call and he finds a quiet place.

"Alison."

"Hi, babe."

"I want you to start traveling with me. To all these events."

"Why?"

"I just need you. I think it'll make me a lot happier. It'll help."

"What about the kids?"

"We can hire someone. Or have some family come down and stay with them. It's just while I'm in the race."

35

"Samantha, if you're going to be in here at this hour, you're going to have to learn how to deal with it." Gail Erickson depresses the top on the can of spray tan and waves it around her legs. The aerosol fumes fill the twelve-by-eight-foot office that Gail and Samantha share.

Samantha keeps reading her computer screen. She hadn't complained and still doesn't. It's Gail trying to establish dominance.

Gail says, "It would be easier on both of us if you were somewhere else between seven and nine a.m. You know I have to get ready and I'm going to be prancing around here in my thong."

Samantha doesn't look up and the more Gail talks to herself, the weaker Gail feels. Gail is a correspondent with a regular segment on the nine a.m. broadcast of UBS-24. No one can know Gail for thirty minutes and not learn from her that she was Miss Nevada eleven years ago.

Gail is all aggression and weakness. Only anchors have their own office and even some anchors share. Office space is generally negotiated in contract terms. Samantha enjoys sharing but not with Gail and her two racks of wardrobe and duffel bag of cosmetics. It would be easier to share with a guy.

The office door starts to open, then there's a knock as a face comes through sideways looking for Gail.

"Jesus, Stacy, I could be naked in here," says Gail louder than for just Stacy.

Stacy is the producer of the nine a.m. show and knows Gail well enough to ignore her. She puts a folder with thirty pages of printed computer paper on Gail's desk. It's eight thirty. "Here's your packet for the segment."

"I don't have time to read this, Stacy." She says the word *Stacy* like it tastes bad.

Stacy leaves and closes the door behind her with no reaction. Most of the fumes are still trapped in the office. Gail slides the folder from her desk and into the wastebasket.

Samantha stops her research. "Don't you do any prep?"

Gail is relieved to have gotten a rise at last. She leans back like she's going to inform the rookie how they operate in the professional leagues. "No, it's better to go out and be natural than to fill your head with preconceived ideas. It's hard, but some people like me can do it and it's more compelling to watch."

"That's ridiculous. You're delivering news. You need to know the news," says Samantha.

"Larry King never did any research before he interviewed his guests. That was the way he could put himself in the place of the viewer at home and ask the questions they wanted to ask."

"That's moronic. There's no way to ask a question that penetrates anything. If his only way to be relatable to people is to preserve ignorance, then he's failing. That's a rationalization for laziness. Or a bloated ego. Anyway, he's interviewing celebrities, not doing a news broadcast."

Gail doesn't like the words *ignorance*, *laziness*, and *failing* but doesn't know how to defend herself. "I just don't need to do a lot of research like you do." She waves the back of her hand at Samantha's computer. "I never have. The main thing I do is watch last night's prime-time shows."

"Last night's prime time," repeats Samantha, and goes back to her computer screen. Not all the correspondents at UBS are this bad. Some work for stories and understand them, but Samantha already has a reputation as a hard worker in a way that she wouldn't have had at a law firm. Everyone works hard at a law firm.

Gail is flustered at the conversation and unhappy that she's lost Samantha's attention again. She says, "Everyone in the building is trying to be like me. Have you noticed that? They're copying my hair, wearing the same style tops. It's so annoying."

This is Gail trying to be relatable. Samantha sees that she has only twenty minutes more until Gail needs to leave for the set, and she can keep her head down that long.

Gail says, "It's ruining my brand."

Samantha's voice is disobedient and she says, "Your brand?" It was unignorable.

"We all have a brand, Sam. You too."

"You're on a daytime show for six minutes a day. Nobody's thinking about your brand but you." Samantha is not normally so cutting as this, but Gail ought to hear it.

Gail's attempts at dominance are undermining her position. The only TV trick she's learned is to bridge away from difficult moments, so she says, "What do you think about Pauley's chances?"

Only a few more minutes until she's gone, thinks Samantha. She's not interested in having a conversation with a person who doesn't care about the answer to her own question, much less have an opinion about it. "He has a shot."

Tom Pauley is a national figure now, though Samantha has not been in touch with Pauley since the years they worked together at Davis Polk. Who knows what national media scrutiny can turn up.

MITCHELL MASON

36

"Mr. President, I recommend we commit resources to prepare a campaign against Governor Pauley."

"How sure are you?"

"He's up five points and all the GOP money is starting to coalesce to him. His lead is going to accelerate. We need to find our angle on him and get the narrative out there," says Ron Stark.

"Alright, open up the spigots a little."

"Things could be a lot worse for us. Pauley's smart and he has a nice-guy thing going, but we can kill him on experience."

"He's holding up fine in the GOP debates," says Mason.

"It's a weak field. Pauley's a good candidate for us. Believe me."

"You're a real optimist, aren't you, Ron?"

"I suppose."

Mason's look is not playful. "Do you think optimism is a virtue, Ron?" Stark doesn't say anything. The president is on one of his riffs and Stark is feeling uncertain where the safe ground is. "Would you want your money manager to be an optimist? Your security guard?"

"I suppose not my security guard."

"No, I suppose not. There are some situations and professions where pessimism is better. Or at least realism."

"Fair enough."

"Twain said there's no sadder sight than a young pessimist, except an old optimist."

"That's pretty good."

"Twain and Churchill already have all the good ones. Ron, I don't want you to be an optimist. I want my wife to be an optimist, not my chief of staff."

"I think a realistic view is that we are in very good stead with Pauley as our opponent." Stark would have done better to let the president's point carry rather than hold his ground on a technicality.

"Start playing like we're behind or we will be."

A light on the president's desk phone flashes with no ring. He picks up the internal call from his secretary. "Yes."

"Susan Fitzgerald is requesting a ten-minute meeting for a matter she says is important and time sensitive." None of his secretaries likes Susan much or anyone telling the president what he needs to consider important.

"Send her in." He turns to Stark. "Ron, would you excuse me." Not a question.

Stark nods and walks out the side door away from the secretaries. He can find out easily enough who's coming in the office another time without having to pass by now.

The doors open and close at the same time as though connected by a lever. Susan Fitzgerald enters from the president's right and looks after the sound of the shutting door across the way, then to the president.

Her facial expression is completely given over to panic, like that of a passenger screaming on a roller coaster; there's no capacity left to govern ordinary physical control.

"What's going on, Susan?"

"Can we talk?"

"Of course we can talk, there's no audio. Just keep your clothes on and take a seat."

She sits, shaking her head side to side, unable to start the horrifying news.

"What the hell is it?"

"Allen knows."

"Allen knows what?"

"About us. Our affair."

The president leans back with distended nostrils. "Exactly what does he know, Susan?"

"I didn't have time to unpack my bags from the New York trip, I had to get directly back here. He's been suspicious lately anyway and he unpacked them."

"And what did he find?"

"The lingerie you bought me."

Mitchell waves his hand like he's brushing away a flying insect that doesn't have a stinger. "Just tell him you bought it. You were missing him, you found a few free moments in New York, so you ran out to buy something to surprise him when you got back."

"They're used." She pauses and chokes on the admission. "And dirty."

"Then tell him you put them on one night in the hotel when you were alone and thinking of him."

She shakes her head no.

"Susan?" He demands eye contact without speaking. "What have you told him already?"

"Nothing! Nothing. He called me, I told him he's crazy and hung up and I haven't answered his calls since. I haven't seen him yet. He suspects it's you but he doesn't know anything for sure."

Mitchell spins his chair ninety degrees to look to the side and think. "Okay."

"I feel sick."

They sit in silence for two minutes until Mitchell says, "What's done is done. I know you feel like a bad person, but you're not. That's beside the point anyway. What matters now is how you handle this. Everything that happened is in the past. How you handle it starts right now. In this moment, you either start to address the problem or you don't."

She's still in a panic and unable to follow any sort of thread. She's more like a schizophrenic skipping between thoughts that are unlinked.

"Susan, are you with me?"

"I am. Yes." She starts to cry.

"The people that matter here are you, Allen, your child, and me. We need to plot the best course for these four people."

"Right."

"Clearly the best course is to save your marriage and your family."

"Okay."

"Allen doesn't want to believe you've had an affair. He wants to believe anything else, so you have to give that to him."

"Okay."

"That's the hard part, Susan. You have to give it to him in a way that can satisfy him. You have to give it to him in a way that can remove all the doubt and ugliness from his life and really help him. You have to do it so well that he wants to apologize to you and love you more than ever."

She nods her head yes.

"That means you need to lie, Susan, and you're a terrible liar. You don't lie well because you're never prepared for it. The secret to lying well is preparation."

The framework for a plan is coming together and Susan is starting to calm down and absorb it.

Mitchell continues. "He's holding used lingerie and suspicions and that's all. You say you bought it and wore it while thinking of him and alone. That's not impossible."

"Right."

"If you bought lingerie to surprise him and wore it thinking of him because you lust for him and he turned around and accused you of an affair, how pissed off would you be?"

"Angry," she says as though guessing at the emotion.

"Very angry! So get there! Get angry. He's an asshole for doing this to you. Yell to me that you're angry."

"I'm angry."

"Louder!"

"I'm angry!" It's louder but the tone is meek and not angry.

"Susan, you have to do better. This only works if you're one hundred percent on offense. There's nothing to defend. He's a jerk who abused your trust and accused you of something awful. How could he?"

She nods.

"Think of something that makes you angry. I don't care what it is." He waits. "Now scream. Just scream at the top of your lungs."

She screams and the light on the desk phone flashes again. "We're rehearsing something. Everything is fine, thanks." He hangs up.

Susan's face is flushed but she's collected herself. She's thinking strategically now, the way she would about White House policy, and at the same time she realizes that is exactly what this is.

"Prepare yourself, Susan. He needs assurances, so that's exactly what you need to give him. He'll ask you to swear on your life, your kids, your country, so that's what you'll do, only you're going to do it one hundred times in front of a mirror first. Make those swears out loud, over and over, until all the sting and hesitation is gone. Don't stop practicing until you want to go find him and yell it at him." Now he smiles at her like a proud and encouraging teacher and his voice gets soft. "Prepare yourself, Susan."

"I will." She's got control of her face again and she looks determined.

"I know you will."

She gives a nod like a military man accepting an order, then has a letdown. "I'm a bad Catholic, Mitchell."

He comes up from his chair and shows fire. "Stop that right here, right now! This is business, Susan. You don't have time for that. You worry about God after you get the job done. Right now you stay focused."

"I'm sorry. I will."

Too many emotions are at the surface for Susan. He knows she's unstable. "Don't talk to Allen tonight. Work an all-nighter here, urgent business. Talk to him tomorrow night when you're ready."

"Okay, good."

"You're really Catholic now, huh? You're raising your kid Catholic?"

"Yes, Allen's devout."

"We just started letting Catholics into the club about five years ago." He laughs and she laughs too. He decides it's a good way to end. "I have a meeting, Susan. Let's talk tomorrow night."

37

Mason had shown no nerves in front of Susan, but the news has thrown him. The angry husband of his communications director going to the press with stories of an affair would be the first major setback for his administration. He's always polled great with women and he could kiss that good-bye, especially if he's running against Pauley. And his wife would believe the affair rumors. He doesn't think any amount of preparation can prevent that.

He changes into his pajamas and slippers. Only men under forty-five sleep in boxer shorts. He steps from the bathroom to the bedroom and his wife enters from the hall at the same time. They had already eaten dinner together two hours earlier and Mitchell was distracted.

"Come here," she demands but looks nervous.

He wonders if she could know anything or maybe has just now heard a rumor. He knows he's the stronger of the two and could crush her by not going to her now. Only the weaker makes a demand in this way. Her words are not planned but are a reaction to fear. He walks to her and gives her a hug. She's relieved and hugs back.

"Are you okay, Mitchell?"

"Of course, just a lot on my mind. As always."

She forces the hug to continue. "I know. You work so hard. You do so much."

"It's the job. I signed up for it."

"Yes, we both did."

"Yes." He relaxes his embrace but she does not so he tightens again.

"Are you happy, Mitchell?"

He pulls his chin back from over her shoulder so he can look at her while still in a hug. "Of course I am, dear. Very happy."

"Good."

"Aren't you?"

"I am," she says. "Sometimes. Most of the time I am." She is happy with Helen but she'd like to have a deeper connection with her husband. She knows she's capable of it and still hopes that he is.

A husband ought to follow up at a time like this but Mitchell wants no part of this conversation and says nothing.

Evelyn continues, "We were born into rich families, went to good schools, got all the breaks our whole lives. If we want something we get it. It's a good lot."

Mitchell's chin is back over her shoulder and he looks at the wall behind her. "A person's happiness and his circumstances overlap by only about ten percent. If you're happy, it isn't because of any of that stuff. If you're unhappy, it isn't because of any of that stuff either."

"I suppose you're right."

"I am," he says.

"So you're happy?"

"I am," he says and holds her tighter. "You're at the heart of that." He says in a whisper, "You're the love of my life, my partner, my soul mate. And you're my First Lady." He pinches her and she smiles. "I couldn't do any of this without you. I'd be lost. With you, I can do it. And I'm happy."

The tension in her arms is static and she stares to the side at their bed. "I am too." He can't read me, she thinks. Or he doesn't want to badly enough. Our relationship, as it is, is well charted and he doesn't want to move beyond that. We work with what we have.

38

The president sits behind the desk in the Oval Office in his morning meeting with the usual group: Ron Stark, Susan Fitzgerald, Press Secretary Ted Knowles, and Senior White House Advisor Armando Gomez. They're joined by Gregory Grey who reports to Armando and is briefing the group on the latest polling information.

Mitchell doesn't know Grey's age but guesses it could be as young as late twenties. He seems like a smart kid. Grey covers the favorability polls on all the branches of government, then reports on the poll results across a dozen social, fiscal, and foreign policy issues.

Mason asks a few questions and makes suggestions for the design of questions in the next round of polling. Grey responds from behind a curtain of notes.

After the third of these responses, the president interrupts him. "Gregory. Is it Greg or Gregory?"

"Either, sir."

"Fine. I need you to look me in the eye when you're talking to me. In some countries people don't look each other in the eye when they're talking to a superior. It's a cultural thing. Koreans. Maybe some families here are that way too. In this office we look each other in the eye. Whatever has you in the habit of not looking me in the eye, break it. I won't have someone work for me who won't look me in the eye." Mason knows a person who deceives is more likely to suspect others of deceit, but he's not going to lay this at his own feet. He just can't tolerate a person who won't look right at him.

"I'm sorry, sir. I will." His head is angled down and to the left but he raises his eyes just enough to make contact with the president.

"Thank you, Gregory. That's all for now."

Gregory Grey stands and leaves through the back of the office into the main hall.

The odd exchange between the president and Gregory Grey leaves the room in an awkward silence. Stark senses the president veering toward a monologue and tries to get the group back on point. "The numbers look good, overall. Nothing alarming for us."

Mitchell ignores Stark and turns to Armando. "How old is Grey?"

"I'll find out. Do you want me to replace him?"

The president pulls his right earlobe with his right thumb and forefinger. "No. You'd wind up with another kid who'd be the same way. He seems fine enough."

"Okay."

They all wait for the president to finish with his thoughts. The release of his earlobe signals this and he speaks again. "Do you realize that as a people, our capacity to survive in a postapocalyptic world is zero. As one issue, we're completely removed from the source of our food. I went to a pig roast last week and it was disgusting. The pig was split from its nose to its ass, legs flayed out to each side over a fire, eyes and mouth still intact. I wouldn't know how to do it. We eat hot dogs and don't think where they come from. Everybody goes nuts today if their social media goes down. Can you imagine actual survival? The human race was more robust during the Stone Age. They could survive and didn't even have unemployment. Someone had to get the nuts and berries, someone had to hunt the meat and fish, someone else had to build the homes and tidy up. People in cities now can't do anything for themselves but call for pizza. We're a race of wimps. We better pray for no bombs or asteroids. God knows what people will do if they can't hang around on the Internet all day."

The president has a light schedule this morning. When he has important meetings he's well read and prepared, but he has blocked out this morning for brainstorming with his team. He wants to set a policy course for heading into the reelection campaign.

Nobody wants to touch the president's critique of the human race. They know it's better not to respond but to let him run out of steam like a toddler in a tantrum.

When nobody comments, Mitchell leans forward and taps his desk as though announcing that this view is now the accepted scientific theory. "Ron, Armando, let's take a walk."

He stands and turns around to look out the window. When the president sits at his desk, to his right is the door outside to the Rose Garden. Just next to that is the door out to the secretaries which most people use. Straight ahead is the fireplace and to his left is the hallway down to his private study and dining room.

Mitchell opens the door to step out in fresh air and view the Rose Garden. Ron Stark, then Armando Gomez follow, closing the door behind them. "It's a macro issue I want to discuss with you two. We're kicking off the reelection bid and we need to decide how to tack, if we tack at all."

Stark knows that when the president wants advice, he asks a question. When he wants to feel good about a decision he's already made, he starts talking. The president has succeeded in more funding for green energy jobs and for the Department of Education but failed in cutting tax breaks for big oil. There's been no bold, signature legislation from his administration but the country is healthy and the public approves of a slow and steady approach. "What are your thoughts?" asks Ron.

"Our numbers are good right now. We're going to run a strong race. We could play it safe, move a bit to the center the way Clinton did coming into reelection. Or we could stand our ground."

Stark says, "Our base is happy with the DOE work and the push on green energy. If we move to the center it would likely be something on tax policy. Reach a compromise with Warren. Make sure we have all the appearances of working closely, announce something jointly, show we can reach across the aisle."

The president says, "We could do that. Or we could tell Warren to pound sand. Clinton moved to the middle because he had to. Our numbers are good. If we move to the middle, we risk losing good numbers, alienating our base. I could be a one-termer. The people elect a person, not a policy. Only a small percentage of the people even look closely enough to be on a policy level, except for fringe social issues, and these days there are too many advertising dollars spent to confuse people for actual policy to matter much. Right now I'm a person people like."

Ron and Armando nod. They're looking over the gardens and hedges and a field of grass cut that morning. A breeze rolls over the earth.

"We're not moving right or left. We stay the course and we win in a landslide. You know I can campaign like hell."

PART THREE

There are no accidents, all things have a deep and calculated purpose; sometimes the methods employed by Providence seem strange and incongruous but we have only to be patient and wait for the result: then we recognize that no others would have answered the purpose, and we are rebuked and humbled.

—Mark Twain, 1835–1910

FACT CHECK

39

Samantha spends twenty minutes on the Internet to find the reporter who covered the hit-and-run and the cop who led the investigation. She starts with the reporter, and he agrees to meet with her for lunch at the Yard House Restaurant in Palm Beach Gardens.

The Yard House is a barn-sized restaurant in a shopping complex developed a decade ago near Military Trail and PGA Boulevard. The inside is open and in the center is a massive square bar with six bartenders handling the siege from all sides. Drop from the ceiling into the center of the bar are 154 pipes, connecting it with 154 different types of keg beer from a back room. The bar pulls a mix of young professional happy hour goers and students from Florida Atlantic University.

At lunchtime it's mild enough and the food isn't bad. Samantha is early and waits in a booth until the hostess leads a man to her table.

He's in his sixties and dressed in sloppy denim. He looks like all the aging, male coastal Florida residents who found out too late that Jimmy Buffett is not a truth teller. Rick Henly had covered the hit-and-run for the *Miami Herald*. He's now semiretired and doing freelance pieces for the *Palm Beach Post*.

"Your party, miss," says the hostess, and directs Rick to the other side of the booth.

Rick sits and picks up the menu but doesn't let the hostess leave. "Before you go, ma'am. Double Mount Gay and tonic. Lime."

"I'll put the order in with your waitress. Thank you."

"Thank you for coming, Mr. Henly," says Samantha. She notices the fleshy face and watery eyes with loose lids. He's not drunk now but has been at some point every day.

"Why, thank you for having me, Ms. Davis." He has a big smile. A drink on the way, pretty woman in front of him who will also pick up the tab. It's already his best day in years. "I hope you like the place."

"They don't make them like this in New York City."

"What we lack in style we make up for in square footage."

She laughs. He seems like a nice guy.

Rick looks to the bar and sees an attractive, tan waitress pick up a tall glass with light-brown rum and a lime. She moves in and out of booths full of people dressed business casual and covers the thirty yards to their table. Rick looks her all the way in without saying anything. It's a mental tractor beam.

The waitress puts down the drink and Rick picks it up and orders a second one just before the glass gets to his mouth.

Samantha thinks as long as he stays conscious, more alcohol can only be a good thing for her cause. The waitress nods and takes Samantha's order for iced tea.

"Rick, I'd like to talk to you about the hit-and-run I mentioned to you on the phone, but let's go ahead and get settled in first."

"Great."

They make small talk and order food and Rick's on his fourth drink when Samantha returns to the case.

"I read the two articles you wrote in the *Herald* about the accident. Is there anything you can tell me about it that's not in the pieces?"

"I dug up my old notebooks. I keep all the notes of my investigative pieces in a composition book. When the book is full, I date it and put it in this big trunk I have. Mementos, I guess. I found the date of this one and there's not a whole lot more than what was published."

"What more is there?"

"Well, the thing that is more is that there really wasn't anything at all to go on. It happened on US One where there's a pretty wide shoulder to the highway. Guy on a bike in the shoulder gets hit. There's no dirt so there aren't any tire tracks to go on and there weren't any skid marks on the pavement either. They figured that meant the driver was drunk. A sober person would have hit the brakes."

Samantha makes a note to call Rick a taxi after lunch.

"There was no automobile paint on the bike that could be identified. No glass or parts of anything to pick up that could lead anywhere. Just a mangled bicycle and a mangled body, but these things might as well have been airlifted in for all the evidence that was left around."

"Is that unusual?"

"I don't think so. The cops didn't think so. Sometimes you get a skid mark, sometimes you don't. Sometimes you find pieces of things, sometimes you don't."

"Did you get the sense they were looking hard for the pieces, or that they just wanted the case to go away?"

"I never saw anything to make me wonder that." He works his drunken face into something thoughtful. He's genuinely reaching back. "They seemed to be working it real. I never had a whiff of anything like that so I guess it was real. Otherwise I might have picked up on something."

Samantha nods. Rick drinks.

"Why do you ask, Ms. Davis?"

"I'm wondering if there's anything interesting about this case. Something like that would be interesting."

"Yes, it would be. Why this case in particular?"

"It's unsolved. And it fits the time period for something else I'm looking at."

Rick looks satisfied and his fifth drink arrives. "I love day drinking. It spreads out the hangover. Start now, then sign off around seven p. I start to feel a little crappy around eight, but by the morning things aren't half bad. If I'm out drinking until two a.m., come the morning I'm suicidal. Much rather be not half bad than suicidal."

Words to live by. Truly. "I should be living in Florida," says Samantha.

"No state income tax." Rick toasts the air and drinks.

"Were there any rumors at all at the time about who might have been involved?"

"No, nothing." Rick is surprised they're back on the topic of the case. "You think it was murder? Something deliberate?"

"Nothing like that. I'm sure it was an accident. I'm just wondering if there was any speculation at the time, even just neighborhood gossip."

"Not that I know of. The whole thing was just a big nothing-burger, from a news perspective. The only newsworthiness of the follow-up report was that there was absolutely zero to report."

Samantha nods. She wants to try one more thing and she wants to catch him off guard. "And Connor Marks?"

Rick is baffled. Drunk and baffled, and Samantha can see it is a real reaction. "I don't think I know any Connor Marks."

Samantha meets the retired cop who had led the investigation of the hit-and-run. They spend an hour in a Starbucks and she confirms everything Rick Henly had told her.

An unsolved hit-and-run. No physical evidence, no eyewitnesses, no suspects. The case never moved forward an inch and has been cold ever since.

The cop is generous with his time, is calm, and is a fan of Samantha. There isn't any indication that the cop was ever pressured to leave the case unsolved. It's just a dead guy and nothing more to go on. Samantha has one more meeting.

40

It's noon, late September, and eighty-six degrees in Palm Beach. Samantha drives alone, east on Okeechobee Boulevard in a rented Toyota sedan. There's little traffic and it moves in a relaxed way. The population won't surge for the season until November.

Her lane bends left to merge into the bridge traffic going on to Palm Beach Island. The superyachts in the harbors by the bridge are an unnatural white and on a clear day are as hard as the sun to look at straight.

The bridge releases to Royal Palm Way, the massive trees lining the broad road that cuts across the island to the ocean on the other side. On her right are the beach cottage versions of major banks. Morgan, Goldman, Bessemer, all with a presence for the high-net-worth locals to drop in for retail business.

Monica Morris had set up the meeting for Samantha. Monica said Reese Kinard is her longtime friend and confidant and met Mitchell Mason when Monica was still seeing him. Samantha and Reese agree to meet at the Brazilian Court.

Samantha turns right from Royal Palm Way to Australian Avenue. The built-in GPS of the rental directs her left from Australian, then she turns left into the semicircle drive of the Brazilian Court and stops for the valet.

Standing in the shade of the entrance is a woman in her midfifties in navy slacks and a cotton blouse. Her brown hair is pulled back and her face and posture look severe. Not aggressive, just unhappy. The only happy people in Florida are the ones who live there less than half the year.

It is a morbid idea to meet at the restaurant that served the drinks the night of the hit-and-run. It was Reese's idea but when Samantha steps from the car Reese says, "Let's not eat here. I hate this place."

"Sure. Anywhere's fine."

"Let's walk a little. It's not too roasting out yet."

They walk Hibiscus to Worth Avenue and turn east toward the ocean. The homes in the blocks behind Worth are a walk to the beach and more modest and mixed among the shops and galleries. Worth Avenue is wide and lined with only stores. The reputation is the Rodeo Drive of the Southeast but Samantha decides there is better shopping in Greenwich, Connecticut. Except for the Ralph Lauren and Saks Fifth Avenue, most of it is odd and tacky. Maybe she'll have time after lunch to drive to the northern part of the island, where the spectacular homes are done with some taste.

Samantha would rather Reese open the topic of Mason and will be patient. "This is Ta-boo," says Reese, pointing to a restaurant on their left. "It's not like it was in the old days but still a pretty good spot for a drink."

The restaurant is dark wood on the outside. Samantha uses her hands as visors to block the glare and she looks through the glass window. It looks like the inside of a cruise ship. "There's a certain look and feel around here that you don't find many places."

"It's not for everyone." Reese says this with no edge as though she hasn't yet decided whether or not it's for herself. "Let's not stop here, though. Let's get a look at the water."

They keep walking and half the stores are closed. One posts a sign that reads "Open when I feel like it, Closed at the same time. Welcome to the Off Season."

"So you'd like to know about Mitchell Mason."

"Did you meet him in person?"

"Three times over about two years."

Samantha says, "Did you like him?"

"He was okay. I know what he was, what that relationship was. But so did he and he was honest about it. Monica may have hoped for more but she knew what it was too."

"Was it an open relationship? Many people knew?"

"No, it was an affair and it was buttoned-up like affairs are. Mitchell was an important politician even then but nobody's as careful as they should be. Enough people knew. If you're looking for more confirmation I can point you to a few people. The manager at the Brazilian Court is still the same and I imagine he'd talk with you."

"Okay." Samantha thinks about pulling out a pad of paper and doesn't.

Worth Avenue dead-ends in a three-way intersection. The fourth side is a sidewalk with a few benches overlooking a drop-off, about a hundred yards of beach, then the ocean. The breeze is stronger and feels good. There's no shade anywhere.

"Let's sit there for a minute," says Reese. Her body is better trained for the climate. Samantha is sweating but agrees.

They sit. "Did you see Monica or Mitchell the night of the accident?"

Samantha looks sideways at Reese and Reese looks out over the ocean. "I love the water. Always puts things right for me. And I love sailors. People who sail have a real perspective on the world and they're humble, humble people. If you spend enough time in a boat out on an ocean like that, you come to learn who the boss is. And it isn't us."

Monica had mentioned that Reese is a psychologist. Reese seems the type that was so immersed in therapy in younger years that she decided it was a calling. A few breakthroughs for herself and she decided she would feel even better giving breakthroughs to others so she skipped medical school and went directly to psychology.

Samantha nods.

Reese says, "Some people have these fears of superstorms or famine or war. They buy some acres in upstate New York to build a bunker and grow vegetables. Me? I just make sure I always have a full tank of gasoline. Probably anybody that's seen a few Florida hurricanes does that."

Samantha nods again.

"No, I didn't see them that day. Monica called me the following morning around seven thirty. She was hysterical crying, talking about the accident, talking about the guilt of leaving the scene. She said Mitchell pressed her to leave it, that nothing could be done at the time and no good could come of it anyway. That morning he was saying that what was done was done, and that going back then would be worse than having stayed the night before."

Reese's voice sounds robotic and has taken on a tone of duty. It sounds rehearsed to Samantha but then it would since Reese knew these questions were coming.

"Did you talk with Mitchell Mason after the accident?"

"No, never. I never saw him or talked with him again after that. Monica saw him only one more time. After that, only his aides had anything to do with her."

"Does Mason know that Monica told you about the accident?"

"No, she says he doesn't know about that. He told her to tell no one, but she trusted him less after he told her to leave the scene that night. So she told me, but I believe her that she never let him know she told me."

"I'm sorry. That's a lot to carry around."

"I'm a psychologist. I carry people's stuff around for a living."

Some pedestrians pass behind them. The sun is brutal. The surf is rough and only four people are within sight getting sun on the sand.

"You and Monica have stayed close all these years?"

"We have. She changed after Mason. Fundamental changes, but we've always been in close touch." Reese looks mostly at the ocean and only a little at Samantha.

"Anything else you can tell me?"

Reese reaches for the pocketbook on the bench next to her but keeps her eyes up and unfocused the way a blind person would. She pulls out a photograph that had been loose in the pocketbook and hands it to Samantha.

Samantha holds it up. It's a younger Mitchell Mason with his arm around a younger Monica Morris and on his other side is a younger

Reese Kinard. They're seated in a restaurant and the table is crowded with wine and glasses and plates of desserts. "May I borrow this?"

"Yes."

"For a few weeks." Samantha will get someone to test the authenticity of the photo.

"That's fine."

"May I use it? If I do a piece, this may be useful. Do I have your permission to use it?"

"That's why I brought it."

Reese seems resigned, like a person who is doing a bad thing but has given up hope there is anything better.

"Thank you, Reese. I'm sure this is very hard. I can only imagine."

"What you don't know is that it's worse than what you're imagining." Again Samantha sees a hopelessness in Reese that is a point beyond tears.

"I'm sorry."

"You know that I'm a psychologist."

"Yes."

"Do you think humans are basically good or basically bad?"

"Depends on the human," says Samantha.

"Do you think society is basically good or bad?"

"Depends on the society," says Samantha.

"That's because the truth is that human nature is evil. The only societies that are good are those with a political system that holds human nature in check."

Samantha doesn't say anything.

Reese says, "Carl Jung said that as a people we are now intimidated and endangered by the military techniques that are supposed to safeguard our physical, spiritual, and moral freedoms." She says this in the voice people use for quotations. Then she says, "You can say the same of an aging democracy. Over time, people figure a way to make it dangerous to the point that it no longer safeguards us. Political systems evolve and it's human nature that forces the evolution. No political system can survive that for very long."

Samantha is back in New York for two weeks. Reese's photo is real. She has scanned it and kept copies for her files, calls to arrange the return of the photo and ask some follow-up questions.

Reese's office is a partnership of practitioners, each with their own space and phone line that goes to shared reception.

"Reese Kinard, please."

A female voice says, "Are you a patient?"

"No."

"Friend or family?"

"Friend. Has something happened?"

"I'm sorry to inform you that Ms. Kinard passed away last week."

Samantha is silent for a moment. "I just saw her. How did it happen?"

"I'm sorry, ma'am, I don't know any of the details."

"She's young and healthy. I was just there. Was there some accident? Is there anything you can tell me?"

The woman clears her throat then talks in a whisper. "If you read the papers, and it's probably all on the Internet anyway so I'm not saying anything that hasn't already been said, it was a suicide. In her car, in her garage."

"Oh, God."

"I'm sorry, ma'am." Silence for ten seconds. "Is there anything I can help you with?"

ON THE ROAD

41

Dan Cullen walks up the steps at the corner of Twelfth and I Street into Bobby Van's Grill in Washington, DC. Cullen is chief of advance for the Pauley campaign which means he has some responsibility for deciding which cities the campaign should visit and all the responsibility for making sure there is a team set up in those cities to see that the visit comes off without any problems.

The election is in fifty days. For campaign teams and the press on the road with them, this is like studying through the night for a life-altering final exam the next day, then repeating this for the next fifty consecutive days. Campaigns will visit three or four cities each day during this period. In the morning, Dan has a flight to Columbus, Ohio, and he won't be back to his DC home until after election day.

Dan is blond and handsome. If he were merely chief of advance, he'd sleep with most of the interns. The interns need to sleep with someone of power in the campaign but don't want to admit to themselves that power is the only reason for going to bed, so they race to the only man, aside from Pauley, who is also handsome. Dan has slept with every decent-looking intern without having to make a false promise or make any effort at all. It's understood that no strings are attached and they're fortunate for a night with him rather than the fat and sweaty communications director.

Dan steps into Bobby Van's past the host desk to the bar and lounge with navel-high cocktail tables and tall bar stools. There are a dozen people in the bar, all men, all in dark suits, all DC lobbyists or consultants.

A few heads turn to see Dan, then there's a backhand to their buddy's triceps and a moment of shame that they weren't more cool about spotting Dan Cullen. Dan is respected in political circles and unknown outside them. He does TV appearances on political shows and being in a room with someone normally seen on TV can do funny things to the person doing the looking.

Now most heads are turned to Dan and there are a few nods from people he may have met before. Anyone he really knew would have come right over. He's at the peak of his political career today. He smiles back and everyone sees that his teeth look even more white in person.

He walks down the middle of the narrow lounge to the stairs that lead down to the private dining rooms. He likes knowing eyes are on him. At forty-six, this is likely to be the last presidential campaign he plays a major role in. The schedule is too demanding. Most people are in their twenties and even senior people are only in their thirties. Dan enjoys his role as the veteran, which he can establish by referencing campaigns he worked in two decades ago when his listeners were just learning to read. He can imply that they have no real frame of reference, that everything they're seeing today is just a prop in the background of a grand painting and until they can step back to see the painting with twenty years' experience, they can't even know what the painting is of.

The downstairs level seems empty. At the base of the stairs are double doors to a private dining room with a round table that seats twelve. Around the bend is a small bar that is closed. Across from the bar is a windowless door. Dan opens the door and steps into a small conference room with a table in the middle and a bottle of Dewar's scotch on it. On the other side of the bottle is Jack Boothe, strategist for the campaign to reelect Mitchell Mason.

"Dan the Man."

"That's right. You remember that."

"Ha. Nobody will remember that after your guy loses."

Dan knows plenty of people will remember him, whether Pauley wins or loses. The difference will be a few hundred thousand dollars in a signing bonus from a lobbying firm. If he's deeply connected to the administration in power, he'll be worth more. Or he could take a job in the administration. "My guy's not going to lose."

"Bullshit."

Dan pours half a rocks glass with scotch and no ice and drinks a mouthful at room temperature. "This guy's riding the wave, Jack. This guy could do it. The campaign just has the energy winning campaigns have."

Jack is Dan's age, trim with dark hair and also handsome. Appearances matter at their level. They're trying to close the world's greatest sale, which happens only twenty-five times in a century. Their expensive suits are pressed, shirt collars are flawless, and the tie knots are fat and right down the middle. "It's not the year for the GOP. Mason is too strong."

"I don't know. Remember us trying to get Romney through the primary in 'twelve. We had to push like hell. It was like getting a handful of Play-Doh through a keyhole. We barely had to push Pauley. He got pulled through the primary like a magnet. If anyone can take Mason, it's Pauley."

"That's just it. No one can. Not this year."

"We'll see. You're up four points and that's all convention bounce. The debates are what matter."

Jack has an early morning flight to Tampa, so tonight is the last time the two will be able to meet before the election. The irony is that as partisan as the nation is, it is the people who work in the business of politics who are the most friendly across party lines. They recognize that it is a job and they need to live and to send their kids to schools. They're like players who shake hands and get a drink after a sporting event even though they're on rival teams. "Dan, you're a true believer. And you're not objective at all."

"And you are?" Dan sits at the table now. He refills his glass to the halfway point and pours some in Jack's glass. "Pauley's for real. I think he came up so fast he hasn't had the time to become a jaded prick like

Mason. And he hasn't had to make any soul-selling compromises either."

"Mason may be a prick on the outside but you can't argue that he has a vision for making this country better. And the man is a genius," says Jack.

"A genius or an insane person?"

"Both. Not all insane people are geniuses, but all geniuses are a little insane. It's lightning in a bottle."

"That's the last defense of an asshole."

"You'd be surprised at what a deep thinker he is. His inner circle has dubbed him the Asshole Philosopher. Both parts of that are true, and whether you like him or not, at least he's real."

"He's an asshole. That's real. And his vision for the country sucks."

"You GOP guys crack me up." Jack makes a high-pitched voice. "Don't tax the millionaires more, it'll shrink the economy and we'll lose jobs." His voice returns to normal. "You think if taxes on millionaires go up two points they're all going to fire the maid?"

"Not tonight, Jack. I don't want to get into platforms. You believe yours, I believe mine, let's just drink scotch."

"Yeah, fine." Jack sips. "You getting laid?"

"Plenty. Too much." Dan is divorced with a seventeen-year-old daughter who lives with her mom while she finishes her senior year. "I need less sex and more sleep if I'm going to survive the next fifty days."

"Tell me about it." Jack is also divorced but no kids. "Couple nights ago we're in Scranton and there's this forty-three-year-old gal who's a staffer in communications. She's been around campaigns forever and this is her last go unless someone makes her a mistress and gives her a spot. She's always turning up around me because she thinks we have a connection being the same age around all these kids. So at two in the morning I run into her in the lobby of the hotel. She says the last fifty days are about to start. 'If you're ever going to fuck me, tonight might be your last chance.'"

"Attagirl. What'd you say?"

"I said I'm sorry but I am just not going to be able to fuck you to-night."

"You're a dick. You should've fucked her. A gentleman would have."

"She's good-looking for forty-three but I was so tired. If either one of us had been twenty years younger, I would have done it."

Dan laughs but feels depression behind it. He has to laugh because it's been his whole life and he's chosen a sick profession. "What's the word in your campaign?"

Jack takes another sip. He and Dan have exchanged information for years. Nothing big or illegal. Like Cold War–era intelligence agents who develop a secret friendship, they share little bits that are interesting and can make each other look good. "The team from four years ago is pretty much intact, only now you're looking at the chief strategist."

"Bully for you."

"That's Mr. Bully, thank you."

"What else?"

"Distant wife, rumors of wandering eye. Stuff you've heard."

"Any ideas where it's wandering to?"

"Nothing for you there, pal. Suffice to say it's not in the league of Kennedy or Clinton."

"Nothing else?"

"Look, Mason's the real deal." Jack takes a drink of scotch, pulling in two swallows the way a young person drinks milk. "Twelve years ago I was running a campaign and we're flying to Reagan National. I'm sitting in the seat next to the principal. As we're about to touch down, it hits the news wire that there's a rumor of a coup in Venezuela. So I turn to my guy who shall remain nameless—"

"I know who you were working for twelve years ago."

Jack winks. "And I say, the press is going to mob you on this the moment your toes are out of this plane." Jack sips again. "He turns to me like a scared teenager. He says to me, What do I say?"

"Yeah, that wasn't your best campaign."

"Right then, I knew I was backing the wrong horse."

"Yeah."

"Mason's not like that. He knows what the fuck he's talking about, on almost everything. And when you think he's being aloof or not listening in a briefing, he actually is paying attention. He retains it and he does something with it."

Dan grunts. "No doubt he's a smart guy." There'll be no convincing Dan that Mason isn't an asshole.

"What about you guys? You're the fresh new story in town."

Dan takes another mouthful of scotch. "Some of the clichéd stuff is playing out. Repeating shit he hears from the body guy." A candidate has an assistant who tends to all the personal needs and is constantly at his side. It's not a political position and is usually a young scrapper. The role is informally titled body guy, and for candidates who are otherwise surrounded by political professionals, it can be his only conduit to normal. "This kid's about twenty-four and a couple weeks ago he's bringing coffee and papers to Pauley and he starts talking about how the price of a gallon of milk and some magazine he reads just went up. So Pauley goes on this three-day obsession with the Consumer Price Index and every morning we have to wrestle him back into the daily message."

This is the perfect thing for Dan to share. It gives Jack an inner circle story to retell but doesn't give away the cause. "I heard the body guy is gay."

"I don't think so. I haven't heard anything about that." Jack probably hasn't either, thinks Dan. He's just feeling around for something better. "And we have the usual old buddies showing up and riding on the planes, whispering nonsense in his ear."

"Oh, that's the worst. Thank God Mason's over that." Candidates often travel with an old and trusted friend because that can make them feel calm and centered. These friends are usually not political professionals but will opine as though they are.

Dan wants something to take back. "Who's playing Pauley in your debate prep?"

"Probably David Larson," says Jack. Larson is the Democratic governor from Massachusetts.

"I can see that. He'll be good. You guys started mock debates yet?"

"Last week. Mason's a little paranoid of the curse of the incumbent's first debate." Jack doesn't need to add the word confidentially. He knows how the information will be used. It's for Pauley's inner circle and not the media. "You guys?"

"Senator Bale to start. I'm pushing the team to find a real Democrat though. Bale can play the part but I think it would be more effective to have a true believer."

"Where are you going to find a true believer to help you out? Doesn't sound like he could be so true."

"Enough money might solve it. Or maybe just someone Mason has personally pissed off bad enough."

"That's political suicide. Anyway, if he's a true believer he won't betray us over personal reasons." Jack finishes his drink.

"It's worth a shot."

"How's Pauley's prep so far?"

"You know how it goes. You just have to help them operate inside the lane they're comfortable in. But I'll tell you, Pauley's good. He studies hard and he's got his facts and stats, but he's also got style and a sense of timing. Sometimes you get just one or the other, but he has both."

"I've seen him. He's good, but it's different getting out there for the big show. Mason's like a middleweight boxer and he knows how to get to his lines naturally. It's jab, jab, jab, then bam, he lands the big one. Mason's one of those guys who does it better without too much coaching."

Dan and Jack almost finish the bottle and complain about each other's super PAC. After the last sip Jack says, "Let's meet up here for dinner in mid-November. Loser buys."

"You're on."

42

The room has no light. It's silent. At 4:08 a.m., Randy Newhope's iPhone alarm chimes. His head is to the side of the pillow and he's open-mouthed with face down against the mattress, which pushes his jaw out of alignment. Just his left arm moves, as though it's the only part of his body that hears the noise. His hand wraps the phone and his thumb sweeps the screen to make silence. At 4:10 a.m. the hotel phone rings. Randy opens his eyes. Each day the hotel room is different, so he needs to find the landline and get into the shower. He lifts the phone from its cradle and drops it. It's not a person calling, just a machine to wake him.

He stands and drops his chin to his chest to think and to try to remain standing. Conshohocken, Pennsylvania, he thinks. We're at a Marriott. Bag call time is 4:30 a.m. He remembers more from last night.

"Time to get up," Randy says.

The sheets behind him move and are noisy. He remembers how rough they were, like brown wrapping paper. "What?" Twenty-three-year-old vocal cords strained by liquor, sex, and lack of sleep. She sounds gravelly and sexy.

He doesn't repeat the remark. He walks into the bathroom and into the shower without turning on the lights. His breathing is heavy, not from physical exertion but from the exertion to stay awake. He puts the ridge of his eyebrows into the blast of the showerhead, slaps the liquid hotel soap around his neck and his armpits, and he pees into the drain without the aid of his hands, the way a horse does.

Randy is thirty-five and a columnist for *Newsweek* magazine, and he has promised himself and his wife that this will be the last time he travels with a campaign. In four years he wants to be covering things from a bureau, maybe running it.

He's about average size and average-looking and is now a veteran reporter with *Newsweek* and that status is currency he can trade for youth and hotness when choosing someone to sleep with. He's been sleeping with Tara Altman every night for the last week.

Randy comes out of the bathroom with a toothbrush in his mouth and no towel. The room is still dark except for the glow of the TV Tara turned on and she is standing by the bed in a white spaghetti-strap tank top and a black thong. Her face is in her hands and she looks unsteady.

"Gotta have your bag in the hall in fifteen minutes."

She nods and says through her palms, "I know. When is pool call time?"

"Five fifteen."

"Okay," she says, and drops her hands. She looks amazing, he thinks. Lack of sleep can make people under thirty look sexier. People over thirty just look like crap. Her young body is immune to the road lifestyle. He can still pinch only skin on her waist and her ass is hard. "I'm going." She pulls on the sweatpants that she had worn over the night before. No one dresses up for anyone at night on the campaign. A girl like her looks just as good in sweatpants and a tank top anyway. She walks to leave and pushes down the handle of the heavy door. "See you at pool call." There's no touch or eye contact. It's all anyone can do to stay awake.

"Okay." With a few more hours' sleep he'd feel aroused by her, but not now. Tara is a blogger for a conservative website with a mandate of getting out the youth vote. Young conservatives are far better sex partners than young liberals. One of life's ironies, and a generalization that holds.

Randy uses an army-green duffel bag. Most people use a hard rectangular bag with wheels but he likes the feel of throwing a bag over his shoulder. It makes him feel younger. He drops the bag on the floor outside his hotel room and walks the hall to the elevator. It won't be light outside for a couple hours. There aren't windows but it somehow feels like nighttime in the hall.

He steps into the lobby that looks like every other goddamn lobby he's been in. False light with hard floors and walls that are too white with the kind of odd lobby art that happens when someone tries to be fancy on too small a budget. He gets a banana, a muffin, coffee, and water, which is what he has every morning.

The campaign takes care of everything. They divvy it all up and send a monthly bill back to the media companies that have embedded reporters, but Randy never has to plan his hotel or food or anything. He just needs to work his ass off and get his stories in.

The lobby elevator door starts to open and close with a rhythm now and the buffet table of breakfast food and coffee gets crowded. He sees Tara come in and now he wants to find a way to sleep with her somewhere today. Maybe she'll be up for something in the bathroom on the plane ride to Palm Beach.

Randy always wears khaki pants, button-down shirt, and a blazer. Most of the journalists dress business casual and the campaign staff does too. The cameramen, sound guys, and other techs wear jeans, sweatshirts, and sneakers. As people pour into the lobby, it's easy to tell who does what.

He's not feeling ready for more conversation until he's had more coffee but he circulates the group to nod hellos and he comes around to squeeze Tara's ass. He should keep it more private since he's married but he doubts anyone notices or cares much. Other people do it too. She lifts one side of her butt to give him a better angle for a squeeze. It's as close to real affection as can happen this close to election day and on this little sleep.

The group starts to move outside in a listless way like zombies that received an unspoken command. A caravan is waiting for them. In front are three black Suburbans. Governor Pauley will go in one of them, along with senior staff and some Secret Service. Behind the Suburbans are four vans for the rest of the staff and the press pool and behind the vans are three tour buses that look like Greyhounds but are covered in Pauley logos. Every vehicle will have at least one Secret Service agent and every-one will be frisked before getting in.

The press pool in the van stays close to the candidate. They go every-where when the rest of the media cannot, and they have to share all their coverage with the rest of the group. The journalists and techs in the pool rotate each day. Randy does pool again tomorrow. Today he's back in one of the tour buses.

A few of the media stand around the outside of the tour buses and vans waiting to see Pauley come from the hotel. Maybe they'll get a de-cent photo or he'll say a few words in his stride that are worthy of print. Probably not. Randy's been at it too many days to loiter hoping for that. He carries his coffee with him to be frisked then gets on the bus.

The Secret Service guys look different from regular military. Military guys have a spine like a spike and their back muscles have formed to hold it straight whether sitting or standing. Their ears line up in a plane over their shoulder blades and their hair is so short you can't tell what color it is. Secret Service guys have to blend in. They wear business suits, their hair is neat but normal and there's no surface tension in their stance. But you come to notice after a moment that their eyes are always moving and they never face the candidate. They always look out and around him.

The bus is a quarter full and Randy takes a seat by a window facing the hotel entrance. Dan Cullen walks out with an aide just behind his left elbow who's walking in steps that are quicker and shorter than those of his boss. Dan's hair is perfect at 5:45 a.m. It must know where to go all by itself. Ev-eryone knows he's slept with all the girls, except Tara as far as Randy knows.

Twenty minutes later the point man of Pauley's detail comes through the door. Tom has six agents around him and he emerges like a kickoff returner behind the wedge. The body guy comes out last, just outside the human perimeter of security. Pauley smiles and waves to everyone. He says a few things that Randy can't hear through the glass but it's probably about what a great day they're all going to have. He likes to say what a great day it is for the human race and he says it in his Southern accent. The guy can't help being friendly.

Pauley gets into the second Suburban. The lead car is the dummy today. The caravan is flanked by a squad car in front and four motorcycle cops, then two more motorcycle cops in back. They hit the sirens and the campaign moves out.

Heads turn and civilian cars clear off the roads and the massive convoy speeds on, bringing the sound of a terrible fire alarm. The local cops love it. They gun their bikes up the sides of the buses, then fall back again, circling the campaign like small fighter planes defending the Death Star. Randy has done this a hundred times and it's still fucking cool.

Pauley has a sunrise rally scheduled at the gym of the Haverford School which is a ten-minute drive from the hotel.

They pull into the campus of the all-boys' school. The sirens stop and Randy's shoulders drop an inch, no longer resisting the weight of the sound.

An advance team of campaign workers and Secret Service is already in the gym setting the podium and getting the area prepared. Randy sees a paper sign taped to a tree and the sign says Press File and has an arrow. He follows the direction of the arrow to another sign with another arrow, and again and again until he gets to the school cafeteria where the press file is set up.

The cafeteria tables are covered with white plastic sheets. Power cords trace the tables and are taped to the floor. A whiteboard rests on an easel. It says "Sunday, October 1, Haverford, Pennsylvania." By the end of the day, with fatigue and a third or fourth city, these posts are useful when filing stories.

Randy keeps a soft leather briefcase with a laptop, a notebook, chargers for all his devices, and a power strip. He needs to get his story filed before the eight a.m. rally. He swings the bag onto the table and takes out his laptop. Only a few other press people have come into the cafeteria.

Randy powers up. The story is mostly written but he wants it as perfect as it can be to stave off his editor's paw prints. He's reading and polishing and notices his battery power indicator move to low. It's an old battery and when this light comes on he has about five minutes more. "Fuck."

He reaches in his bag but the power strip is gone. "Fuck."

He looks around. There are about twenty people in the room, either on their laptops or fumbling for another coffee and bagel. "Anyone have a Dell power strip I can borrow for ten minutes?" He says this loud enough to carry but not to startle.

Nobody moves to react. He can tell that some move deeper into whatever else they were doing. This is a combination of sleepiness, not giving a shit about a fellow reporter, and the fact that power strips are gold on the road.

Randy has about four minutes left. Theatrics might get him to a yes so he steps on the bench seat then to the top of the table so his head is about nine feet off the ground. He raises his hands to make a trumpet and yells, "I fucking need a fucking power strip for ten fucking minutes! Who's going to fucking give me one? *Fuck!*"

He lowers his hands expecting someone to laugh and toss him one and he sees Tom Pauley standing at the cafeteria entrance staring at him.

"Governor," says Randy, trying to strike a balance that is funny but not smart-ass.

"Too much coffee, Randy?"

Son of a bitch, he remembers my name. Randy had been press pool for a bowling event the week before and that was the only time they formally met. "No, sir. I think maybe not enough."

"Well, I don't have a power strip for you, but allow me. Black?"

"Yes, sir."

Pauley pours a cup and walks it to Randy, who is still standing on the table top and not composed enough to step down.

"Thank you, sir."

"You folks are all working hard. Just wanted to step in and see that you're all doing okay."

Randy gets down and bows but only from the neck up. "Doing great, thank you, sir." Randy clears his throat. Love this guy, he thinks. I may just vote for him.

43

Tom hangs up his phone. "Asshole," he says to himself. Peter Brand is seated next to him in the car.

"Okay, Governor. The plane's loaded up," says Peter. The day had started with a sunrise rally at the Haverford School outside Philadelphia, then a short flight to Pittsburgh for a one p.m. lunchtime rally. Now they're at a small private airfield outside Pittsburgh to get a flight to Palm Beach for an evening fund-raiser at the Breakers, after which they'll drive in a similar-looking convoy of vehicles across the state to Tampa, where they'll spend the night and be ready at eight a.m. for a sunrise rally on the Gulf side of Florida. The schedule takes a toll, but like drinking, a person can build a tolerance. Also like drinking, if a person does it too long, the body breaks. "What did he want?"

"The son of a bitch wanted to offer me a job at Google. If I lose. I'm in the middle of working my ass off to win. I'm not interested in discussing consolation prizes."

"Shit, I should have vetted that better before letting them in. They've been good to the campaign and they've been asking for a short call for weeks."

"In the future, tell them to pound sand."

"What's the job?"

"They're launching a cable news network. They've actually got the resources and the brand appeal. Probably one of the only companies out there that can pull it off. They want me to join up as a founding partner with equity because they think I'll add gravitas and connections and all that crap. Not expressing much confidence in me winning this election though."

"Put it out of your mind. We have other things to focus on. Like the White House."

"He said my deal would be worth two hundred million in year one."

"You'll be needing an assistant, I assume." They laugh. "Flight plan is booked. We have a few hours in the air."

"Good," says Tom. "I want to close my eyes for an hour or so. Try to keep people off me."

Peter nods. In the Suburban with them are Dan Cullen, chief of advance, Darren Slater, a law school friend of Tom's who has taken a leave of absence from his firm to travel with Tom, and two Secret Service agents.

The last of the press are at the top of the mobile staircase stepping into the Boeing 757 that has "Pauley" painted down the sides of the fuselage.

Pauley pulls his trench coat tight. It's a cold day for early October in Pittsburgh. The trench coat was given to him that morning by his body guy who had looked up the weather. Tom has no idea where the coat came from. He never has to think about clothes, meals, or cars. At airports he never touches a bag or sees a TSA agent. Nor do any of the journalists or techs traveling with the campaign. They move in a government-sponsored bubble. The vehicles pull up to within yards of a gassed-up 757. Everyone steps out and climbs stairs to the plane and they're cleared for takeoff. Pauley is the last on the plane. They can be in the air five minutes from stepping out of the Suburban. When he lands in the new weather of Palm Beach, the body guy will give him a new set of clothes.

It's a tiny, private field. Pauley doesn't know the name but it must have a runway long enough for the 757. He takes the steps and tries to look full of energy. He's watched and photographed at all times, but at the top stair he stops and takes a moment just for himself. Only a Secret Service agent is behind Tom and the agent stops three steps back while Tom looks across the strips of concrete that divide the grass and a backdrop of deciduous trees turning color. He pays attention to his breath because that always relaxes him. He counts five deep inhales which is about thirty seconds and he feels the muscles of his chest unclench and his posture returns to something sustainable.

Tom steps inside thinking he can never get any sleep inside this madhouse. These flights aren't like anything he'd seen before. The plane is refitted for the campaign. There is an extended amount of first-class seating in the two-by-two configuration where twenty-five campaign staffers sit then about a dozen Secret Service who act as a buffer between the campaign and the media. Backing up to the Secret Service is a stocked wet bar. The reporters feel it's part of the tradition to be a little drunk in the daylight and the techs are just happy to be drunk anytime. Also there's something in the human spirit that compels the ingestion of free things.

Behind the bar the configuration changes to coach class with three-by-three seating for about forty reporters and forty techs.

Tom scans the back of the plane and sees Randy Newhope with a cute young girl sitting in his lap. He's sure they'll sit like that all through the takeoff without a lap belt. It's part of traveling in the government bubble that no rules apply, and people like to flaunt their new liberties. Nobody will bother to power down their cell phones either. That safety request is actually just a lot of bullshit.

Tom sits in the first row starboard side by the window and his law school friend Darren Slater takes the aisle seat next to him. Normally Tom would sit back a row so more people can circle in front of him for a conversation but he doesn't want to talk much now and this helps to prevent it. The seat next to him is the one people want and Darren had to cut off Peter Brand to get it. That will hold until Brand gets frustrated enough to tell Darren to move, like cutting in on a dance partner.

"You're doing great, buddy, you're doing great." Darren slaps Tom's knee. Tom could overrule any of the seating arrangements, but now he just wants a rest. Short of sleeping he chooses a conversation with Darren over others. It's relaxing to talk about sports teams and their old law school professors.

"Thanks, Darren."

"You tired?"

"I'm okay. The hard part is having to be up, then come down, then be up again. It's hard to fire up the adrenaline more than once in a day."

"I want to talk to you about that, Tom." The jet engines strain and send vibrations through everyone as the plane accelerates down the runway and pushes the passengers into their chairs. Tom reclines his all the way. A few people are still standing by the bar pouring drinks and they widen their stance for balance. "These events shouldn't take up energy, they should give you energy. If you're being yourself. The only reason you would even have to build up to something is if you're putting on something that you're not. Don't get overcoached."

Tom would much rather talk about the Tar Heel basketball recruiting class. "I don't know, Darren."

"I do. I saw you speak in law school. That wasn't exhausting, it was fun."

"This is a lot different."

"It doesn't have to be. You're making points and persuading people. It's just more people."

"I appreciate what you're trying to do, Darren, but I'd like to see you do this for a few days and tell me it's the same thing."

"Look, I know it's a lot more and it's more intense, but it will be easier when you get out there if you let you be you."

"I don't get it. How am I not being me?" This is getting annoying. Tom would rather be talking Arab-Israeli relations with a policy wonk. He's not interested in Darren's psychology revelations.

"You're all guts and fire. Normally. Like the way you reacted to that glitter bomb. Get out there and do that, be that guy. If you do that, these events will feed you energy rather than sap it from you. You'll be hungry for more of them. Besides, we're a few points behind. We need some Pauley fire to shake things up." An in-flight crew member hands them each a bottle of water and a glass of red wine which is what Tom has on almost every flight. "What do you think, Tom?"

"I think you're spending too much time on the toilet."

"Oh, please."

"Try more fiber."

Darren laughs. "Fuck you." He drinks the wine. "Sir," he adds. Darren knows he's there to be a comfortable place for Tom but he also thinks he knows best in certain matters, as do most people around politics and cable TV.

"I'm sure there's something to it. Let me think about it." Tom extends his legs, pressing his shoulders hard into the seat back, and he closes his eyes.

Peter Brand had been listening to the conversation and decides this is a good time. He comes from the seat behind Darren. "Governor, we need to do a bit of debate review." The first debate with Mitchell Mason is in four days. They'll spend the next three days in Tampa so Tom can prepare with no travel. It'll give the staff and reporters time to do laundry. "Darren, do you mind switching?"

"For Christ's sake, Peter," says Tom. "Would you give me an hour?"

Darren smiles and doesn't move. He's actually not such a jerk but people can't help but jockey for Tom's wing.

"Okay, get some rest, sir." Peter sits down and closes his eyes. Both he and Tom sleep for almost two hours while Darren plays Pac-Man on his iPhone.

The announcement of the plane's descent wakes them both. There's only twenty minutes left in the flight and Peter curses for having slept so much. "Darren, hop up, please."

Tom is still asleep and Darren moves without argument. Peter nudges Tom awake then doesn't speak for a few minutes while Tom gets ready to engage. Tom presses his palms to his face then runs his fingers through his hair and drinks half the bottle of water. Someone will be by to fix his hair again before he gets off the plane. "Okay, Peter. I'm yours."

"Okay. We have three solid days in Tampa to prepare. There's a morning rally tomorrow, then you go off-line. There are eight policy areas and we're going to do forty-five-minute review sessions on each. Every day. That's six hours of review and we're going to have a different team assigned to each policy area. We're also going to do two full ninety-minute mock debates each day. We'll break them up, one at noon and one at nine p.m., which is the time of the actual debate on Thursday. We'll fill in the time around the mock debates with the policy review modules. We'll also block out time for exercise and casual reading."

"Good. And how about a siesta?"

"You have one scheduled for November seventh."

"Right."

"The key to the next few days is two things. One, to know the information cold so you never have to worry about searching your brain for it, and two, to role-play all scenarios Mason will throw at you so you're ready and relaxed. You know I think Darren's full of shit"—he turns his head to the side and says this louder so Darren knows he's at least half kidding—"but he's onto something in that you need to be as relaxed as you can be. It's a big night and no one can think on his feet when he's stressed."

"Okay."

"Chuck Knoll said it best. Pressure is something that you feel only when you don't know what you're doing."

"Alright. I feel good. I'm pretty far up the curve on the issues already. We'll put the work in and get there."

"Good." Peter holds up eight manila envelopes. "This is the review material for tomorrow's policy sessions. I'll get this to you for the drive from Palm Beach to Tampa tonight."

"Wonderful."

There's about two minutes before landing. Peter stands and turns around. "Darren, you want to switch back?" Peter looks up to the back of the plane and sees a bearded kid standing against the lavatory door holding a plastic serving tray and facing forward. He's the sort of young person who grows a beard because his features are too round and boyish for people to see him the way he wants to be seen. Aisle surfing has gotten popular on this campaign. When the landing gear touches and the plane rapidly decelerates the kid will run a few steps then drop the tray in the aisle and jump on as though skimboarding the slick sand at the edge of an ocean wave.

"Sure," says Darren.

"Hang on. I want to see this."

Darren stands too and they hold the same seat back while watching the bearded kid at the back of the plane. Tom twists in his seat to look.

The gear hits and the plane lurches then rises into the air again. The kid starts his run to time the next contact of wheel to ground. He takes four long steps then crouches and flips the tray in front of him. He makes an unafraid hop and sticks both feet to the tray while looking forward but with shoulders squared to the port windows and toes pointed in the same direction. Everyone is watching, including Secret Service.

His feet touch the tray a micro second after the wheels touch the ground which is perfect. In two seconds the plane has decelerated by forty miles per hour and there's a near-complete lack of friction between the tray and the short carpet in the aisle. The look on the kid's face shows that his precision was more than he'd hoped for. He stays true to the middle of the aisle, clearing the coach seating a second later.

Rather than bailing out to one side, he decides to brace for frontal impact with the wet bar. He rises a few inches from his crouch with open hands in front. His palms catch the countertop of the bar and vault his body up and forward over the fulcrum of his wrists so that he leads with his chin and chest, like a sprinter crossing the finish tape, and passes toward the rows of the Secret Service.

An agent made of muscle and bone stands to prevent the incoming. The agent's body has had a lifetime of contact and knows by instinct how to gauge a physical action and prepare the reaction. He braces his feet and leans all his body weight behind his raised forearm that catches the kid in the sternum. There is a sickening reversal to the movement of the kid's torso and his head snaps forward and back like a crash test dummy's. The agent's body is unmoving and unforgiving.

The boy's body collapses on the coach side of the wet bar. The landing gear maintains contact with the ground and the plane slows to taxi speed. The engines ease and stop drowning out the smaller noises in time for people nearby to hear the plastic tray rattle and come to rest on a metal beam of the floor, reminding everyone that this violence started with a little horsing around.

"Jesus," says Tom. "That boy's seriously hurt." He moves out of his row and starts back to check on the boy.

Peter puts a hand on Tom's shoulder. "It was an accident."

"I know that. I'm not angry with anyone. He's goofing around and the Secret Service has a job to do."

Dan Cullen stands with his hand on his own chest. It looks like the boy is breathing fine and starting to move a bit. Dan says to Peter, "These kids come into campaigns. It's a crazy place. They're not kids very long."

44

"Sir, I understand where Ron wants to spend money in this last month, but I need to highlight to you that we're running low. If we do everything Ron says, we're going to dip below a zero balance." Derek Hamilton is budget director for Mitchell Mason's campaign. He's in the back of the Suburban with Mason and Ron Stark for a private conversation. For Mason to have an audience this small at this stage of the campaign that includes the budget director is rare. The only others in the car are Secret Service, who for the purposes of the content of the meeting are deaf and mute.

"Then pull in some money." Mason says this in the tone of telling a thirsty child to pour himself some water from the enormous pitcher in front of his face.

"We're trying." The funding for Mason's campaign is down from four years ago, in part because he hasn't put in the time for as many fundraisers and in part because the enthusiasm is down a bit as well. He now finds himself in a race that's a few points closer than he expected it to be with only one month to go and he wants money.

"You're not looking in the right places."

"I'm sorry, sir. Where do you mean?" Derek is a thirty-six-year-old investment banker from Goldman Sachs on leave to help the campaign in the hopes of making enough contacts to return to Goldman as a rainmaker of new business. He looks like a Goldman banker. Perfect haircut, perfect shave, nice suit, precision to his movements and mind. He never makes wild gestures. His hands never go beyond the span of his shoulders and when he talks his forehead tips out over his nose and he talks in a clear, quiet voice.

"Ron, I'm going to read the paper for a moment while you and Derek talk privately." This is mostly a joke since they are all three just inches away from each other but Mason actually picks up the *Wall Street Journal*.

"From the PAC, you jackass," says Ron Stark.

Derek sits with his hands in his lap, realizing in stages that are each separated by a few seconds that he's been told to do something illegal and the president is in the car but he's reading the paper and this is a private conversation with Ron Stark. "How should I go about that? I'm not supposed to have even a conversation with them."

"You find a way," says Ron. "Your job is to find a way. That's why we hired you. Has this campaign hired a person who can't do his job?"

"I can do my job," says Derek. He finds some haughtiness for his voice, remembering he's a Goldman man. "I'm a banker so I know how to manage your finances. I don't know the outer edges of campaign fund-raising law."

Ron pulls out his iPhone. "Skadden Arps has a good Federal Election Commission practice. I'm emailing you the contact information for an attorney there. Call him, get to know the important parts of the law. I'm also going to put you in touch with a couple campaign veterans who are creative thinkers."

"Okay."

Ron hits send on the email. "From there you figure it out, Derek. The next thing the president and I want to hear on this is that there's plenty of gas in the tank. Nothing from you before then, and I want to hear it soon."

"Yes, sir."

Mitchell crumples the paper in his lap. "You boys finished?"

"Yes, sir," says Ron. Derek nods.

"Derek, let me tell you a little story," says the president. He doesn't look at Derek. He looks out the window. "A couple decades ago I was an active surrogate for a candidate in a tight race. At that time, there was a one-point-three-million spending cap in Iowa. We needed Iowa. We needed it for momentum and we viewed it as key and we were going to be goddamned if we weren't going to spend a hell of a lot more than one-point-three million on Iowa. So you know what we did?"

It's rhetorical but Derek is so rapt that he says no and Mitchell had left enough time for the response.

"We booked all campaign flights into Illinois, then rented cars in Illinois and drove into Iowa. That was all billed against Illinois, where we knew we'd never spend near the cap. We set up our phone banks in Missouri and that was billed against Missouri, not Iowa. We did that every turn we could. We spent more than ten million dollars on Iowa and exactly one-point-three million was billed against Iowa."

Derek smiles.

Mitchell continues. "Now this was all legal to the letter of the law. I hope you'll be as fortunate. The following year, campaign finance law caught up to these tricks and shut them down, but my point is that where there's a will, there's a way. Or should I say, where there's greater determination, there's a way."

"I'll find a way, sir."

The president is enjoying his talk too much to stop. "A smart campaign is always ahead of the campaign finance law. It's the same as with steroids in sports. Think of all the hundreds of billions of dollars to be had through success in sports. Add up all the prize money and endorsements for all the sports from humans to horses. Globally, it could be trillions. And how much money is spent policing the cheating? Maybe a few tens of millions? There's much more will, read will as money, on the side of cheating than on the side of policing. Barry Bonds was getting his steroids from a few guys in a lab that was basically a garage, and they managed to design something undetectable. The only reason Bonds got caught was a whistle-blower."

Derek nods again.

"You are determined and you have resources, Derek. You stay one step ahead." The president is smiling as he says this, then he stops smiling and points a finger at Derek. "Get me that money."

The Suburban is driving south on the Florida Turnpike to Miami. The president is going underground for two days of preparation before the debate in Tampa. He travels in greater style and with greater security than Pauley. He also has a full-time job but his focus for the next month is to keep the job.

The ride is smooth and safe behind the bullet- and soundproof glass. The sun through the window is on Mason's lap and it makes him hot. "I'm looking forward to November when all this crap is behind us. Four years isn't much time when you factor in all the hell you have to endure to get and then keep the damned job."

The Suburban passes exits for Fort Lauderdale and Mason thinks of all the people living different lives and wonders if those are happier lives or if that's just the kind of pitiful thinking a person has in a weak moment.

45

The campaign to reelect Mitchell Mason pulls into the Tampa Intercontinental Hotel at three p.m. The convoy is bigger and more glamorous than Pauley's but has all the same building blocks. The notion of checking into the hotel is absurd. The Secret Service advance team has been at the location for more than a week.

There is enough daylight between Mason and his entourage for only a tight photograph. Otherwise he moves at the center of a mass of bodies that provide the propulsion so Mason doesn't have to. He feels his feet don't touch the ground.

Once inside, security fans out, knowing where to go and staying in touch wirelessly. The president's agenda is known by security and aides so Mason follows the lead man but the pace is set by Mason.

Hotel employees keep their distance and stare at their elected leader. Everyone is frozen except for the eyeballs moving across the white space of their eyes as he moves by.

The first meeting is an emergency core staff meeting called by Ron Stark. The meeting will include only the president and Stark along with Jack Boothe, chief strategist, and Ted Knowles, press secretary. Others are excluded, which has offended them.

The president follows the lead agent to the lobby-level conference room of the hotel. The entire hotel has only campaign staff, Secret Service, and hotel employees screened by Secret Service.

"What's this all about, Ron?"

"I'll make it quick. Problem, solution." The four men sit around a table too big so there are unusual distances between them and an awkward moment as they select chairs. Stark sits next to Mason who sat first. Jack Boothe sits across the narrow side of the rectangular table from Mason and Ted Knowles sits a couple chairs down from Boothe. "The problem is that the *Standard* is going to run a story in two days outlining your extramarital activity."

"All this crap was vetted by the media four years ago!"

"I'm hearing they have new stuff."

"Susan?"

"I don't think she's the source, but she's the topic."

"You're sure?"

"Yes."

"Well, if she's not the source, they don't have crap." Mitchell wonders how Susan's conversation with her husband went. It would have been a few years ago. She never mentioned it again and he never followed up. Hammermill crosses his mind too. That son of a bitch.

"I'm hearing they will claim sources inside the administration."

"Unnamed, of course," says Mitchell. The entire conversation is between Mason and Stark. Knowles and Boothe seem uncertain if it's safe to speak.

"Yes."

"Cowards." Mitchell picks up a bottle of water that has been placed at his seat. "Fuck." He twists the cap and drinks. "You said something about a solution."

"There's only one play," says Stark. He looks at Press Secretary Knowles. "We get out in front of the story. We anticipate that it's coming out and we shape it before it even gets there."

"Absolutely," says Ted.

"We need a friendly," Stark says back to him, still looking right at Knowles. "Who have you got?"

Knowles leans back, trying to think of a person at a credible outlet he could hit up for a big favor. Someone who would let him craft the writing. "I don't know," he says. "There are certainly some people favorable to the campaign, but I don't think you're going to get the level of control you're looking for. Not from anyone with a good reputation." Knowles comes from the media and values journalistic standards. He has never been on the campaign side of things before.

Jack Boothe leans forward with determination. The other three notice his physical entry to the conversation and look at him before he speaks. "I have an idea."

"Out with it, Jack," says Mason.

"It's tricky and I'll have to think of the best way to present it to him, but it may work the best. It's actually karmicly correct."

"Please tell us the idea, Jack," says Stark, saving Mason the trouble.

"Randy Newhope at *Newsweek*."

"Heard of him," says Stark. "Why him?"

"Because I happen to know something about him."

The three men are sick of pulling the information from him so they wait.

"I know that he's married," says Jack. "I also know that he's taken up with a hot little gal following the Pauley campaign."

"How do you know it?" asks Ted Knowles.

"Doesn't matter. I know it. It's certain."

"So you want to use this?" asks Stark. Stark will take over the questions so Mason doesn't have to speak while the plan is formed. It doesn't absolve Mason, but it's something.

"I'll just let Randy know in a very kind and humorous way that I know he's having a good time. I'll then let him know that the *Standard* is planning a story about the president having a good time. I'll give him some good ideas for a story to come out in the next twenty-four hours. Maybe that the days of the media judging a president by his personal life are long over and that only hacks do that. Maybe that citing unnamed sources in an administration is classic bullshit journalism. We'll craft a few things. Then I'll remind him that I met his wife at a reception one time and what a nice lady I thought she was."

Mason stays staring at Booth with his expression unchanged but nodding.

Knowles puts his palms flat to the table. He's angry. "Blackmail? Your plan is to blackmail Randy Newhope?"

Nobody wants to put words to the affirmative, but Jack nods yes. He's certain this is three to one against Knowles.

"Mr. President," says Knowles, "this is a very dangerous strategy. If this backfires, we're screwed." Knowles is smart enough not to argue this on moral grounds, even though that is what persuaded him.

Stark answers instead of Mason. "Like Jack says, it all depends on how we present it to Randy Newhope. It doesn't have to be blackmail. Newhope is having an extramarital affair right now. This could be just a meeting of the minds that an affair is not such a big deal, especially when it comes to judging a sitting president on his job performance."

"Wow," says Knowles. He never says "shit" or "Christ" at any time. It's a self-discipline he practices so that he doesn't say those words in a White House press briefing in front of the media.

All four are silent. The case is laid out and they're waiting for the verdict from the boss.

After a moment, the president leans back in his chair, clasps his hands across his stomach, and looks at the ceiling. "Ted, let me tell you something about politics." He loves not to look at a person when he talks to him. "This is something I know to be true." He makes a closed-lip smile to himself. "In the beginning, a young person will come to a campaign because he believes in a cause. If that cause doesn't move forward, there will be real harm to the country. So he believes. He'll volunteer for a campaign because he'll find the candidate who can champion that cause. Soon, he'll come to think that only this candidate can be the real champion for the cause. He'll love his cause and his candidate equally, and put them first."

The president pauses for water then continues. "This young man will be dedicated to victory. Remember, his guy needs to win or the whole country's in trouble. This young man will come to believe in the philosophy of whatever it takes. That in elections for which the country is at stake, the ends justify the means. You see, the ends are what we all live with every day. Who wins the election, what makes it to the news headlines. It's what everyone sees and lives. Only a few of us get to see the means. And have to live with it.

"So our young man who was cause-driven and wide-eyed and innocent at the start will come to face a series of moral decisions, a series of crossroads. He will cross them. Believe me. People on Pauley's campaign are crossing them right now. Derek Hamilton, our own budget director, is crossing over one right now. You, Ted, need to cross over." Mason sits forward to look right at Knowles. "Barack Obama won elections because people around him wanted it more. They felt a moral duty to get him elected and they placed that moral duty above all other moral duties. David Axelrod is not a wimp."

Boothe and Stark look back and forth between the president and Knowles. They're not sure if they're watching an education or an execution. Knowles looks uncomfortable.

The president breaks the silence. "Let me tell you something else! And this is something I've never told anyone. There's more to it, because the craziest thing happens next." He sips his water again. "The candidate comes to believe he's the only person who can serve the cause. And he crosses over. I crossed over. I don't mean crossing over on little moral issues. I mean crossing over to true indoctrination. Self-indoctrination." Mason looks across the three of them. He knows this must sound crazy but he tries to sound calm and not crazy.

They stare back until Mason laughs again. "Everyone who has ever held the nomination of his party has crossed over. Reagan, Obama, both Bushes. Clinton, both Clintons actually. The only difference among us is self-awareness. I know I crossed over. The Bushes knew. Bill Clinton crossed and kept going. He thinks he's the fulcrum point in the history of mankind, but he knows he's crossed. I don't think Obama knows. Hammermill either."

Now everyone is uncomfortable. It's fascinating but nobody wants more of this. But one thing in common that the three listeners think at once is that the man is fucking honest.

The president brings the conversation back to the main point. "Ted, what do you think is the relationship between our political system and human nature? Is it containment? Is it promotion? Is it a bad system rescued by good people? Or, Ted, is it the best we can do given who we always turn out to be?"

Ted Knowles hopes this is all rhetorical and he can wait it out and not have to answer. Boothe knows that his plan is approved and that Knowles will support it. Time to speak with Randy Newhope.

46

Jack Boothe can get the cell phone number of anyone in the press through the aid that manages media relations. He sends a text message to Randy Newhope.

Room 1507. 11 p.m. tonight. Keep it quiet. Jack Boothe

Jack likes how cloak-and-dagger it seems, though it could also seem gay. None of the press has rooms on the fifteenth floor but they're always trying to get meetings with campaign officials, so if anyone sees Randy on fifteen at a weird hour they'll assume that's all he's doing there.

At exactly eleven p.m. Randy knocks on Jack's door. Randy has on jeans and an untucked dress shirt. Jack says, "Take a seat." He's in a suite with a writing desk and sofas for meeting that are separate from the bedroom. "Before we get started, you should know that the president doesn't know anything about this meeting. This is coming from me." Jack's words are clipped. There's nothing social or friendly.

Randy sits and keeps his eyes on Jack. He's been in the business long enough to know that the president might know at least the intent of what's about to be said, if not the details. People lie a lot. "Okay." He sits and leans forward. He doesn't want to look cocky yet.

Jack keeps standing. He has a drink and doesn't offer one. "Randy, where do you stand on the topic of infidelity?" He pauses to watch the expression go blank. "Of presidents?"

Randy shrugs. "I don't think about it much. I don't know if there's been a president who didn't play around, so it doesn't factor in, really. Unless it's egregious."

Jack doesn't look at Randy. He paces back and forth with slow steps like each footfall has a plan. Randy is at the edge of what he knows to be the inner sanctum and would like to be let in. He's the junior man of the two and would like a handout. Jack likes how the meeting has started. He sips his scotch and says, "I think that's right. It's a nonissue. I'm glad to hear you say that." He points at Randy when he says this as though directing a stenographer to put Randy on the record.

Randy would like to point out that he made a caveat for egregious behavior but doesn't. He'd like a glass of scotch too.

Jack says, "Some media have made a fuss with speculations about the president's fidelity, but it's only those who want to attack him. They don't like where he stands on the real issues so they go after him on a nonissue. Wouldn't you agree that's a distraction?"

"I guess so."

"Good." Jack takes another sip and sits down on the sofa across from Randy. "You have a chance to do something positive for the national conversation. You can get out in front with a piece that reminds everyone to keep their eyes on the ball and exposes the cheap games that some media frauds play."

Randy now knows there's no nugget of information coming to him. Boothe just wants some help. Randy feels more power so he takes his forearms off his knees and sits back in the sofa. "I don't know, Jack. It's a busy news cycle now on campaign issues. I've got a bunch of other pieces in the works and I don't have room for a highbrow opinion piece like this. I don't think I'm your guy for this."

Jack expected this and says, "This topic may come to the front of the news cycle very soon and you have a chance to get in front of it. You like a drink?"

"Sure, I'll have what you're having."

Jack stands and walks to the mini fridge behind the desk. He puts three ice cubes in a short glass and empties an airplane-sized bottle of Dewar's into it. From the desk he picks up a manila folder then hands the glass and the folder to Randy.

Randy drinks and holds up the folder. "What's this?"

"I would consider it a favor, Randy. It's some copy that could help you with a piece like this. I'll be well placed over the next four years and I remember favors."

Randy puts the folder down on the desk in front of him and finishes the scotch in a large drink. It's not the nervous drink of a person who needs the edge off. It's a show of dominance. "Jack, that's crazy. I'm not even going to open that folder. You can have it back."

"You won't do the piece?" says Jack.

"I will not. I'm a journalist. This whole conversation is inappropriate."

Jack crosses his legs and looks over the room as though musing until he's sure Randy is about to excuse himself. "It's interesting that you use the word 'inappropriate.'"

"Excuse me?"

"You remember I met your wife one time, don't you? What's her name?" Randy doesn't say anything.

"Emily, isn't it? Emily. She seems very nice. Kids?"

"Two," says Randy.

"She's a lobbyist at Parks and Solomon, right? I've done some work with that firm."

"What's this about?" says Randy.

"Has Emily ever met Tara Altman?"

Randy is forward on the edge of the sofa now. "You're an asshole."

"Randy, I'm not judging you. I think your fidelity has nothing to do with your job performance. Don't you see the parallels here?"

Randy is thinking about what leverage he has that he can throw back at Boothe. He keeps coming up with nothing and his anger rises. "This could ruin me."

"When you say this, which of your problems are you referring to?"

"This," and he picks up the folder. "This." He has no play with Boothe, just anger. He stands and throws it hard overhand but it's only a few papers and it flaps in a frantic pattern then lands back at his own feet to mock his powerlessness. Randy looks for something heavier and finds the phone. He takes it in both hands, then spins like a discus thrower and hurls it across the room. He raises a ceramic lamp over his head, then crashes it to the floor.

Jack still sits with legs crossed. He knew this could happen too. Everyone's under a lot of stress and underrested. Randy needs to feel strong and in control for a moment while he takes his emasculation.

There's a knock at the door which freezes Randy. Jack opens the door only a few inches and says, "Everything's fine, just a slip." Jack closes the door and says, "Secret Service. They're very good."

Now he'll reposition the issue with Randy to make it easier to swallow. Jack picks up the empty glasses and fills them while Randy stands, breathing heavy and uncertain.

He hands the scotch to Randy and they stand next to each other. "Randy, I don't see any problems here. This is a story you believe in, you said so yourself. Your readers might like a story like this and I'd still like to look at this as a favor."

"With a gun to my head," says Randy.

"There is the unfortunate situation that I know your wife and I have this other information."

"And you'd use it."

"I need something, Randy. My campaign does. You put yourself in this position."

"If this gets out, I'm done as a journalist."

"It won't get out. Anyway, moving on from journalism might be a good thing. I told you I remember favors. If you raise your hand, you might get a nice spot in the next administration."

"Like what?"

"I can't make any promises, but I've always thought Ted Knowles is a pussy."

Randy's felt too many emotions in the last five minutes to think clearly.

Jack says, "Why don't you take the drink with you?" He bends down to pick up the folder and hands it to Randy. "And don't forget this."

47

Mason is sick of reading notes in his hotel suite. It's eleven p.m. "Call down and have them fix a cheeseburger medium with fries." An agent picks up the phone for the restaurant. Mason changes into jeans and a sweater and puts on shoes. He leaves the suite and walks to the elevator and the agents follow without a word.

The elevator doors open to the lobby level and as Mason steps forward a shopping cart with four cases of beer pushes him back inside. He looks at the hands on the shopping cart handle and follows the arms up to Jack Boothe's face. "What the fuck are you doing, Jack?"

Boothe can't get out a word. He backs up the cart to make room for the president to leave the elevator. "Excuse me, sir."

Mason steps out and stops by the side of the cart. "You're a little old for this, Jack. And a little too senior in my staff."

"Sorry, sir. Just getting this up to some of the younger folks." The idea that Jack won't be in the center of the drinking is so clearly bullshit that they both just leave it right there.

Mason walks on to the Shula's restaurant in the hotel and Boothe escapes to the elevator wishing he could do over the last two minutes.

Steps from the door to the restaurant, Mason's personal cell phone rings. Incoming calls are rare and he answers it.

"Hello, Ron."

"Sir, I have some troubling news."

"Let's get it out." Mitchell stops walking and covers his open ear with his free hand.

"You know who Samantha Davis is."

"UBS-24."

"Yes. She's been a bit underground the last couple months, working on a story."

"So?"

"You're the story."

"How much more of this infidelity crap are we going to deal with?"

"This one's different. I'm hearing that she has enough that the executives at UBS have decided to go with it. It likely hits in a few days. Maybe right after the debate. Maybe before."

"Jesus Christ, Ron, how bad can it be?"

"We need to talk."

48

"The jury's back with a verdict."

Samantha Davis, Ken Harper, and David Mueller are in Mueller's office. Mueller is behind his desk and can see the muted television screens on the wall behind Samantha and Ken. Mueller reads the lower third of the screen again. "The jury reached a verdict in less than three hours."

"That's not good for Meadow," says Samantha.

Every network had given over hours each day to cover the trial. The state had made a strong case against her though the media reported that she had developed an in-courtroom flirtation with one of the jurors. A three-hour deliberation indicates there was nobody speaking up for her, though.

"Not at all," says Mueller. "It'll be twenty minutes before they all get seated and read through everything. Let's get back to it."

"Take us through what you have, Samantha," says Ken Harper.

"I have the affair. Plenty of details from Monica Morris and this is corroborated by letters, emails, eyewitness accounts, and photographs."

"Okay, fine," says Mueller.

"I have them in Florida, together, on the night of the hit-and-run. Again, plenty of details from Monica and there are emails that back up that exact night. The restaurant manager is still there today. He doesn't have reservation records going back that far but he remembers Mason as governor of New York, coming in with Monica, and says that date makes sense."

"Alright," says Mueller.

"That restaurant puts them fourteen miles from the hit-and-run, which occurred around midnight that evening. The route from the restaurant to Jupiter would have taken them right along US One where the hit-and-run happened. There aren't eyewitnesses or records addressing it but everything Monica Morris says is plausible."

Both men exhale. "Christ," says Mueller.

Ken Harper says, "I think I know how Woodward and Bernstein's editor felt. It's like we just crested the highest part of the roller coaster and are looking down. It's supposed to be fun but I feel like I'm going to throw up."

"The only thing I don't have is the two of them at the hit-and-run at the time of the hit-and-run."

"You have Monica Morris's confession," says Ken.

"And that's all I have, so we need to report it carefully."

"Are you a lawyer or a reporter?" says Ken.

"She's a damn good reporter," says Mueller for her.

"You're not seriously questioning whether or not we go with this?" says Ken.

"It's a hell of a thing to go with the day before the debate," says Mueller.

Samantha says, "I think we go with all of it but tread lightly around the hit-and-run."

"We have a responsibility to go with it," says Ken.

They all nod. Decision made.

Samantha leans back. She takes a deep breath through her nose and holds it, then forces it out the way people do when trying to raise courage. "There's one more wrinkle I need to tell you about."

"Hang on." Mueller interrupts, standing with remote in hand to come around and sit on the front of his desk. He turns the volume up on UBS. The reporter is reading a text message from her producer inside the courtroom.

"Guilty."

Ken Harper says, "They'll probably hold sentencing in about a week. Now it's just a question of life or death for her."

"Jesus," says Mueller. There's a head shot of Meadow Jones up on the screen, looking like a beautiful little girl, and Mueller is trying to reconcile that picture with a murderer who used a steak knife. He mutes the TV. "What's the wrinkle, Sam?"

THE DEBATE

49

"Gin."

"Jesus." Tom lays his cards down on the coffee table in front of him. "Alison, you know you're supposed to be pumping me up before I go out there. Don't you know how to tank a damned card game?"

Alison stands from a leather armchair that a staffer had pulled to the other side of the coffee table and comes around to sit next to Tom on the sofa. The walls are bare. The room is a rectangle, thirty feet by twenty. There are a leather sofa and chair, both cheap, and a dozen folding chairs that are metal with a plastic-covered pad on the seat.

Their son and daughter are in a corner of the room drinking soda. Tom and Alison drink water and stay calm. Peter Brand and eight others from the campaign staff drink coffee as fast as it can arrive to the room and try to project confidence in their man.

An hour before the debate, Brand ushers in a camera crew to take still shots behind the scenes. Tom's family knows what to do at this point of the campaign. They get on the couch together the way they would for a Christmas card photo. They make sure the playing cards are visible. Then they try for some candid-looking shots. The kids stack the cards to a three-level house, then they all laugh when Tom huffs and puffs and blows the house in. Perfect.

Peter Brand thanks the three-person camera crew and ushers them back out. He refills his coffee and sits next to Tom on the couch. Alison sits on Tom's other side, their hands clasped together and resting on the top of Tom's thigh.

"You're ready," says Peter. "You're as ready for this moment as any candidate I've ever seen. You have all the talent and all the preparation. Go out there and execute, and you will change the face of this election."

"Thanks, Peter. I feel ready. I'm relaxed, I have all the information and I have conviction."

Peter nods. He slaps Tom's knee. "You know, there's a moment when I knew you had it. That you could be in a debate in the general for the White House." Peter sips his coffee and looks at the wall across from them like he's just hit the switch on a projector so they can all watch the moment replay together. "The greatest gift of a politician is knowing how to handle the moments with strangers who know him. You have that gift. We were at a campaign event at Durham High School and a man came up to you and told you he'd lost his job the year before and the bank was foreclosing on his home. You asked that guy what his job was, what he'd been doing to find a new one, how his wife and kids were doing, where the home was, what changes they were making in their grocery shopping. The whole time you were looking him in the eye and you really wanted to know the answers. By the end of it, you knew more about that guy than his own brother would. I watched the whole thing and I knew you'd be our next governor and I was pretty sure you'd get to be right here."

"I remember that conversation. It feels like a couple decades ago."

"You're the better man on that stage tonight, Tom."

Tom sips his water.

"Now listen. No home runs. Just get out there and swing nice and easy. Let it come to you and you'll probably hit one or two out of the park anyway. Just stay firm the whole ninety minutes. Don't do any on-the-one-hand-on-the-other-hand bullshit. For the first time you're going to stand onstage next to the president of the United States. You need to stay strong. Stay decisive. Stay presidential. If he doesn't push you around and you can stay tough, you win and you win big. Tonight will elevate you to presidential status. This is a simple, conservative game plan that gets a big win."

"Got it." Tom sips more water. His last coffee was three hours ago because he doesn't want to be jittery onstage and caffeine can do that to him.

At 8:50 p.m. Tom gives his kids a kiss then walks with Alison down the hallway behind the stage of the Tampa Convention Center. The children will take their seats in the audience where Alison will meet them, then after the debate they'll all surround Tom onstage. The hallways have naked concrete floors with a shine and are empty except for security and debate commission personnel telling people where to go.

Tom doesn't realize how hard he's squeezing Alison's hand and she refuses to tell him. They get to the west side of the stage and Tom gives her a hug and kiss and waits to be called out by the moderator.

50

Evelyn feels that her husband shouldn't have to stoop to a debate with this young man from North Carolina. Pauley's presence on the same stage as Mitchell is an undeserved badge of honor that she would never have bestowed, and for Mitchell actually to have to defend his record of four years is so distasteful that the mere act of it is a political downside. And it's just a pain in the ass. They belong in the White House, not in some godforsaken convention center in Florida, forced into a circus to answer challenges from a novice from the cheap seats.

Evelyn and Mitchell sit on a couch in a room identical to Pauley's but on the other wing of the backstage hallway. They both have legs crossed, his elevated foot pointing away and in the opposite direction from hers. They're not in love but they're loyal as hell in other matters. It's a partnership and it's effective and they both have decided it's more than many marriages have.

It's 8:30 p.m. Thirty minutes to go. "Remember who you are, dear."

Mitchell knows exactly how she means this. It's not a reference to a moral compass or values or anything in his character. It's a reference to a title. You're the goddamned president of the United States. Go out there and act like it and send this charlatan back where he came from. It's the kind of support that Mitchell expects and appreciates from Evelyn.

None of the aides approach Mason. He's made it clear over the years that at moments like this he doesn't want anyone in his ear. They all have had plenty of time for that and now he wants an hour of quiet and calm.

He sits up straight and closes his eyes and experiments if he can think of nothing at all.

"Ten minutes, Mr. President," says Ron Stark from the doorway. He says it in the lowest possible tone and there is complete silence from the dozen people in the room so his voice carries to the president.

Mason nods and keeps his eyes closed. He waits two more minutes, then stands, kisses Evelyn, and takes quick steps to the door. Evelyn will go directly to the seats in the audience and Stark will walk with Mason to the east edge of the debate stage to wait for introductions.

Stark says, "Randy Newhope's piece will run tomorrow so we're out in front of that issue. Given that and what we have on Pauley, it should be a nonissue for us going forward."

Their dress shoes knock the concrete floors as they pass Secret Service who whisper into their jacket lapels. Mason and Stark stop at the edge of the stage and look across the empty podiums to see Pauley and his wife already waiting and holding hands at the opposite edge of the stage.

The lighting is dim but enough to make eye contact. They do, and after a moment of a stare down that Mason is determined not to lose, Pauley winks at him.

"That cheeky little son of a bitch," Mason whispers to Stark.

"Sir, remember, this is likely to come up early. You need to jam him, right up front. Jam him hard. Outraged and indignant."

Mason nods. That wink was plenty enough to outrage him.

51

"We welcome President Mitchell Mason and Governor Tom Pauley," says the debate moderator, David Hennings. The crowd stands for their one chance at applause. There are twelve hundred folding chairs arranged in the auditorium which is a lot for a general election debate audience but not many for this room to hold. It allows plenty of space for media equipment and security buffers.

The two men advance from opposite sides of the stage and shake hands with the right and also grip each other's right biceps with the left. They manage to coordinate an untangling of this, then shake hands with Hennings, Mason first.

The format is for the two men to stand at podiums with David Hennings seated at a table in front of them. Hennings asks a question and each man is given two minutes to respond, followed by five minutes of discussion before the next question. The candidates alternate who gets the first two-minute response. A coin flip has determined that Mason will respond first to the first question.

"Mr. President, this question is new to the campaigns, and I'm going to give you the opportunity to address it here and now. About an hour ago, UBS released the byline for a story they will run tomorrow detailing allegations that you were involved in a hit-and-run incident some thirteen years ago that led to a fatality. Would you please comment on these allegations and on what impact this may have on your presidency?" Hennings and his team had been in shouting matches for the last hour about whether to use this question. It is sensational and maybe a cheap shot, but it is from UBS and real news that's out there and he felt he had an obligation to address it. It would also guarantee the greatest debate moment in history.

Tom's face muscles go slack and his lips part as his jaw relaxes. He looks from Hennings to the president. His mind is no longer debating. He's a spectator like everyone else. What the hell is going on here?

Mason leans into the podium. He looks ready to strike and happy about it. "First of all, David, let me say that the idea that you would open a national debate for the presidency of the United States with such a baseless and scurrilous allegation, thereby giving it credence, is disgraceful." He stops and points right at Hennings. "You should be ashamed of yourself. As for UBS, both their timing and their reporting are shameful and irresponsible. This is not journalism."

The president is rolling. The words are coming easily but don't sound rehearsed. He sounds pissed off. He continues, "Second of all, let me do a bit of journalism for you. This report was concocted by Samantha Davis at UBS-24. The same Samantha Davis who is a former litigator at Davis Polk." Mason turns and stretches an upturned palm toward Tom to introduce him to the conversation. "My opponent, Governor Pauley, is also a former litigator at Davis Polk. David, you've given me no choice but to level this true charge to defend myself against a false one. It is a fact that Governor Pauley and Samantha Davis were lovers. I can't comment on the present."

The president changes his tone from indignant to compassionate. His shoulders back off the podium a few inches. He lifts his eyebrows and looks apologetic. "I'm not interested in anyone's personal affairs, but I will not be a victim of such outrageous media bias."

The president nods to Hennings, giving back the floor, satisfied that seventy million people around the country are as stunned as Hennings and Pauley. UBS had disclosed in the report that Samantha Davis and Tom Pauley briefly dated during their time together at Davis Polk. Samantha had called the Pauley campaign to give them notice that this disclosure would be made. Samantha had left four messages with campaign staff and had stressed that the message was urgent but the messages were treated the same as the many other calls from media organizations that want time with the candidate. Pauley's staff never passed on the message and figured he'd return the call when he wanted to make an appearance on UBS.

Hennings's job is easy. "Governor Pauley?"

Poor Tom actually has to have a response. What the hell just happened? He was still replaying the words *hit-and-run fatality* in his head when he got clobbered by the Samantha Davis affair.

"Well." He clears his throat, even bringing a fist to his mouth as he does it. He knows he's already lost the composure war. The president looked sure of himself and indignant. Tom looks lost and confused. Regardless of facts, people will walk away with that visual. "I can't comment on the hit-and-run allegations. I'm sure authorities will pursue a thorough investigation and the facts will come out. If in fact President Mason has committed a homicide, we'll deal with that eventuality but there is no sense in hypothesizing on such a matter at this point." Tom is glad he got the word *homicide* into his response.

Tom sips his water then looks back at Hennings. "Regarding the other matter, Samantha Davis was an excellent lawyer and, to my knowledge, is a fair journalist. I've had no contact with her in many years. She and I had a friendship and briefly dated many years ago." This has the same evidential effect on the audience as playing the sex tape. Given that Samantha is an on-air reporter with a well-known face, the imagery is complete.

It's the truthful answer and Tom believes that should be the end of it but knows it won't be. He's never mentioned Samantha to Alison because it wasn't worth mentioning. They both met people after law school and before they were married and neither Tom nor Alison wanted to give or receive a full accounting of that period. Now he's angry about the humiliation he knows she must be feeling only a couple dozen feet away from him.

He and Samantha haven't spoken but had been on good terms and he's angry that she didn't let him know this was coming.

Hennings is back in control. "Thank you, gentlemen. We will forgo the five-minute discussion period on this topic and move right to the next question."

The debate moves to the economy where Pauley presses that the number of unemployed and people on welfare is up and that the economy is stalling. Mason counters that the price of gas is down, the stock market and GDP are up, and that the economy is strong.

On foreign policy, Pauley argues that our military is less capable and that our alliances around the world are less close. Mason argues the opposite.

Nobody cares. Pundits are already halfway through the draft of their editorials and viewers are still recovering and it's all about the first two minutes of the debate.

52

"What the fuck, Peter! What the fuck!" Tom has kicked everyone out of the backstage room at the convention center but it makes no difference. They can hear his shouts from the hallway. He takes the seat back of a metal chair and flings it into the wall, losing his balance like a bad golfer. "Why was I the only asshole out there who didn't know what was going on?"

"I'm sorry, Tom. I'm sorry. The UBS thing hit late. Hennings had it. I don't know how Mason was prepared."

"Should I tell them my dog ate my homework, Peter?"

"Okay, okay." Peter has both hands up with palms forward like he's trying to push Tom's anger into a box. "There are two issues here, so let's think this through. First is the hit-and-run with Mason. The president could face jail time if this is real. I'll make sure we're completely informed on the investigation."

"Good." Tom is pissed but he's done throwing chairs.

"The second matter is this thing with Samantha Davis."

Tom sits and breathes hard out his nose.

"What was the nature of the relationship?"

"We dated for about three weeks; it started while we were working a case together. It was before I was married, she wasn't married, it was innocent fooling around."

"Okay." Peter crosses his arms and walks in a wide circle. "Okay." He keeps walking then stops by Tom. "Tom, I have to say this is an area where you could have been more free with the information."

"What do you mean?"

"Well, she's in the media now. We might have booked an interview with her and we should know that ahead of time."

"I would have said something before it came to that. We're not booking a lot of interviews with freshman correspondents."

"Have you had any correspondence with her in the last several years?"

"None."

"Mason's going to try to show that you have."

"Let him try."

"Alright. Look, the press will have some fun with this for a while, but there's no impropriety so it'll blow itself out pretty fast."

"Fine."

"So let's drop that for now. All of this is out of our hands. His scandal is the much bigger issue and the facts are going to fall, but probably not until after the election."

Tom's mind hadn't worked its way around to that yet. "True."

"So this election will hinge on whether or not that scandal is believable. And which campaign can spend more to make it so."

Tom nods. Everything the election was about two hours ago no longer matters.

"He has a real scandal. You just have a bad TV moment. That footage with you looking like you just swallowed a cockroach is going to play in every battleground state around the clock. That imagery is going to be tough, but only in the short term." Brand continues, "If this allegation on Mason holds any water, nobody will care about an affair. Mason's had a million of them anyway. If the hit-and-run isn't immediately discredited, if it can stay in the news cycle for a week, then Mason will lose this election."

53

"Pitch perfect, Mr. President," says Stark. "You knocked the scandal on its heels and turned the focus right around to Samantha Davis and Pauley." Stark believes they can no longer win the election but he can't start talking that way.

"Man, it felt good to unload. On Hennings too. What a twerp that guy is."

"You had better intelligence than anyone out there. Nobody else had the complete story." Stark notes the value add of his sources.

"It's working. For now," says Mason.

Stark and Mason are back in their debate prep room, having a similar meeting as Brand and Pauley. Mason also evacuated the rest of his staff to talk in private with Stark. Both men are standing with hearts beating too fast to sit down.

"Here's what we know," says Stark. "There are numerous correspondences, email and handwritten, between you and Monica Morris. They easily have established a romantic link between you two."

The president picks up an unopened bottle of water and throws it into the trash. He's annoyed he ever put anything in writing to Monica. "So what. I had a romance, he has a romance plus conspiracy with the media to set me up."

"There's no evidence yet that they've been in collusion, but we'll certainly play it that way."

"They're lovers, for Christ's sake," says Mason, getting into the narrative he wants.

"It's going to look like a conspiracy only if we can cast enough doubt that you had any role in the hit-and-run. So far it's not a very strong criminal case."

"Of course not."

"Public opinion is something else. There's enough there to raise eyebrows."

"Like what?"

"There's an unsolved roadside death in Jupiter. A guy on a bicycle hit by a car. At a time when correspondence confirms you were with Monica in Jupiter. Driving from a dinner in Palm Beach."

"Fuck."

"Look, all that is circumstantial. That's why I say it's a weak criminal case, but the fact is it doesn't have good optics for you." Stark sips his water bottle. "There's no real evidence, so a lot will depend on how this woman presents. She hasn't owned the car in question for eleven years and nobody has located it yet. Might be in scrap parts by now. There were no witnesses. There are no traces of anything anymore on the roadside where the body was found. We'll paint old Monica as a crackpot." Stark shrugs his shoulders. "If she can come across as credible, she can do real harm, though."

"Christ."

"The real issue is that there's a news peg based on the affair that's already established. If she just turned up with a fourteen-year-old hit-and-run story and nothing else, this would never make it to your doorstep. We'd only have the piece from the *Standard* to contend with. But once Monica's on camera about an affair, she can go on about whatever the hell she wants. Apparently she's decided to go after this."

The president drops into the sofa, leaning forward over his lap with bent elbows pressed against his thighs. The adrenaline is still flowing but turning to nausea and causing a metallic and inflexible feeling in his muscles. Mitchell is silent.

"Sir, it's all a he-said, she-said. We just need to outspin the other team. The public likes you. Hanging a homicide around your neck is going to be a tough sell." Stark needs to say this to his candidate but he doubts the message is true. He knows the only sell that needs to be achieved is to cast enough doubt around the allegation to swing only a few percent of the voters.

The president stands to his full height, remembering who he is. In a soft voice he says, "Ron, you need to crush her. Crush Monica Morris and then crush Samantha Davis. Then I want you to take their blood and guts and smear it on Pauley."

"Yes, sir."

"You need to make the connection between Pauley and Samantha Davis. You understand me? You need to make the connection."

Only a few weeks to November sixth. "Yes, sir."

THE END

54

"It would have been nice to win on the issues," says Pauley.

"They're all issues. Watergate was an issue," says Brand.

"You know what I mean. Policy issues." Tom looks distant. It's nine hours before the close of the voting booths in North Carolina. Pauley is up eight points in the Real Clear Politics average of the national polls. Mason has no path on the electoral map to a win. There's no drama. No suspense. Tom, Alison, and Peter are in the back of a Suburban on the way to vote.

"I repeat. They're all issues."

"Will you hear what I'm saying for Christ's sake? I would rather it didn't come down to this. I'd rather win on something positive from my side, not negative from his."

Brand says, "You did plenty positive or you wouldn't have been in the position for a win. You're great and you deserve it and the Monica Morris piece was one small factor." He pats Tom on the knee. "Tom, all of history is made by the macro forces. Single events and individuals are just particles on a stream. No one man led the civil rights movement or caused the fall of Rome any more than did a single organism take credit for the march of a world of amphibious organisms to land. It's just that we need some names for our history books."

"That may be true from the perspective of millennia," says Tom. "From the perspective of a decade, or the twenty-four-hour news cycle, that's not true. Everyone with a soapbox says the Monica Morris scandal is my whole margin of victory."

Alison squeezes Tom's hand. "Tom, it isn't the scandal so much as there is a very attractive alternative. Very attractive." She kisses his ear. "No one likes to fire anyone and that's what people had to do to Mason. This just gave people an excuse to do what they already wanted to do. Vote for you."

Tom kisses her cheek.

She says, "This is a happy day. Get happy, you ass."

"You're right."

The Suburban pulls up to the public library in Chapel Hill designated for Tom's and Alison's vote. Secret Service and the national media surround the Suburban, then layers of the public look on from behind the waist-high portable metal fencing used for parade routes.

Tom doesn't plan any remarks here. He just waves, gives the thumbs-up sign, and hugs his wife. They enter the library together through a corridor of Secret Service. There are a dozen individual voting booths, each with a purple curtain. No other voters are in the library.

Tom and Alison are holding hands. "Race you?" she says.

He drops her hand and jogs to a booth. He looks at the screen and is amused that he is so struck at the sight of his own name. He taps the buttons on the touch screen and votes for himself for president.

Alison finishes a moment before him. "You ready?" she says from inside her booth.

"I am."

They step out together, high-five, then hug.

Brand is registered in New York State, which will hold for Mason. Evenso, Brand will leave the library for the airport and fly to New York to vote this afternoon.

Tom and Alison, and a security detail and the press, will drive to a farm near Winston-Salem for Tom's final speech of the campaign. As a boy, he loved the images of Ronald Reagan splitting wood on a farm and he thinks this will be the way to end his campaign and start his presidency.

He changes into jeans and a flannel shirt on the way. As he steps from the Suburban onto the farm, he gets the medieval smell of animal manure and open fires and he thinks, This is the country I love.

Mason spent the entire day in Westchester, New York. He had continued to campaign hard around the country up to the day before to keep the appearance that he was not despondent or a quitter. But the Monica Morris news was too big and there were not enough campaign days left to run out the clock on the scandal.

Mitchell and his wife voted and then went to his friend Jason Parr's estate and horse farm in Bedford to relax in privacy. Parr is seventy, an age between Mitchell Mason and his father, and Parr was a friend to both.

"Son of a bitch," Mason says to himself, looking down at his third rocks glass of scotch. Jason Parr stands by the window. His wife, Penelope, sits by Evelyn on the sofa and Mason sits alone in a deep leather chair. They're in Parr's library with the television on but muted.

Parr inherited the thirty-acre estate from his father. Parr has always been wealthy and never worked much.

They're all watching for signals from Mason for how to act. Parr wants to lighten the mood but Mason needs to be the first not to be somber and he won't do it.

Parr says, "It's almost five o'clock. I need to do it before it gets too dark."

Mason thinks, Jesus, he's actually going to do it. I'm going to get fewer than a hundred electoral votes and he's still going to do it.

Parr puts on a white wig with a three-cornered hat and Colonial coat so he looks like George Washington in the paintings of the Potomac crossing. He walks out of the library and across the field to his stables.

Every election day Parr does a celebration ride on horseback in Colonial getup. It's not the kind of thing he naturally does, but he did it once when he was drunk and then declared it a tradition so now he has to do it always because to stop would be to concede he was drunk and a fool.

"For crying out loud," says Mason, and he groans over his knees to stand and walk to the ladies by the window to watch Jason come out of the stables. Penelope is too uncomfortable to speak so she watches her husband harder.

Parr takes the horse out in a slow trot. He lifts his hat by one corner and smiles at the three faces in the library window. He works the horse to a cantor.

Evelyn comes around to take Mason's hand that doesn't hold scotch. She says, "This will be better for us, dear. No more piranhas at your heels. Or mine. You've given your service up to the limit you can give and now we can live our lives in some peace."

Mason looks straight out the window at the trees but not at Parr. The host is riding in loops and waving like a jackass and Mason doesn't want to see it. "We live in a great mirage, Evelyn. There's no substance to anything, there's just what your brain gets tricked into believing. That's what matters more than what's actually true."

She squeezes his hand and brings her body against his. The affection is real.

He says, "The press held the narrative and never left it, everywhere I went. Things in my past that never warranted comment are now context for how this whole thing is possible." Mason won't say the name Monica Morris.

"It's unfair, darling." Evelyn believes her husband and doesn't believe the charges. Her husband has been under siege for more than a month and the two have developed a codependent bunker mentality.

Parr moves out of his circular pattern and makes straight for a three-foot-high hedge bordering the field. The horse moves faster and Parr pulls the horse up too soon. The front hooves clear the hedge but the back hooves clip it so that the front of the horse lands hard and Parr's chest and face crash into the back of the horse's neck. His hat flies off and the wig comes to his eyebrows. Parr straightens up with a dazed look and is otherwise okay. Penelope laughs. Mason turns for more scotch.

He likes Parr well enough but is uncomfortable around him, not for how he is but for who he is. Parr is a Democrat and his position in New York society makes him a natural connection but Mason is uncomfortable with how Parr acquired that position and what he has chosen to do with it. Parr is a dandy who gets by on wealth and pretension. He can see through Parr, and in moments of doubt and defeat Mason hopes he isn't just a little better at doing the same things Parr does.

55

Pauley wins with 319 electoral votes. The White House changes occupants and this time changes parties too. Mason and Pauley exchange only brief and formal communications. Mason writes the traditional letter for Pauley to unseal after inauguration.

The scandals increased the outrage over a political process that is broken and attracts the wrong sort of men and women. Pundits joked that it was a choice between a Republican or Democrat, small government or big government, a hand up or a hand out, and a civil or criminal case.

In America the cynics always take control over time but Americans love beginnings, and for the beginnings Americans always rationalize optimism. People find that Pauley seems like a good man, a good father and husband.

Pauley never addressed the relationship with Samantha Davis. He talked only of his vision for the country. Samantha Davis never spoke out and so reporters were left with a fourteen-year-old tryst and nothing more and the story passed as Brand had predicted.

Mason's scandal fared worse among the independents. Most who began as Mason supporters remained Mason supporters and unbelieving of the allegation. They opened their minds to the idea of conspiracy. Just as the nation had watched the trial of O. J. Simpson, all seeing the same facts in evidence and the same arguments made, then falling along predictable lines, each with a moral certainty, so did the Democrats and Republicans divide. There was negligible party crossover and the election was determined by the true independents, the ten percent of society that rules.

56

Samantha Davis stays an extra day in Washington, DC, to see a girl-friend from college for a drink. They decide to meet at the Ritz-Carlton in Georgetown because the bar there offers a compromise between good people-watching and a place quiet enough to talk.

At the time of the inauguration, it takes more than just wealth to get a room at the Ritz. It also requires either connections or extreme advanced planning. The people-watching might be very good.

Samantha always determines her first drink ahead of time. It's too cold out for gin and tonic and wine won't be enough. A vodka martini, up. She takes a taxi to the hotel, enters the lobby and walks left to the bar and lounge. It's mostly wood and dark red fabrics and has a warm feeling. The lounge is crowded but in a calm state, full of many private conversations. People who have come to meet someone they know, not someone new.

Samantha sees a single open stool at the bar and starts for it. She'll take it so her friend can sit later because Samantha would rather stand anyway. The bartender is serving two men in the far corner. One has a thick neck and thick face with a sports coat that is tight on his shoulders. The other is slender and neat and handsome in a manicured way.

She takes her seat and puts her jacket on the short backrest of the stool. She looks again to the bartender who is finishing with the two men.

The thick man recognizes her before she recognizes him and he's smiling. He is Connor Marks. She's stunned to see him in a context other than Miami Beach and she calculates it's been well over a year. She had called him twice after he gave her the lead on Monica Morris and he had returned neither call. She smiles and waves just as the bartender puts a gin and tonic in front of her. Another gift from Connor.

Wrong season, she thinks, and drinks it anyway. Connor looks very pleased to see her but the other man looks agitated. He looks from her to Connor and back, then says a word to Connor and walks out making eye contact with only the exit. The man looks familiar to Samantha but she doesn't know why.

Connor had nodded to the man but never stopped looking at Samantha. He picks up his drink and turns the corner of the long bar to join her.

She's a journalist at heart and curious to know what the hell he's doing here. She makes a quarter turn in her bar stool to greet him. "A long way from Miami, Mr. Marks."

"Just a short flight to celebrate our new president. The least I can do."

"I had no idea you were so motivated by politics."

"It's not politics so much that motivates me," he says. He smiles but it's not flirtatious or even friendly. It's triumphant and smug.

"What happened to your date?"

Connor laughs for real this time. "He decided to hustle off."

"Who was that?"

"Kenny Landers."

Of course, she thinks. He's the billionaire CEO of the private security firm who donates fortunes to the GOP. "Stepping up in the world, are we?"

"We've been friendly for a while now. For two years."

He wants to tell her more. He's bursting and Samantha is getting alarmed but wants to let him tell her. "I see."

"He hired me for a little piece of work."

"I didn't realize you were a mercenary too."

"I'm nothing like a mercenary," he says.

"Do tell."

"I could never. But you're welcome to venture a guess. Of course, I can't confirm or deny anything. All I'll say is that sometimes the country needs a little repointing."

Samantha starts to turn things over piece by piece. "And how did you manage that?"

"You tell me," he says.

"Monica Morris?"

He sips his drink and it seems like confirmation.

"Was Monica Morris real? There were photos and witnesses to the affair." He keeps smiling. "Or was she just real enough?" Each time she turns a thing over, it leads to another, worse thing. "She had the affair with Mason but not the hit-and-run." She's not asking anymore, she's declaring a story. "Monica was angry with Mason who had moved on from her, or you just paid her enough to work with you. You did a bunch of legwork on his old affairs, you found one you could prove, you got her on your team." She imagines Marks sitting in the file room of a Florida police station, let through a locked door by a buddy, taking photos with a little camera then making a wisecrack on his way out the door to go tell Monica what to say and how to play it. "Then you searched around for an unsolved hit-and-run that fit a timeline you could match with Monica."

She stares at him. His expression is the same. "My, my, you're a devious one. Hypothetically."

"Just like that, you bring down an innocent man."

"I don't know what you're talking about. But that's an interesting story."

"Then you sent me in like a military drone. I break the story."

"Ha. I like that."

"How do you think this doesn't catch up with you?"

"Let's depersonalize this because, as I said, I don't know what the fuck you're talking about. But in the context of your interesting story, how would anything catch up with anyone?"

"You coerced false testimony. Conspiracy."

"In your fantasy land, let's assume that happened. This is a fourteen-year-old incident. You've read everything about it that I have. There isn't enough evidence to convict Mason and there isn't enough to exonerate him. And so there isn't enough to go after Monica, either. Nobody can prove anything so people just have to make up their own minds." He smiles. "Anyway, you're missing the point. Again. It's not about going to jail, for anyone. That was never going to happen. It's about politics, winning elections. If the other side could have made some of America think Tom Pauley is a bad guy who might commit a crime and doesn't deserve your vote, of course they would do it. It's their moral duty to do it." He points at her. "You think Terry Stanton at the NEA wasn't out to get Pauley? We're all doing the same thing, Sam."

"And Reese Kinard?"

"Are you suggesting I murdered her? Absolutely not. She took herself out of the picture all by herself."

"What about Monica? Isn't she a loose end? You going to kill her?"

"I suppose the character in your fiction could have been motivated by a number of things. Maybe hate, maybe money, maybe both. It's all in public records that there's a website set up to help her through this hardship. Maybe some big donations came in from people concerned that she was a victim of a man like Mason, but that's all aboveboard and public information. There's no lid to blow off, sweetheart."

Asshole. "What if she talks?"

"So what? Her credibility is already on a cliff's edge. Then she reverses her story? With no evidence to point in either direction?" He wants to say "sweetheart" again. "Would you unseat a sitting president on that?"

Samantha is silent.

"What's done is done. In your little story."

Samantha doesn't notice her friend until she leans into the space between Samantha and Connor and says hello. Barbara Conrad is still wearing her purple puffy coat stuffed with down that comes below the knee. She's taken off a pair of earmuffs that wrap behind her head so her hair is still in good shape.

"Barbie, hi." Samantha draws herself and her energy back from Connor for a moment and decides not to introduce them. She decides that when Connor is gone she won't tell Barbie about any of it. It would sound like an improbable conspiracy theory and a waste of time for a responsible journalist. A work of dark fiction.

Barbara presses her cheek against Samantha's to say hi and wonders what she's just interrupted.

"Barbie, I need one more minute. I'm sorry." Barbara nods, not feeling put out at all. Unpleasant things happen with men all the time and she's looking forward to hearing the details after this guy is gone. She walks to the other end of the bar.

Connor watches her go, thinking of her as a civilian following a false god and that she'll be happier that way. He knows Samantha is not a civilian anymore.

Samantha watches Connor. He turns back to her and he says, "I told you I'm a fixer. Look it up. In the dictionary. It means to mend, repair." He takes the last sip of his scotch. "It also means to adjust or arrange." This is the part of the job he loves the most. Finding a person he can tell just enough about it. He says, "Don't question the methods employed by Providence, Sam. You just need to know that it couldn't be any other way." His gloating is almost complete. "What's done is done. Don't you think Pauley is the better man anyway?"

"Maybe what's done is done and maybe not. Even I can name four people who know everything. Three of them were in this room tonight."

This sounds desperate and hollow. People with power don't make vague threats. They let the power speak for itself. Samantha knows this. Connor knows this exactly. "Sure thing, sweetheart. You broke the story. What are you going to do, unbreak it? That wouldn't look very good." He puts down his empty glass. "By the way, I think you're damn good on TV."

This is just how he wants to leave the conversation so he does and walks right off through the exit. Samantha refuses to watch him go. She stares through the space where he had been standing. She sips the gin and tonic which has too much tonic that is flat and tastes sweet, then looks at Barbara.

Barbie is still in her unzipped purple coat, watching Samantha, knowing something is wrong and waiting for a signal about what to do. Samantha creates a story in her mind that Connor is a lobbyist for the NRA and was sharing off-the-record information about pending gun control legislation.

She doesn't want to talk about what Connor has done. Someone like Barbara couldn't know from her far distance that the system that succeeds every time in the election of officials and the transfer of power is, from up close, so ugly.

57

Something Connor Marks said stayed with Samantha. Every media organization reported on the hit-and-run allegation. She doesn't need to unbreak that story, she needs to break the real story.

The mistake Connor made is the same that all narcissists make. Narcissists are capable of anticipating the behavior of another only by anticipating what their own behavior would be if in the other's position.

Samantha gets to work. She finds the Miami cop from the Delano Hotel who first introduced her to Connor Marks and who had been angry with her for her part in the Meadow Jones case. He can identify Connor Marks as a fixer but nothing more.

She finds Charlie Keating, her driver and photographer in Miami, who relates the way in which Connor Marks manipulated the Meadow Jones interviews.

She reaches the office of Kenny Landers who had been at the bar in Georgetown with Connor Marks the night of the inauguration, but he does not respond.

Monica Morris does not respond. Samantha digs up all she can on the fund-raising website in support of Monica, and who the donors are.

There are few tracks left by Connor himself. Samantha has cell phone records proving they spoke on several occasions, and she has contemporaneous notes that describe where Connor pointed her and the mission he gave her.

There's no smoking gun. It's her interviews, supported by her notes

and emails along with a few stories from people like Charlie Keating that
fit a pattern.

It's not enough. There's no story. There's nothing for anyone to go on
unless she can link Connor Marks with Monica Morris, and Monica has
either been paid enough or is scared enough not to cooperate.

Then Samantha has an idea.

58

"I need to vent." Samantha sits across the unsteady wood table from Robin in Le Grainne Cafe in Chelsea. Her college friend is a safe person to share a load with.

"I already ordered the bottle of Sancerre," says Robin. Ethan Hawke is a few tables behind them in his usual place of prominence by the window, attracting gawkers. The café is the right amount of bohemian for his image.

"It's important that you know me this well." The waitress pours the wine into two glasses that are spotty but clean enough.

They touch glasses in a silent toast and Robin waits for Samantha.

"I have so much to tell you. Some of it I should keep confidential. For now, because I'm going to report on it, but those are just small details."

"I hope you'll start by telling me about Tom Pauley. You never mentioned that one to me before and he's hot. Usually they don't look like Harry Hamlin in real life."

"He's a good man. It was just one of those things that happens when you're working too hard and then drinking too much. I was his associate on a case so we had a few months of working those crazy hours together. It happened and it was over almost as fast."

"I don't care about that. I want to know how the sex was."

Samantha laughs and drinks. "Nine."

"Pretty good for a head of state. And that was before he was head of state. The extra cachet could put him over the top." Robin catches herself talking too loudly. She leans in and whispers, "Sorry," then pours more wine.

"This issue doesn't have to do with Pauley. It's Mason." Samantha is whispering too. At 3:30 p.m. it's between mealtimes so the café is only half full with coffee drinkers and a few crepe eaters. Nobody is near enough to hear a whisper.

"Okay."

"He didn't do it. The hit-and-run."

"I figured there's a good chance that woman is a crackpot."

"It's more than that. She was a piece in a plan. People organized a lot of pieces to make this seem credible."

"What people?"

"That's the confidential part, but they organized me. They gave me facts but all organized, secondhand information."

"But facts are facts."

"Presentation matters. It's like wearing the preprinted T-shirts with the wrong Super Bowl champs on them."

Robin frowns. "It's not like that. Those are factually wrong. We donate them to third world countries."

"Monica Morris is factually wrong. I put her story out without enough skepticism."

"Her story was going to get out no matter what. Everyone reported on it and nobody could show it was a lie. Still nobody can show it's a lie."

"But I broke the story. I let it out with a bang but now I have an idea how to close it down with a bang."

The waitress comes back and they each order a Nutella crepe. Ethan Hawke is people-watching the people watching him. "He wouldn't have settled on you for the leak if he'd ever seen you litigate a case." Robin sips her wine with one hand. With the other hand the tips of her fingers caress her collarbone and she looks at Samantha, worried. "Don't do anything dangerous."

"I don't think I'm in danger. Any daylight would make these people go underground, not attack."

"Don't be so sure you know who you're dealing with."

"I'm not worried about danger from those people. They're not part of my plan anyway. I just need to talk with Monica Morris, but to your point, I'm not sure I know who I'm dealing with."

"That's easy. She's crazy."

"She's at least a little crazy, but I don't know if she's a malicious opportunist who knew what she was doing. If she is, that'll make this easy. If she's a broken woman who was exploited and didn't understand the consequences of what she was doing, it'll be harder. I don't want to hurt her. I'll have to weigh whether or not to use anything I get because right now I don't know another way to set this right. I'm actually hoping she has no remorse. I'll feel better about going after her."

Robin smiles. "I said you'd be right in the middle of it all."

"For better or worse."

"I know you. For better."

59

"Round trip to Rye," says Samantha. She had looked for thirty seconds for a ticket kiosk in the massive Grand Central lobby before doing it the old-fashioned way.

"Track twenty-one." The attendant hands her a credit-card-sized piece of paper.

It's fifty minutes on the local Metro North train to Rye. Samantha then walks Purchase Street to Boston Post Road and it takes her twenty minutes to get to Rye High School.

She shows her press credentials to the administrator at reception, who recognizes her anyway and knows that about twenty-five years ago on *Latch Key*, Samantha played the younger sister of the Rye High drama teacher.

"How fun. Melissa is in the auditorium now, finishing a class. I'll take you over there." Security at suburban schools is tight but a little celebrity goes a long way.

They enter the auditorium from the back and look down the stadium-style seating to the stage where Melissa Evers and about twenty students are sprawled in a cluster.

"I'll wait here and watch, thank you." Samantha sits in the dim light of the back row.

The students are reclined around Melissa on the stage. She reviews a rehearsal schedule then dismisses the class and all the bodies stand and move off the sides of the stage then up the steps past Samantha.

Melissa is three years older than Samantha, both on the show and in real life. When *Latch Key* ended, Melissa was fifteen. She stayed around the loop of acting in L.A. for ten years trying to make her transition from child actor to actor. It was ten years of nervousness and rejection, of having to create an image of herself for herself, then picking up the pieces after each audition.

Watching dozens of friends live the same reality, it became harder to rationalize an alternate reality for her own life. She moved to New York to find work in daytime soaps. She found unsteady work, did guest appearances on *Law & Order*, and tried stand-up comedy. Then the work stopped coming at all. She was banished from the dreams that used to nourish her and she took the job at Rye High. She became happy for the first time in two decades.

Samantha claps from the back row. Melissa squints toward the noise and doesn't recognize her. Samantha starts down the steps, still clapping.

"Bravo." The voice gives her up.

"Samantha?"

"You're as beautiful as ever." Melissa is blond with blue eyes and no less beautiful than any of the five hundred thousand other women her age that have wanted to be in the movies.

"So are you. What a nice surprise to see you."

Samantha doesn't want to ask the favor just yet. "It's great to see you. It transports me back twenty-five years."

"Please. Don't depress me."

Samantha holds up her arms. "This is beautiful."

"It's suburbia." This is not an endorsement.

"I walked here from the train. Quite a town."

"I live in Port Chester. The town over. Much more affordable. This is a pretty wealthy set here, but nice-enough people."

Samantha says, "Do you have a few minutes to catch up?"

"Sure. I have about an hour. Do you want coffee?"

"No."

"Then let's stay here. I usually hide down here most of the day." She pulls two wooden chairs together on the stage. "I've seen you on TV a few times. You're doing great."

"Thanks."

"The first time I saw you was on the Meadow Jones murder case. You were all over the place. And your reporting on President Mason and the hit-and-run caused a big stir. I haven't followed that since the election. What's happening with that now?"

"He's innocent."

"Really? I knew it! I hadn't heard that yet."

"It's not really out there yet."

Melissa frowns. "Why not?"

"That's why I'm here. I need your help."

"My help?"

"I need a talented actress."

"For what?"

"If I spring for JetBlue tickets, would you take a flight with me to Palm Beach? The whole thing is probably two days."

"When?"

"How about next week?"

"Is this for UBS?"

"Sort of, but it's unofficial, which is why I'm here."

"This has to do with President Mason?"

"I can't guarantee there's no danger to you."

Melissa would take a bullet for a great role. She brushes away the warning with a hand motion.

Samantha believes her plan will pose little danger to Melissa. "If you're in, I'll give you the details."

"I'm in."

60

"How is Connor?"

"He's fine. He's doing well and he wants to make sure you're okay too."

"When do you think I can see him?"

"It may be a while, Monica. Maybe a couple years. Maybe more. I'm sorry." Melissa does feel a little sorry for Monica Morris. The woman is alone and upset and though she must have known on some level what she was getting involved with, she couldn't have known what it would feel like to have media stationed outside her condo for weeks, following her movements around town. The last she had heard from Connor was not to travel, not to do anything different, so she has stayed immobile in the center of chaos. "Connor wants everything to go through me for now," Melissa says.

"Okay."

"This must be so hard for you, Monica." Melissa's goal to start is to be sympathetic. Monica is scared and isolated. Melissa needs to be a shoulder for her, build trust, get her talking, and be vague about everything in return. Don't go for anything until Monica likes Melissa enough that she wants the meeting to be longer rather than shorter.

"It's been horrible." It feels good for Monica to be able to say that to another person. For someone to hear that and understand it. To validate her. Monica has another thought. "So I won't see Alan anymore? Did something happen to him?"

Melissa leans back and thinks, Shit. The most important rule in improv and stand-up comedy is never to shut anything down. When the dialogue passes to you, you don't drop it, you take it and do something with it. No is not an answer. "You'll still see Alan. He's still there for you."

"Good. At least he's someone familiar, even if he does scare the dickens out of me when he appears out of nowhere. It's gotten so every time I come out of the Starbucks into the parking lot, I hope he'll show up. Tell him to come more often."

Melissa smiles. "I'll pass that along. I'll be here for you too. Connor wants to make sure you're getting what you need."

"What I need is for this mess to go away. I'm barely sleeping." Monica is relaxing and venting and showing some anger. "What do you do for Connor? Have you known him long?"

Be vague, be vague. "It's better that you don't know. I'm sorry to be secretive, but it's better for you and it's better for me."

Shutting down the question diminishes the trust that has been developing. Melissa and Samantha had role-played this interview the way they would rehearse lines for a show, trying out different emotions and emphases. They had anticipated this question and giving a nonanswer seemed the realistic response for the fictional character Carol Shaw that Melissa is playing. But Melissa sees the damage this answer causes because she and Samantha didn't anticipate the effects of the isolation and paranoia on Monica Morris. Melissa changes course.

Playing Carol Shaw, Melissa smiles. "I've known Connor for years. We've worked together a long time. I'm a field person, not his accountant." She smiles wider. "No harm in you knowing that."

Monica takes this as a gift and she's happy.

"Nicely done," says Samantha from the adjoining room in the DoubleTree.

She's watching two screens in black-and-white. One is from a camera in Melissa's lapel pin that gives a close-up of Monica, and the other is from a camera in a clock on the wall that shows a side view of the two women talking. The sound quality is good.

They had considered miking up Melissa's ear so they could speak with her but decided it would be too risky and possibly distracting to Melissa anyway. Melissa's on her own but she's rehearsed and she's a pro.

"Keep your routine with Alan the same as it has been. Nothing changes there, but Connor wanted to give you someone you could talk to more easily."

The information on Alan has given her something credible to run with and sets things up for where she wants to go.

"She's doing great. Calm, even. Sympathetic body language." Samantha's directing a movie except she can't yell cut. They just roll tape.

"She's good." Tim Hart is a freelance audio tech that Samantha has met in her work with UBS. Hart had wired the room for the meeting. He sits next to Samantha, leaning over the two laptop screens that receive the camera signals and record them.

They're at the DoubleTree Hotel on the corner of PGA Boulevard and Military Trail. Melissa had called Monica the day before, saying her name is Carol Shaw and that she works for Connor Marks. Only a handful of people know of her connection to Connor and Monica believed her. Melissa told her to drive to Palm Beach International in the morning, park, get a taxi at the airport, and get to the DoubleTree at eleven a.m. That would lose any media vans. Don't speak to anyone until then.

Samantha and Melissa don't care if Monica's phones are tapped by law enforcement. They're on the side of law enforcement. And they know Connor wouldn't risk putting a tap on the line and getting found out. They knew there was a chance that Connor had set up a code word with Monica to verify anyone contacting her, but they had to hope that the name Connor Marks would satisfy as verification.

"Well, I appreciate you meeting me. This has been a worse hell than I thought it would be. I just want it all to stop. I'm angry and I'm scared for my son."

The comment surprises Melissa and instead of nodding her understanding she says, "Why?"

"Alan was very clear. These are powerful people. If anything goes wrong, if I do anything wrong, it'll be bad for Sean."

"Well, nothing's going to go wrong, Monica." Melissa has recovered. "I'm here to help make sure of that."

Samantha and Melissa think at the same time that there could be collateral damage in releasing the tape of this interview, but in the case of Sean Morris, the tape making national news will be the best outcome for his safety.

Monica covers her face with her hands and presses back the emotion. "I'm just so angry," she says. There is a single cry that is muffled and when she pulls her hands down, there are tears and saliva and a runny nose mixed together.

Melissa leans forward and reaches a hand to Monica's knee and thinks, Maybe you shouldn't have lied to the FBI. This is one of the openings she and Samantha had rehearsed.

"Here it is, Melissa. Gentle," says Samantha to the laptop.

"Monica, I have a background as a therapist. Healthy, successful people talk things out with a psychologist all the time, in addition to friends and family, and they do this when they're under one-tenth the pressure you are. I know your friend was a psychologist. You haven't had anyone to talk with. You're under enormous strain. Let's just talk a bit. It might make you feel better."

"I know, I know. Connor thinks I'm turning into some basket case that's going to crack. You need to come here and manage me or it's going to mess up your whole disgusting plan." She twirls her fingers by her ears in the crazy motion when she says the word "manage."

Melissa sees the woman is already unhinged and not remorseful. "We know you're under a lot of stress, as would anyone be in your position. I'm here to help. I've helped people in tight spots before."

Monica makes a big exhale. She has the bratty way of a person who always thinks the world has singled her out for unfair treatment. "Okay." Monica is gathering herself. This seems like an idea worth trying.

"What emotions are you feeling, besides anger and fear?"

"Oh, my gosh, Carol." Monica rolls her head back. "I couldn't possibly say. All of them at once, I guess, but mostly anger and fear. And exhaustion, if that counts as emotion."

"Exhaustion is a real thing. It's a major force on us. Rest is the most recuperative thing our bodies can do, and you need it. You should think about a sleep aid."

"I'm all over that."

"Any other emotions? Guilt?"

Monica nods sideways to acknowledge a maybe but says nothing.

"Guilt is a powerful emotion."

"Yes."

"You need to address that. For yourself. Or it doesn't go away, believe me, I know."

Monica nods.

"You need to talk it through, Monica. Do you feel guilty that this damaged a man or stirred up the election?"

"Mitchell Mason is not a good man."

"Maybe, maybe not. But this is about you, not him." Melissa needs to get back on Monica's side. "I'm here to help you through this, Monica. That's why Connor had me come here."

"I know."

Now feels like the time to take a shot. "It's too late to change anything that's happened. I'm sure Connor and Alan have made that clear. But it's not too late to deal with what you're feeling. Are you feeling guilt or remorse that you invented the hit-and-run?"

"I suppose I am. He's a bad person but I wish now it didn't come to all that."

"Are you angry with him?"

Monica thinks about this, considering a question she hasn't asked herself in a while. "No, not anymore. I really loved him. He treated me like trash, but I loved him."

"Monica, this is strictly between us. Are you angry with Connor Marks?"

Monica is surprised by the question and takes a moment to check with herself for the true answer. "No, I'm not angry with Connor. He didn't do anything wrong, and he explained everything to me. I was just naïve, and it's a lot of money. And Mason is such a prick."

This is her true answer though she's also a little afraid of Connor and thinks Carol will share the answer.

"Okay, good." Melissa is close to the end and wants to run out the door. "Connor has a lot of years in with the Miami Police Department. He'll know how to take care of you. Over the long haul as well." This is a comment scripted by Samantha. If it gets this far, she wants to make sure there is no doubt about which Connor Marks on the planet they're talking about.

"I know. Connor has been a friend."

"We got it," says Samantha from the next room.

61

Samantha finds a few photos of Connor Marks from his time with Miami PD. She chooses the one that has his neck the thickest and his face the most thuggish. She prepares the forty-five-minute package and mentions Pauley once to say he had no connection with Connor Marks. She mentions Mason once to say she is convinced of his innocence. The rest highlights Monica Morris and Connor Marks the Fixer and it plays the video of Carol Shaw and Monica Morris in full.

Samantha introduces the forty-five-minute piece on Candace Park's nine p.m. show on UBS-24. "You may not know the name Connor Marks, but it is a name the world will come to know. The allegation of hit-and-run against President Mason was false. It was a fraud created by Connor Marks." The piece runs then the camera cuts back to Samantha and Candace.

Candace makes a dramatic pause on camera, looking at Samantha. "Where is Connor Marks today?"

"I don't know."

"Will charges be brought against him?"

"I expect conspiracy as a start. Maybe more once they've investigated everything."

"Reese Kinard?"

"At this time that is still classified as a suicide but the police are re-examining the case."

"And Monica Morris?"

"She's in custody and I understand is cooperating."

The broadcast moves to a split screen to include the photo of Connor Marks. Samantha says, "He is out there and I suppose others like him are out there. People who are focused on an objective and who will leverage any perversion, use whatever means to achieve it."

62

The day after Samantha Davis's report, the headline of the *New York Times* is "Monica Morris a Fraud, Changes Election."

The *New York Daily News*: "The Fixer Is In."

The *Washington Post*: "Morris Scandal Upends Washington."

The *New York Post*: "The Lady Is a Tramp . . . and a Liar."

There are seventy million Democrats who will never forget the faces of Monica Morris and Connor Marks, though the national outrage over the scandal is nonpartisan. While no one suggests that Pauley had any hand in the manipulation, his administration is taking incoming from all sides. His victory is legally unchallenged but is relegated to practical illegitimacy.

"I can't govern this way, Peter."

"You can't resign and we're not going to do the election over again. You're the president of the United States. This'll pass."

"This is a stain that won't go away. The country's just going to wait out a four-year clock to take away something it thinks I should never have had. And anytime I try to push a policy agenda, the people are going to ask me by what right."

"It'll pass."

"No, we need to do something."

"There's nothing to do, Tom. We can't have copresidents."

"Maybe a team-of-rivals gesture."

"No. You want to make him secretary of state? That'd be an insult."

"Of course not, but we need to change the media conversation."

"I'll call Mason's people. Maybe he'll make some statement of support for you. The fact that you're president isn't going to change in the next four years, so getting you past this is the right thing for the country. He may decide it's a gesture that'll make him look good."

Tom sits behind the desk of his upstairs study in the private residence of the White House. It's past midnight. Alison is asleep. His belongings are unpacked and arranged except for two cardboard boxes of old personal items that Tom has now opened up.

Tom is looking through some old photos then stops on one and puts it down on the desk.

His elbows are down on the desk and he leans forward and rubs deep into his eyes with the end digits of his fingers. He's president now, but at a price. Everything that had to happen to get him to the goal now hangs around his neck like a weight too great to carry. He's impotent because of the process. The price was too high.

He stands to go to bed and leaves the pictures where they are. Nobody goes in here but Tom.

The picture on top is faded with age. It's a group photo from the Camp Arrowhead summer camp for boys. Six boys, ten years old, are in the photo. Four standing and holding fishing rods. Two are kneeling. The last sentence of the caption reads, *Kneeling: Tom Pauley, Connor Marks.*

In the actions of all men, and especially of princes,
where there is no court to appeal to, one looks to the end.
For that reason, let the prince win and maintain his state:
the means will always be judged honorable,
and he will be praised by everyone.

Niccolò Machiavelli, 1469–1527

Acknowledgments

Two people who deserve a special thanks are Dana Perino and Chris Stirewalt. Not only did they meet with me on several occasions to help with this book, but they introduced me to people well-placed to continue aspects of the research. They also read an early draft of the novel and provided great feedback. I ignored some of the corrections they offered in order to preserve pieces of the story I want to tell. If you find something you'd like to change, they probably found it too.

Many others were generous with their time and expertise, including: Joe Trippi, Charlie Hurt, Terry Holt, Marc Lampkin, John Murray, Melissa Francis, Arthur Aidala, Jared Weinstein, Tom Rooney, Pat Brosnan.

My agents, Lane Zachary and Todd Shuster, once again helped me through the process and had thoughtful suggestions for the book. I'm grateful for their hard work and friendship.

Stacy Creamer has been an early believer in my writing and has had great advice for both of my books. It has been a pleasure working with Sally Kim, a great editor and advisor. Also at Touchstone, Meredith Vilarello, Melissa Vipperman-Cohen, Courtney Brach, Jessica Roth, and Lisa Healy.

My wife Megyn is my most trusted reader, and her feedback means the most. She is kind, brilliant, funny, and strong. I know a few people who are so talented they can do anything they want, but she is the only one who can do anything she wants with excellence. I'm lucky that she's my love story. Together we've done amazing things, and the best of these we call Yates, Yardley, and our new baby Thatcher. Now everyone is here.

About the Author

Until 2011, Douglas Brunt was CEO of Authentium, Inc., a security company. His first novel, *Ghosts of Manhattan*, was a *New York Times* bestseller. A Philadelphia native, he lives in New York with his wife and three children.